A Picture of Distance - Copyright 2015 © by F. Bradley Reaume

Penshurst Publishing   First edition - May 2015

ISBN   978-0-9734452-7-5

A Picture of Distance

A novel of perspective

By F. Bradley Reaume

Chapter One - 1999

Like most other days that summer it was memorably hot. Summer in Toronto isn't always that way.

There had been little rain, so lawns and parks were parched, crinkly and brown. Many days were humid and uncomfortably sticky, notable only if you had to spend much time outside.

It was not at all the type of day I would have thought my mother would choose to die. I'm sure she would have wanted the hundred-year storm of pounding rain, thunder and lightning flashes, just to emphasize the point of her passing.

She was old. And while her death did not come as a surprise, the void of her presence did. For years she had simply slowed down bit by bit, almost imperceptibly. There was no real warning, save a few weeks of rapid decline. With a heart attack or accident, the surprise of death is its sudden appearance. It meets us seemingly out of nowhere, even though we know it is always lurking.

In my mother's case the surprise came in trying to cope with the knowledge she would not be there anymore. It was not in the death but the reordering of life in its aftermath.

There was a rapid decline but no other warning other than her great age. Once someone surpasses the expectation of death it is like they will always be there - because to virtually everyone alive, they always have been. However, in her 99th year, her death could hardly be considered shocking.

Still it profoundly shocked me, as I found out there were truths about her and our family, barely hinted at. Truths that I did not know that I did not know. I am still trying to find meaning in the truth of things I did not know were untrue.

My mother was an outgoing woman who, as did most women of her generation, had put her family first. She had long outlived her husband and all of her other contemporaries. She had her family of six children, 12 grandchildren and numerous great-grandchildren. A good life but not one without its bumps.

My father came from a prosperous, well-known family that had parlayed the skilled trades of three brothers into a company that built industrial and commercial buildings, mostly in the Toronto area.

My father had been trained as a carpenter in his youth and as an accountant after the Great War. As the family business grew he took on more of the accounting tasks and would only henceforth lend his talents to the building of beautiful furniture. Most family members had at least one of his creations in their homes or offices. He built with very little middle ground, usually with functional austerity or on rare occasion with an opulent extravagance that was fascinating and almost nauseating in its wild complication and splendor.

In his youth he was a dashing young man, with dreams for the future and a plan to get there. Building Stuart Construction and reaping the financial security it brought was part of the plan. His intricate woodworking gave him the creative outlet so many people crave but let fade as obligations and duties pile up.

As he aged he came to believe his efforts in life were empty of meaning. He had helped build a successful family business. He had built most of his progeny an intricate one-of-a-kind desk, shelving unit or armoire as an heirloom. But it wasn't enough.

With most people the depression over their aging and accomplishments is a passing phase. One realizes their biggest dreams were not achieved but they are able to see the value of the path they took. My father never grasped the meaning or value of his life and he retreated into the church to try to find it.

As an old man he withdrew even deeper into his few interests, chief of which became horticulture and daily mass.

I always wondered at his choices, the apparent nurturing of life and preparing for death.

But it wasn't always that way, he had been young once. After a short time in the family carpentry business, my father had convinced his own father that a short adventure with the troops was necessary for his education.

He entered the army in the summer of 1916 getting his basic training at

Camp Borden, and serving overseas with the Canadians defending France in the Great War. He used his carpentry skills to help construct and reconstruct the trenches and command posts along his sector of the front line. He was wounded at Vimy Ridge in April 1917 and sent to England to recuperate. He rejoined his unit for the duration though rarely spoke of any action he had witnessed.

Though he never really exhibited the classic symptoms I wondered if he hadn't felt a touch of poison gas at some point as he was never robust in person or in pictures.

Ever after the war, sudden loud noises would cause him to tense and sweat. Sometimes he would simply stop; becoming glassy-eyed for long minutes until the present world encroached on his reverie and he slowly came back to the present.

He never spoke of battles or engagements of his wartime experience except to tell amusing tales of those times between battles. Only once did he speak of any sadness.

We all had heard the tale of a stray dog that had been adopted by his company which one day entered no-man's land responding to the sound of a wounded man. Watching the dog and sending a few messages back and forth from the trenches to a wounded man via the dog, those safe in the trench knew where the wounded man would be found, amongst the barbed wire and bomb craters. And the wounded man knew that they would come for him.

As they sent the dog out one last time with a message that they would attempt a rescue that night, the dog was killed by a single shot - presumably from the German lines.

He said the men were so upset by the killing of the dog that they planned their revenge. They knew that the German trench was about 50 yards beyond where the wounded man lay. The usual practice was to wait until dark and stealthily crawl and scrabble into no man's land and drag the wounded back. This time it would be different.

The men quietly assembled a large group to go and recover the waiting wounded. Normally only a few would go for speed and so the Germans would know it was not a general attack. This time unbeknownst to their officers 20 men lined up, each with four grenades.

They moved out quietly with two assigned to the wounded man who was about 75 yards from their trench. When they were prepared to move that man they gave a signal to the rest and then jumped up and threw their grenades at the German trench. Upon receiving the signal all the other men did the same while the corpsmen used the cover to run back to their trench with the wounded man. With four grenades each there were waves of explosions and no return fire - everyone retreated to the trench unhurt. Of course there was no indication of any German casualties as they might have been attacking empty trenches.

Their officers were particularly concerned about the hijack of authority and their lack of knowledge of the attack. Their concern was proved real two days later when the Germans conducted a short but intense bombardment of their section of the line.

My father never indicated if anyone was killed in the attack and never acknowledged any regret for their unilateral action. He quietly avoided all things German during his life.

In the end my parents had six children between the wars. William was the first, born in 1920, he enlisted after the Battle of Britain and served overseas in England, France, Holland and Germany. Charles born a year later, looked and sounded so much like my father that he was pin-pointed as a Stuart in his daily travels. He enlisted a year later than his older brother and served as a munitions supply driver and mechanic in England, France and Holland.

My oldest sister Helen was 16 when the war broke out. Lithe, but plain of face, she bore a mild resemblance to both my parents. She took a job at a local bank during the early stages of the war, quickly gaining a reputation for diligence, detail and accuracy.

At the time my second sister Charlotte, was 14. She trained as a nurse as the war was winding down but was much too young to serve and completed her training only as the war was ending.

Next in line, Mary, was born in 1930 and like me was just a kid for the duration. I was born in 1935 and had little understanding of the war, even the privation and rationing that took place, as I was too young to be aware of any other way of living.

Both Charlotte and Mary were enrolled in a private girls' school at the start of hostilities. Both were indebted to my mother for their good looks and keen sense. As the youngest child, by the time the war ended I was properly and totally in awe of my older brothers.

We lived in one of the most peaceful and prosperous places on earth, had a solid if not enviable family background, connections, and while not rich, we were comfortable and self sufficient. As the promise of each of our lives approached we had an almost unlimited horizon. And yet, the foundation of our lives would be molded by war, by circumstance and by fate.

With the chasm of history the war created in our world, we would be the grist of progress for the twentieth century.

Chapter Two - 1914

Eddy grabbed the weathered metal knob and pulled the heavy oak door open. A bell jangled deeply, clanking more than ringing as it hit the wooden frame. The bell redoubled its warning in a slightly different tone, on the door's reverse pass.

Eddy entered the office. It was really just one big room, with a counter, desks, and people with their heads down, working furiously at their tasks. There were a few large oak doors leading to private offices in the back but Eddy had never even seen the big boss, Mr. Pimlico. He only rarely saw Mr. Hardbottle, who ran the operation, and who always looked at Eddy like he shouldn't be behind the counter, apparently unaware that he worked there as a runner.

It was hot in late June and sweat was on every brow. Much of the day's work was done for the regulars but as a runner, Ed's job was just beginning.

People had long ceased to look up from their tasks despite the metallic clanky ring when Eddy arrived at the telegraph office six days a week. He came in like clockwork, five minutes after the school bell sounded just down the street.

He walked over to Skip Driscoll's desk where the youngish man, sporting black suspenders over his white shirt, a bushy moustache and a head of unruly dark hair was hunched over the telegraph. Ed tucked his school books on an empty corner shelf. Skip looked up and with a smile acknowledged his young charge while he kept writing.

"We gotta busy one today, kid," said Skip, still scribbling. "Take this to Frankie in sports and this one to your uncle." Skip tore off two notes. "And then get back here, lickety-split. This thing hasn't stopped all day."

Eddy grabbed the notes, he knew better than to read them while Skip was watching.

The telegraph rang and started to hammer out its statacco tune again, but Eddy knew that Skip was watching out of the corner of his eye. Eddy adjusted his cap, acknowledged the instructions and moved quickly back onto the street.

It was the news. He loved knowing. It didn't matter if it was New York or London, or from somewhere else across the country, Eddy wanted to know. He even got a little shiver when one bit of news came through that connected with another from days or months before.

A fire here, a new law there, Eddy saw it all. He'd even contributed a bit of background when the men at the newspaper wanted to talk about the connections of various events. Mostly he just listened to their talk when they put events into perspective or context.

When three houses had burned down on the south side in May, the reporter shook his head and said it was inevitable as the City of Hamilton had refused to fund a bigger fire department even though the city was getting larger every day.

When the Boston Red Sox sold George Ruth to the Yankees it wasn't much talked about in Hamilton, a minor league town, but Ed knew. He knew who George Ruth was, only the best lefthander in the American League.

And while Ed loved baseball, even that came in behind just knowing and piecing the news and events together, one thing causes another, and then in turn affects another. It was a grand parade where the solid ground of expectation could shift at any moment.

Eddy loved his after school job running tickertape messages to the newspaper office. His Uncle Frank had got him the job when he needed someone to run back and forth between the telegraph office and the newspaper when big games were being played out of town. They would post frequent updates of football, baseball and hockey games in the office windows.

Little Eddy would also run final game details to the local paper to be included with the next day's news. There were other messages that he would have to deliver, birthday wishes, birth and death notices, and the like, but the news was what made it fun. It felt good being the only one other than Skip to know what had happened in the world – unless it was a really big deal and then Skip told the whole office as it came in.

Skip was a wiz with code. Of course Morse Code was the standard but Skip and a few of his regular contacts used some shorthand they developed among themselves. It was especially effective for sporting contests.

Perhaps the worst thing that ever happened to Skip was when his counterpart in Buffalo took ill for several months and he had to revert to the more laborious full code because the replacement didn't know the shortcuts.

Eddy adjusted his cap and looked at the messages. He had a personal delivery of a sealed message – personal stuff was always sealed. But the news stuff was on open pages – the Chicago Cubs beat the Boston Braves 4-1 at Wrigley Field with Hippo Vaughan throwing a two-hitter for the win and third baseman Heinie Zimmerman getting four hits.

The Cards were in New York and the game had just begun – he was running the first inning to a new fangled radio station in town. Owned and operated by his uncle it broadcast voices to special boxes that people could buy. Amazing stuff thought Eddy. He would bring updates to the station until the game was over. Hamilton's minor league team supplied players to St. Louis, so locals were Cards fans by default.

The Cards were tied 0-0 with both teams going down 1-2-3. His uncle wouldn't like that, he liked busy first innings, so he would have plenty of time to get the next update before he ran out of things to say.

"It looks like there will be a lot of foul balls in this inning," Eddy thought with a smile.

Of course Uncle Frank and his son Charlie always moaned about a huge second inning which took forever to play, meaning the update after the quick inning didn't come in until the next lengthy inning was complete. Uncle Frank could be downright upset when that happened – the skies might open up. Eddy looked up at the sky - clear blue. He stifled a laugh.

Eddy ran the messages out all afternoon, thankful that school was nearly over for the summer as the end of June was just around the corner.

Late in the day he had his final run to the newspaper. Skip gave him the folded notes and he was almost through the door when the ticker tape bell rung, and the machine started hammering out a lengthy message. He waited for the final message to be transcribed.

Skip waited patiently to give the machine a head start and then began transcribing code as the ticker tape hammered out more. When it finished Skip was only a couple of moments behind on his transcription.

"I thought it might be the final from that Philadelphia game but it's just a bit of news."

Eddy grabbed his school books, tied them together with a cord, jammed them in his leather satchel, looped it over his head and took the completed sheet with him and headed for his final run. He could hardly wait for dinner, riding around town was hungry work.
He reached the nearby corner where he waited patiently for a few large carriages to plod by and idly looked at the messages. A couple more personal deliveries. He groaned inwardly because one was all the way out on the edge of town, and he'd have a long way to ride. The others were some stray scores for the newspaper and some news from Washington.

The final sheet was on the bottom. It seemed some Austrian noble and his wife were shot and killed by an assassin.

"Oh, my who would do anything like that," thought Eddy. "I wonder what their children will do?"

He crossed the street, dodging some horse droppings on the way. "At least those automobiles don't mess up the street so much," he said out loud. "I daresay there hasn't been a street cleaner here all day."

Eddy moved down the block. He made his deliveries in the order specified by Skip with a little local geographic trickery tossed in to shorten the route. Actually Skip only told him which of the messages were at the top and Ed was free to choose his own route as long as the priority messages were delivered quickly.

There had only ever been one complaint and that came from old Miss Galtenburg, who saw Eddy run up the front steps of her neighbour's house half a block down the street before coming to her home with a priority message. Eddy had been worried that he was going to catch an earful or worse but even Mr. Hardbottle only harrumphed when told of Miss Galtenburg's concern.

"The other one was on the way," Eddy explained to Skip after Mr. Hardbottle contributed his thoughts. "It takes more time to double back, so if I do, other deliveries are much later. Miss Galtenburg may have had to wait an extra two minutes but the last five deliveries were done half an hour earlier by doing it my way."

"Hey kid, I know, I used to be a runner. Just remember who complains and how loudly they do it, and adjust your route accordingly," said Skip. The next day, Eddy went to the telegraph office as usual. And as usual nobody noticed, until Skip handed him a small sheaf of papers. Eddy left and according to his custom walked quickly down the block to the main intersection, reading the interesting press and organizing the messages into his route for the run. His first run was usually reserved for nearby addresses and priorities. He usually did these on foot.

As he approached the intersection, another of the big slow carriages lumbered through the crossing. With two more just down the block. Eddy thought of running across the street ahead of the carriages but he was still juggling the messages, and was unsure of his route. So he stood on the corner piecing his plans together. A large man passed him, knocking Eddy's shoulder as he stepped out into the street.

The man looked back at Eddy and scowled as he moved away from him. He was unaware that Eddy had a handful of messages to organize and was thinking that the kid had stopped unnaturally.

The well dressed man, turned back to face the street as he approached the intersection. He saw the approaching slow moving carriages. He took a few quick steps to get across the street before being cut off by the horses, but as he tried to avoid one pile of horse droppings he stepped on another causing him to slip and fall. Just as he made his decision to dash across the street an automobile had careered around the corner, also trying to cross in front of the horses before turning up the street in advance of being cut off.

The car struck the fallen man hard and bounced over and away from him. He lay sprawled on the street partly on top of one pile of horse manure, not moving.
The horses shied.

One of the occupants of the car had been thrown out of it and was pulling himself up into a sitting position. Blood gushed from a wound on his head and his arm was scraped badly.
Eddy ran into the street and looked at the man who had collided with him. His neck rested at an unnatural angle and his leg was also badly and obviously broken. He had several cuts and was bleeding from a gash in his leg.

He mumbled a few words and was still.

A mounted policeman was on the scene quickly. He directed Eddy to get help and took charge of the situation, tending to the sitting man, deciding after a quick examination that there was nothing he could do for the man who had been struck. He was dead.

Eddy was in the middle of the news, interviewed by a newspaper reporter. He enjoyed speaking to the newspapers but he wasn't too happy with the attention from those who knew him. They wanted all the gory details, and were disappointed when Eddy said there really weren't any.

Chapter Three - 1918

She walked through the chill streets. Her basket was filled with vegetables from the market for the evening meal. It was her job to make the vegetable purchases every two days.

She walked through the city streets from business and commercial streets to a more residential area. Downtown the permanent city was made of stone and brick. Wooden frame construction was more common in nearby residential areas.

Despite the absence of wind it was cold as buildings blocked the warmth of the low, late-afternoon sun. The dampness in the air and grey looming clouds gave the impression that snow was coming but the temperatures still warded off the white. Without direct sunshine winter was very near, even if the calendar said November had barely begun.

The brick and stone echoed the cobbled streets which were often laid with the same bricks that graced the buildings and homes. By the end of the second decade of the twentieth century automobiles had grasped the fancy of the masses. Horses were still common and in evidence, by sight and smell.

Still, as she walked, she marveled at how much cleaner the streets had become in just a few short years as the automobile grew in popularity. She pulled her heavy shawl closer over her wool coat to battle the chill and hurried home.

She lived in the dormitory of an all-girls school. Boarding there with Anne, her sister, Kate Lewis was in her final year at the Academy. She was preparing for life as a wife and mother. However, the school provided enough education that should she be unsuccessful in attracting a husband, or ill fate left her in need, she could teach or become a nurse. It was a hedge should no husband be forthcoming or some other unfortunate circumstances arise. It was also a good training for raising a family.

It was Kate's job to purchase the necessary vegetables from the market for the dormitory's kitchen. As the harvest season ran out she brought more and more back to the dormitory as the girls had a constant autumn effort to preserve their foodstuffs for use in the winter. Most of the hard work was done but the dormitory mother was still trying to get the last few jars filled.

Kate turned the street corner and picked out the third walkway. She carefully replaced the wrought iron gate and scrambled up the steps. The door was flung open, light and noise poured out and Kate was greeted by a throng of girls, led by her sister.

"The war is over!" they squealed in something approaching unison.

"They stopped at 11 a.m.," said Ann, as everyone else nodded, "fighting that is."

"Let her in and close the door, we are not trying to heat the whole city," came the scolding voice of the dormitory mother from deep inside the house.

"It was on the radio," said one of the other girls, then deepening her voice to mimic a radio announcer, "The guns have fallen silent across Europe."

Kate heard snippets of detail from whoever first remembered it - an announcement was to be made that evening at city hall, troops would be coming home and a few apparent details of the armistice. It was an excited group of girls who pitched in with the dormitory mother and prepared the evening meal.

The radio news confirmed that the mayor would say a few words at City Hall at 8 p.m. about the armistice and capitulation of the Kaiser, Germany and its allies. The girls wanted to go but the dormitory mother would have none of it, citing the cold, the throngs and the lack of proper supervision.

"Having their daughters tramping about on a cold autumn evening is not what your parents paid for when they enrolled you here," said the dormitory mother. "I daresay your attendance will not speed the return to normalcy nor will your absence lengthen it unnecessarily."

The girls grumbled but they knew she was right. Most of them gathered around the radio for snippets of news as they repaired clothing, checked their workbooks or did puzzles. As it was her assigned task, Anne had excused herself to do laundry and asked Kate to join her.

As they reached the room they shared Kate said, "Anne, I know you. How are you going to get out?"

"Me?" asked Anne innocently. And then she smiled sweetly, "Don't you mean 'we'?"

Kate knew her sister was a bit wild but refused to acknowledge the bits of evidence suggested anything more. As she neared graduation from the Academy her curiosity matched her determination to become a bit more worldly.

Anne revealed her secret. She explained that nobody ever checked the lock on the dormitory's cellar access. It was used for deliveries and it was locked from the inside after each delivery was made. Deliveries were first reported to the front door and the dormitory mother opened the back cellar access so she could direct where goods should go. The wide staircase and hallway leading from the back of the house into the cellars was used as a storage area.

"But what if they lock it once you've left?" asked Kate.

"Who is going to know it needs locking if there hasn't been a delivery? Besides, who goes down there after dinner? Nobody, that's who. Anyway I've never had a problem and I've used it many . . ."

"I don't want to know," said Kate quickly, stuffing her fists in her ears.

"Well, let's get busy with our laundry. We need to do a lot of it to make it look as if we've been hard at work. You can think about it as we work, we won't be going for a while yet."

"Why do you want to go? What's so interesting about hearing a few musty old people drone on about stuff you have nothing to do with?"

"It's a once in a lifetime event," said Anne. "If you don't want to go, I'll go by myself."

But Kate went. She couldn't leave Anne to go alone and her own curiosity over Anne's methods got the better of her.

First the girls filled a tub with water and soap and scrubbed their dirty clothes before rinsing them and leaving them hanging to dry. They left some in the soapy water. Then they went into the parlor and engaged several girls in short conversations to establish their presence and both told one girl they were going to read before retiring early.

They quietly left the parlour with most of the girls still listening intently to radio news bulletins interrupting the musical variety shows.

Quickly collecting their coats they slipped down the basement steps, negotiated the piles of boxes and other supplies in the hallway before quietly slipping out the cellar access door, up the steps and into the night.

There was no keyed lock. There was only three slide locks on the inside. Anne quietly shut the door and expertly wedged a fist sized rock in front and under the heavy door to keep it closed and keep telltale cold air out. Kate shook her head as it was apparent that Anne had the rock there for just this reason.

City Hall was not far away. The girls were careful to leave the locale of their house quietly. Anne choose a practiced route in the shadows, by trees and along alleyways that got the girls a quarter mile from the school dormitory with minimal chance of being seen or heard.

Once they were on city streets Kate thought to herself how different they seemed in the night compared to her daytime travels. Quieter and somehow disquieting but the sensation soon passed.

As they approached City Hall the atmosphere was charged. From the moment they turned onto Jarvis Street, two blocks from the dormitory, crowds thickened, people chatted and the girls knew they could weave into the growing throng. People were loud and chatty, certainly unusual, and an almost frightening aspect in a town known for its dour demeanor.

The girls were swept along with the streams of people making their way toward City Hall and they barely spoke as they took in the unusual scene. There were many men in uniform, some of them horribly mutilated. Sadly it wasn't unusual thought Kate, except in their sheer numbers. Their shadows danced oddly in the glow of the gas lights.

Seeing so many in one place made Kate shudder at the individual horror of what she saw and because of the obvious extent of the carnage endured by these men and all the nations involved.

"Come on," urged Anne, "quick, follow me." Anne grabbed Kate's arm and started running down a side street. "This will get us close to the mayor."

Sure enough Anne's route behind City Hall brought the girls out on Bay Street into a celebratory throng moving south to gather in the centre of town awaiting an address by the mayor.

People seemed in a great hurry to go nowhere. They rushed about hugging each other, with young men snatching a kiss whenever a girl of a certain look happened by. Once the girls found a likely spot they stood rooted as they were close to the speaker's podium. However, it soon became obvious that they had the certain look that many of the young men were searching for and they barely had time to plan any escape.

Kate had kissed a boy once before. She had ducked into an equipment room during a sudden downpour at a tennis club back home. A tall boy whom see had seen but never spoken to was already there sheltering from the rain. As the rain fell they settled into introductions. A game of truth or dare forced her to accept a harmless kiss or lose face. She took the kiss and enjoyed it enough to be disappointed when the rain quickly let up and her father had come looking for her.

At City Hall things were different. So many boys grabbed the girls by their shoulders and moved in for quick kiss that puckering up seemed the only defense to soften the blow. More than once Kate had clashed teeth, and worried about a chipped tooth, but the boys were gone as fast as they appeared with another one stepping in to fill the breech.

Anne took Kate by the arm again and moved her up the wide staircase of City Hall where the steps kept the young men at bay as the difficulty of lining up a kiss and escaping without turning an ankle was very real. The girls ended up partly behind a pillar at the top of the staircase to avoid the stream of happy young men who wanted to shed some of their happiness on the sisters.

Not long after they had fled to their defensive position another commotion began nearby. From a thick crowd emerged Mayor Thomas Langdon Church. A man of slightly shorter than average stature Tom Church commanded respect with his deliberate movements, quick smile and serious reputation. Tonight he wore the ceremonial chain of office around his neck.

He moved to a podium which had been set up for his address. He was shaking hands and waving greetings as he moved down a few steps to a landing halfway up the main staircase of the great stone City Hall edifice. He held out his hands palms out appealing silently for quiet and waited patiently as the crowd simmered.

A skilled orator, he waited. Once he had virtual quiet, he waited longer still to enhance the dramatic effect and create a higher level of expectation. Anne just thought he was tongue-tied in his joy.

"Ladies and gentlemen, good citizens of Toronto; the Great War is over! The Prime Minister cabled me directly with the details most of you already know. The Germans and their allies signed a cease-fire that took effect at 11 a.m. today. We need to prepare for peacetime. Our boys will be home in the next several months as operations wind down in Europe. God save the King!"

The crowds cheered. As the mayor spoke several newspaper photographers who had been positioned in front of the podium set off their flashes and got their photos for the next day's newspapers. Mayor Church outlined the city's approach to the coming peace. He provided a bit of news, announcing a convalescent hospital for returning wounded soldiers. In fact it was already under construction but would be built with an extra wing for the expected need.

Tom Church spoke about the valor of the soldiers, their commitment to King and Country, and about Toronto's growing place in the Empire. He spoke at length about the difficulties of reorienting society and business to a peace time footing.

He wrapped up his comments and started to wade into the crowd that quickly returned to its happy frenzy.

"Well, I guess we'd be best getting back before we're missed," said Kate. Anne nodded and the two moved down the steps into the relatively quiet wake left by the mayor who was now 50 yards in front of them shaking hands, pulling the crowd with him as he patted people on the back and was otherwise officially pleased in a dignified manner.

The streets were quieter on their way back to the dormitory.

"Wait here," said Anne as she turned to race up the walk of one particularly imposing Victorian style home. She stood on the porch, tucked her head into her coat and looked around furtively.

She reached up for the huge iron doorknocker. Watching, Kate started to move up the path toward her sister to investigate why she wanted to call at this particular house. The doorknocker crashed once and then again before Anne sped down the path, a little fear in her eyes. The sound echoed in the quiet street.

"Why are you calling here?" asked Kate. Anne sped passed her and grabbed at her arm, spinning her around.

"Run, run, and hide," called Anne, beckoning with her arm.

Kate moved to follow but couldn't quite follow her sister's point and she stopped just as the door opened.

"Can I help you?" inquired a voice.

"Yes, er, no," said Kate as she turned around and looked into the most shocking blue eyes she had ever seen. The eyes belonged to a young man. "Well thank you for answering, I'm, I'm just doing a little survey on the length of time it takes people to answer their doors, at various knocking levels. Yours, I believe was a double knock?"

She fished around in her pocket for a small pencil and notebook she always kept. She pretended to make a note of the address and the double, rather than triple or single knock.

"Yes," said the confused young man. "Yes. I was just working on my ledger when you knocked, I believe it was two knocks. Did I do better or worse than most?"

"Oh, much better," said Kate, as she began to move away. "So sorry to take your time, I have many other stops to make you know."

She quickly turned down the walk and along the street. She didn't want to but she turned to look at the doorway as she had not heard the door close. The young man still stood in the doorway watching her. She turned into the next walkway, and gave the young man a little wave goodbye. She continued up the walkway until she saw the light extinguished from the first home as the door was slowly closed. Kate quickly exited the walkway and ran a few houses down the street. Kate was trying to think of what to say to her annoying sister when Anne leapt out of a nearby hedge laughing.

The giggles broke the tension and Kate began to laugh as well as she recounted her quick thinking.

The girls scurried back to the dormitory, quietly moved through the cellar door and stealthily returned to their own room, dodging a couple of girls on the way. Their coats were sure to give them away if they were caught. Anne fished out a needle and thread from her coat pocket. The girls turned their coats inside out and carried them like they were about to do some repairs with Anne flashing the needle to anyone who they encountered. As long as they weren't touched there was nothing that would give away their short absence.

Once back in the safety of their room they hastened to their tasks to further cover their time tracks. The last of the laundry was completed and hung to dry. The dormitory mother came to check on their progress with the laundry and give them their nightly bed check. They had been gone for less than two hours.

It had all been very exciting and incredibly mundane. However, Kate knew she would not soon forget the frenzy of young men, the large crowd and the happy formality of the evening. Nor would she forget her sister's seeming indifference to the rules that others followed without question and her own willingness to be led.

After a bit of whispered chatter regarding their adventure they stopped talking. Kate tried to think of instances where Anne was inexplicably busy with other tasks and did not join the rest of the girls. She easily identified several and suspected a few more before slipping into dreamless sleep, having gotten away with the harmless jaunt.

The next morning, the girls readied for breakfast before going to class.

Everything was routine and they quickly forgot about their adventure the night before while attending to their usual morning responsibilities.

The day flew by. However that evening, as they took their places at the table for the evening meal it quickly became apparent that the usual routine had been upset. Attributing it to the big news of the day before, the girls paid little attention to the glances being tossed their way.

"The mayor gave a rousing speech at City Hall last night. Kate, did he say he had been informed of the armistice by the Prime Minister?" asked the headmistress.

"I'm afraid I was doing laundry last night, ma'am and didn't hear him speak on the radio," said Kate.

"Anne, did he mention where they new hospital will be located?" asked the headmistress.

"I was with Kate working on the laundry and had no time for the radio."

The headmistress moved to the table and placed the newspaper between Kate and Anne. A photo of the mayor standing on the steps of City Hall was on the front page, and standing behind the mayor, up a small flight of stairs beside a pillar, were Kate and Anne, as plain as day, looking cold and a little wide-eyed.

The headmistress waited a moment to let the gravity of the photo sink in, "As I as saying did he say he had been in touch with the Prime Minister?"

Kate swallowed hard. This was not likely to be a very pleasant few days.

Chapter Four - 1920

"Do you Katharine Marie Wharton Lewis take this man, Charles Makepeace Elliot Stuart as your lawfully wedded husband, to have and to hold, from this day forward until death do you part?"

Kate looked at Charlie, his shocking blue eyes burning into her own. That she should meet this young man again in the street and know him only because of Anne's foolishness and then end up marrying him was hard to believe.

"I do," she said.

Charlie Stuart was a good man. He was a carpenter turned bookkeeper in a business started by his brothers. He was solid, reliable and unfortunately scarred by war.

He had the gift of being able to work with his hands, fashioning several pieces of furniture as a wedding present. He built an exquisite desk /

dressing table for his bride, inlayed with rare wood. It included several ingenious hidden drawers and compartments for safekeeping without locks. Kate had been enchanted by the detail and the attention to design elements - it was her prized possession. She wasn't even sure she could remember all the little nooks that Charlie had showed her.

He also built a huge dining room table out of solid quarter sawn oak. It too had inlay of ebony, maple and ash. In evenings after the wedding Charlie had taken on the project of building the chairs.

He also had a head for figures, so when his brothers, former building tradesmen, had begun to bid on small construction projects they turned to Charlie to work the accounting magic in addition to his day work as a carpenter. The first bids had been a lark as the brothers had been called on to build large portions of some nicer homes. But success followed and soon the brothers had organized a small construction business which had steadily grown and had gained quite an outsized reputation. The company was moving into more commercial building projects and larger, multi-use structures.

Charlie enjoyed demonstrating his wood craft but he was frustrated as most of his daytime efforts were basic construction, frames, walls, floors and ceilings. He preferred the subtlety of craft work on furniture or room detailing. As the business grew he came to spend more time on the books and financial considerations. He preferred the solitude of the books. The calm predictability of the work had been good for him. Pounding hammers had occasionally set him off.

Kate had been apprised of Charlie's war trauma by Charlie himself, who knew she would be faced with it at some time. She saw Charlie's difficulties one evening soon after she had begun being escorted home from school by him as their courtship had been formalized.

When the girls had attended the school formal where graduating students were bid goodbye, Charlie had been there and recognized her.

He asked after her studies and mentioned that his sister attended the school as a day student. They ran into each other in the street that spring as Kate went about her dormitory duties. Charlie would walk a few blocks with her and help deliver her purchases to the dormitory.

After school was finished in June, Charlie called on Kate at her parent's home in distant Burlington, 40 miles west of Toronto. He had taken a trip out there before and eventually declared his intentions. Kate accepted and Charlie was a frequent visitor that summer.

Kate's family lived in a sprawling old home. Once a cottage by the lake, then, with numerous additions and rebuilds, a single storey labyrinth of rooms, storage spaces, living quarters and distant wings for various relations.

The Lewis's were Loyalist stock, originally from New York, relocating to Ontario a generation after the Revolution. It took that long before economic conditions made for a fair and reasonable sale of their American property and goods. They settled at the head of the lake where there was a perfect natural harbour.

As the family matured one branch moved to the agricultural town of Guelph, 40 miles northwest, where some of the Lewis' commercial interests lay. By the mid-1800s the Guelph branch of the family was farming a few large acreages and acting as a purchasing agent for other farmers. They shipped their agricultural produce to their relations who ran the original family business in Hamilton.

As the family prospered they expanded a cottage property on the lakeshore to the north of the harbour and moved full time to the country property. It was in this treed place that Charlie spent time with the Lewis clan.

The courtship was particularly uneventful until eventually his luck caught up to him as tea was being served. Charlie simply sat immobile, a glassy look covering his eyes. Direct entreaties elicited no response.

It was a war reverie. Kate tried to think of a trigger and suspected a dropped cup and saucer in an adjoining room coupled with Charlie's discomfort and unfamiliarity with the house and the family. Such things were hard to avoid entirely.

The whistling kettle and clattering of the dropped china must have sounded to Charlie like shelling and he slipped away to another time and place.

He recovered himself fairly quickly, explained his difficulty and soon it was like nothing had happened. His malady was not uncommon amongst those who had served in the Great War.

Kate wanted to help and on one of their walks shortly there after, she asked him to recount his war experiences, hoping she could find the significance of the strange behavior.

"Oh Kate, the war was something," he said wistfully, his manner not betraying the obvious horrors of war. "Paris, have you ever been to Paris? No, of course not, you're too young. Well, once we were on leave in Paris, that is myself, my good friend Calvin and two other friends from our company who we'd gotten to know in basic training.

"We were staying in a small hotel on the Right Bank not far from the Paris Opera. There are a lot of small, old streets full of inexpensive hotels. It was all a bit seedy now looking back on it, but it had been recommended to us by others we knew who had been on leave. We didn't have a lot of money to spend. We wanted to see the sights.

"We had spent the day looking around art museums and various palaces before we stopped for dinner on the Left Bank, mostly because we heard it was easier to get an inexpensive meal there. It's a little more run down, and home to a couple of universities. So because of the distance, maybe a mile or two, our return to the hotel was later than we anticipated.

"We first heard the voices just before we rounded a corner north of the Opera near our hotel. They were speaking French of course, loudly. Well one voice was yelling. We were walking up the street, remarkably with no one else in sight. One voice was coming out of a doorway while another was getting out of a taxi. The taxi moved off and the first man stepped out of the doorway into view and started yelling from the sidewalk, the second saw something that we did not immediately see because he did not move toward the door.

"Of course we were down the street and could not see much but then the first man lifted a huge butcher knife above his head. It was practically a small sword and looked very substantial. He started to move toward the man in the street yelling at the top of his lungs. The street was empty except for these two and us. We were hemmed in by the buildings and our own ignorance of alternate directions to our hotel. I don't think they saw us, we were well down the street and they had other things on their minds.

"The man with the knife lunged. The second man turned and fled. He just ran right down the center of the street. The man with the knife gave chase. He turned and came right for us. He hadn't gone 20 yards when three more people came running out of a side street and fell in behind the person with the knife. Everyone was yelling. All in French. It was hard to figure out what was going on. The person being chased passed us. As he passed he said, "Help. I know his sister. Only a little."

"The man with the knife came across the street to give chase and the latest addition to the chase, those from the side street, brought up the rear.

"We shrugged at each other and started after this motley race by falling in behind the three chasers. We quickly figured out they were friends of the girl's brother who had the knife. They followed him, running down the middle of the street at full speed, trying to calm him down, in very loud voices. We were all yelling at the top of our lungs too.

"A hundred yards along, the street came to an end at a more important avenue. The quarry turned right and the man with the knife turned left and ran on for a few yards chased by the three who had come out of a side street. As we approached it was obvious our guess was correct that they were friends trying to stop him from his murderous rage. We slowed immediately and turned right casually hoping to catch up to what appeared to be one of our own in a little spot of trouble. We never did find him. When we looked back down the street the guy with the knife had disappeared. We all shrugged wondering if the drama was real and we returned to our hotel without incident."

Charlie had many stories of the unusual, bizarre and curious relating to his time overseas. Often the stories took place on leave or during a quiet time on duty. He always managed to deflect direct requests of more horrible events into a recounting of a funny story or some tidbit about a comrade or a little bit of third party excitement.

He related these stories whenever asked of his time in Europe. It was several years later before Kate realized he never spoke of the real battles of his tour of duty. She heard stories about all the waiting the soldiers did and let the lack of battle stories lull her into believing there was little to tell when it came to battle. Still, she knew of Charlie's shell shock and would occasionally interrupt a reverie.

With marriage came a home. Charlie and his brothers did a wonderful job updating an old building they bought north east of the University. It had been a stable but lay unused for several years when Charlie found it and began renovations. They lived with Charlie's family for a year while construction was completed.

Kate had little trouble with the arrangement as she had just finished several years at the boarding school. She took a great interest in the home as she had the experience of her own family's sprawling cottage. She located rooms, introduced conveniences, or at least maintained the space necessary to include them in the future as her mother-in-law had a very definite and frugal approach to life. However, when something was necessary, such as laundry facilities, Kate was berated into sparing no expense in return for quality.

The children came quickly straining the space in their little abode. Two boys William, the eldest, in 1920, Charles Junior, in 1921. Helen was born in 1923, followed by Charlotte in 1925, and Mary in 1930. Fred was born in 1935.

The stage was set. The Stuarts lives would be entwined in events, push the agenda and reflect the century. They would do it consciously, individually, and sometimes as part of a greater movement of ideas and desires, unaware of what they would ultimately create.

The ultimate in modern, the 20th century, with all its technological innovations, changing attitudes, pressures and ideas was theirs to shape.

Chapter Five - 1920s

The potential economic powerhouse of North America was realized with the end of the Great War. Much of the industrial superstructure of the continent was built to support the war effort and could now be capitalized upon in peacetime.

Immigrants, displaced by years of war in Europe, poured into North America from Italy, England and Germany.

Dreams of automobiles and their siren song of freedom largely fuelled the industrial machine. Many technological advances led to higher productivity on the farm and meant that even more people flocked to the cities.

The rise of organized labour along with huge gains in productivity provided people with more free time, time to enjoy their families or to take on hobby pursuits. The union movement went largely unchecked as companies found it more profitable to buy off their labour problems rather than face shutdowns where no profits were being made.

As the 1920s rolled on prosperity was everywhere and it seemed without end. Great fortunes were made, professional sports took hold of the public imagination and celebrated athletes competed with film stars for the fruits of fame. It was a kind of fame that had been unknown a generation earlier. Fuelled by growing media conglomerates, by breathless newsreels, radio broadcasts and fawning newspapers - fame found those who craved it, and some who did not.

It was an age of innocence, where fame seemed the ultimate desire, and newspapers and newsreels firmly planted accomplishment and character in the popular imagination. In this hurly burly, before disappointment created a general cynicism with fame and hype, one figure attained an almost mythic status – George Herman "Babe" Ruth.

Perhaps the first person to know fame on a dangerous scale, Babe Ruth was a Baltimore roughneck; a child of a broken marriage. He learned to play baseball at an all-boys Catholic school for truants.

Once freed of the shackles of his youth and sold out of Baltimore to Boston and then into New York, a city fast becoming the center of the universe, the exuberant Ruth led the parade that became known as the Roaring Twenties.

Those years of almost unbridled economic growth which fuelled the expansion of the young continent, saw huge steel works in Pittsburgh and Hamilton. They saw the flowering of skyscrapers as high as the sky. They saw the birth of new industries and mediums such as movies and radio.

It was all doomed as an economic bubble swelled along side the exuberant lifestyles to fuel the appetite for more and more excess. An experiment with the prohibition of alcohol proved to have consequences of its own as it fuelled the rise of organized crime. Eventually the experiment of prohibiting alcohol slipped into history as the cure was deemed worse than the disease. The experiment shaped public policy on vice for decades.

By the late 1920's the problems with prohibition were becoming obvious. In Canada it was making and killing fortunes as some brewers and distillers were able to capitalize on the lack of competition to build empires while others fought to serve the underground speakeasy trade in the United States.

At this time Kate and Charlie had three of their four children in school. Mary was on the way and Fred was not yet a consideration. The family had some money and had moved uptown to a lovely home in one of Toronto's northern neighbourhoods at Hogg's Hollow, a natural dell a few miles north of downtown.

The girls attended nearby Loretto Academy. The boys St. Michael's College school.

Kate hired a regular day nurse to help her with the children. Always active in the church, Kate was organizing socials and cajoled Charlie to arrange for favourable terms on construction of a manse for the local priests. As one of the leading families in the parish and owners of a major business, there was much coming and going at the Stuart household.

Everything was looking rosy for the Stuart clan. Business was strong. Yet Charlie sensed a chill. It was almost as if his innate sense of self-preservation demanded that he look over his shoulder. As book keeper for the family business he mentioned it to his brothers who could barely find time between projects to consider his concerns.

"Several of our customers have asked us to take on their projects on credit, they say their money is all tied up in other ventures," Charles told his two brothers. "They are offering reasonable terms but I'm uncomfortable with the arrangement."

"Do we need to provide these terms in order to get contracts and keep busy?" asked Charles' oldest brother.

"No," Charlie said with a nod. "You are right. We can be more accommodating say with a 30 day payment deadline, but we don't need to offer long term credit. That just gets us into a whole administration effort that we don't want to pay for."

"So that settles it then, offer the extended payment terms but decline the credit terms citing high costs and our own cash flow requirements. If business falls off significantly then we'll think on this again."
The construction company didn't experience any real loss of business. Entrepreneurs simply got their credit from other sources, dangerously expanding the bubble economy. However, Stuart Construction continued to be paid and contracts for new buildings were at an all time high when the bubble burst. It's first portent was the crash of the New York Stock Exchange in late October 1929.

While only a few on-going projects were stopped, sometimes with work only half completed, it was the lack of new projects coming in which worried Charlie. Continuing financial shocks, government policy and a lack of confidence in the future economy hampered business growth for years to come. Personally he had taken steps to reduce his family exposure to the down turn and the Stuart family and family business survived with only minor blemishes to their financial concerns.

With business down and a new baby, Mary was born in 1930, the family became even more active in the church. With five small children Kate brought in some help to manage the day to day affairs of her family. Always active in the church she also organized free meals for local families hit hard by the depression, often disguising them as church socials. She made sure those in need took home the carefully created excess food supplies.

One of the local priests, Father David O'Riley, cottoned on to what Kate was doing and helped her with the organization. He was a frequent visitor to the Stuart home. He knew the Stuart family from its involvement in the parish and the Stuart children well from school where he taught music, literature and religion.

Father David helped Kate by canvassing local businesses for small donations that could be used for a stew or soup, as well as other necessary supplies for the church events. A trained pianist Father David often led sing-alongs at these socials. So popular did they become that by 1934 they were a Thursday night regular event.

Chapter Six - 1920s

Harry Derch, was unnaturally tall and generously built. He had played a bit of football in his college years as a tackle on both sides of the ball. Seeing the rise of radio and quickly grasping its potential he had opened a radio station in Hamilton in 1913. It had been a technological marvel which meant it broke down all the time. However, by the early 20s the station was at the cutting edge of broadcast technology and was quite a commercial success.

He broadcast mostly sporting events sponsored by local businesses. Between the sports was music, much of it live broadcasts either in studio or from the local concert or dance halls as technological improvements allowed.

Proprietors of these venues, initially skeptical about the radio broadcasts eating into their attendance figures, were surprised when interest in attending the live performances shot up due to the exposure on radio.

People quickly figured out the broadcast schedule - if there was a game, it was likely on the radio, if there wasn't a game it would be music and regular news shows. He even had a regular Friday night interview with local government officials on how sanitation worked, fire calls, water, and even road maintenance. The radio broadcast a signal pretty much noon through 9 p.m.

His service was popular and it was all local. Businesses clamored to purchase advertising spots, most of which were simply mentions or quick avocations by the station announcers.

Derch had heard of some stations In the United States that were broadcasting radio plays but it all seemed like too much work, and very expensive besides, having to have all those actors, equipment and specialists for sound effects. He did hear from a service which tied stations together to have a larger reach but he was skeptical of the financial arrangements and preferred his local advertisers. He was a bit fearful of outside control, giant amounts of equipment and other impositions on his domain.

"Oh my what a log jam that studio must be," he'd think to himself. The Derch radio studio consisted of a small room, large enough for maybe four people, radio plays just weren't money makers. Sports was.

McMaster University and high school sports were his big draw, as they provided him with what he needed to broadcast the away games to keep fans interested when the teams were out of town. He lined up sponsors and fired up his transmitter at game time. Derch also broadcast some professional games and even local senior leagues as long as he could find a sponsor – which wasn't too difficult, if the price was right.

Derch knew he would be drawn into the future of radio which likely meant a network affiliation. He was already getting calls to broadcast some of the shows like Tom Mix, that were gaining popularity in other markets.

While the future beckoned he was locked in the present and made a good bit of money essentially following the exploits of local teams, which was something of a hobby for him anyway.

For games out of town he'd get a runner to bring him the tickertape description of each half inning or time in possession of the football and then he and his eldest son Charlie Derch, would reconstruct the inning putting together an occasionally compelling account to match the bare bones details of hits, outs and score from far-flung Buffalo, Rochester or Toronto. Football games received the same treatment.

He learned pretty quickly to keep the inning alive until results of the next half inning were available. More than once he'd managed three outs before getting the ticker description of a long, high scoring inning. He would have to invent rain delays, disturbances in the stands, and injuries which were forgotten, just to keep the game alive until new information reached him.

He had to be much less creative when local games were on the schedule as many of his listeners might actually have attended. More than once his credibility had taken a hit when he was a bit too descriptive.

The games filled up the hours, kept the locals tuned in and provided as many opportunities for sponsor spots as they could reasonably put in.

Charlie wasn't a natural announcer but he understood the technical side to the business and besides, Harry thought , he worked cheap, happy to help out his father.

Chapter Seven - 1930

David O'Riley was an accomplished and capable musician but couldn't settle on a path for his life. Having escaped the horrors of the Great War by being too young to serve, he travelled to Europe as a young man. He led a bohemian existence for several years, living cheaply, taking short term or odd jobs and playing piano for money when he could. He wanted something but he wasn't sure what it was.

Inspired by the great cathedrals of Chartres, Paris, Rheims, and Cologne and without the material ambition of many of his peers he gravitated towards the church. The church welcomed him as it tried to rebuild in the aftermath of war.

Many of his contemporaries became rich in the fertile business growth of the 20s but David did not lament his choice. He took on teaching to indulge his love of music and literature and inwardly tried to grasp the mysteries of Catholicism which always seemed to elude him, while outwardly training steadily for his vocation.

Originally from a small Halifax family, once ordained he was posted to Toronto where he took up his parish duties with gusto spending much of his extra time with several large families in the parish. These families were sure to become the backbone of the local church community as the years progressed.

"Good morning Mrs. Stuart," said the priest sticking his head through the back porch door after a quick knock. "I thought I heard someone in here. I hope I find you as well as the weather?"

It was high and glorious June. Flowers were bursting, vegetable gardens planted and bits of green were showing more than just expectation. The strawberry patch looked especially promising. The Stuart children were all atwitter with summer and a release from school duties only days away.

"Ah Father, please come in, the children will be pleased you're here. Kate Stuart moved a chair so Father David could sit at the large kitchen table, which served more as a food preparation station than an eating area. "Billy and Charlie said they were waiting for you to help them build a tree home, or some such thing. Apparently you've discussed this arrangement."

"Before you're off to your construction duties sit and have tea – I've just made some crescent rolls," she said as she stooped and slid a large tray of steaming buns out of the oven and placed them on the table to cool.

He reached to prize one from the tray.

"Just wait," she said with a smile and a mock whack on his reaching hand, "Honestly you are as bad as the children. Let them cool."

Drawn by the aroma of creamy freshness of the newly baked bread, first

Billy, then Charlie then Charlotte, one after another were drawn magically into the kitchen hoping for a bite. And one by one she sent them off to do some chore or another before any of the rolls would be handed out.

The priest accepted his tea and waited only a moment before his hostess indicated the crescents were sufficiently cooled and he could take a bite of bread.

The children returned breathlessly one by one as they completed their assigned tasks and earned their reward.

"Okay," said Mrs. Stuart, "Go and check on baby Mary and then you can have a bun. Be quick and be quiet."

The boys ran off arguing who would be fastest.

"It's funny but they never argue who is quieter," said Mrs. Stuart.

The priest smiled and supped his tea. He would have liked a bit of milk and sugar but was too polite to ask.

"Oh pardon me, Father, would you like a little sugar for your tea?"

The priest looked pensive and then broke down, accepting a half teaspoon of sugar willingly. He topped up his cup with a bit of milk also on offer from a small pitcher Kate produced. His quick stir of the contents produced enough tinkling to sound like a small dinner bell.

"Have you seen the paper?" asked Kate as she put a copy of the Daily Star in the table for the priest to peruse.

"Ah thank you but I'd rather spend my time here speaking to you, unless of course you have things to attend to? If Mr. Stuart has finished with it, I'll take it with me after I'm done with my obligations to the boys and their project."

The boys bounded back in claiming in unison that each had won the challenge, and that Mary was smelly but still sleeping.

"Okay I've a babe to clean up and you three have some business outside no doubt," said Mrs. Stuart as she swept out of the room to the noisy bustle of bun battles.

Chapter Eight - 1931

"Come Father, this way," Billy yelled as he ran on ahead.

"Yes, it's this way," parroted little Charlie, barely being able to contain his excitement.

The priest was directed to a copse of trees in a deep corner of the yard. Stepping among the trees he saw a rudimentary work area with two saw horses, bits of lumber and some scraps of metal sheeting littering the ground.

"Father, we need some help getting started. If you could help us we could do the rest," implored Billy.

"Yeah, just get us started and we can do the rest," said little Charlie.

The priest surveyed the area.

"What about your father, have you asked him?"

"He said he was too unsteady to get into the tree. He said if you would help it is alright to go ahead and build. He said we could use any scrap in the shed."

Cornered, Father David, picked up a hammer. "Well first we have to build steps up the trunk."

The three set to work. First thin strips of wood were nailed into the tree as a ladder. Then the priest climbed into the tree and had the boys hand him several two by fours which he fashioned into a frame for a platform. Filling in the frame produced a sturdy platform secured to the main truck and lying between two large branches, while supported and steadied by a third.

"Pretty good work for one day," said the priest, with a hand on his hip. To avoid hitting himself with the hammer he used the back of the other hand to wipe a bit of sweat from his forehead.

"Yes Father, it looks real fine," said Billy surveying the project and mimicking the priest's wipe of his forehead. "What do we do next?"

"I think we need some walls and a roof, but it's going to have to wait a few days as I'm busy at school. Once the summer starts I'll have a bit more time. You should begin to collect up some wood we can use for walls and see if there is some metal sheeting left over from the hot house your father built."

True to his word the priest arrived again the next week and met the boys in the back yard. They went straight to work on the walls and a second smaller platform which would be placed higher in the tree. This time Father David set Billy to laying it out on the ground as they could haul it

56

up to the first platform once it was built. Charlie helped by hauling and fetching pieces of wood where needed.

The second platform took a bit of skill as it surrounded the main trunk and with the addition of three foot walls and a roof made a wonderful crow's nest for keeping watch over much of the immediate neighbourhood.

In fact the boys had worked out much of the detail, and with the priest's help had managed to hammer some of the frame together by the time they finished for the evening.

Going out to survey their work the next morning, Charlie came running back, "Look at the house, look at the house!"

It took everyone a few minutes to guess that he meant the tree house. Billy could not believe his eyes - the circular platform was completed in two half-circle pieces which fit together ingeniously and even had drill holes lined up where reinforcing screws could be added to hold the edifice together. It was supported underneath by strong wooden poles running from the platform downwards about 10 feet into the tree trunk.

One of the more prominent poles near the main entrance bore some dark wood inlay with the same numbers as the main house followed by 1/2.

"Wow, it's a miracle," said Kate. "Somebody had put in a lot of effort."

"It wasn't me," said Charlie.

In the ensuing weeks old sheet metal walls and a roof sprung up on the main platform creating a perfect hideaway for adventurous boys.

Father David made many trips to the Stuart tree house, stopping by to pitch in and to measure the progress with Katharine and Charles Stuart. On one occasion the elder Charles seemed miffed that the boys, and by extension the priest, were using some choice pieces of loose lumber but he quickly retreated into a compliment on the quality of construction and the safety measures the priest had thought to incorporate.

Mrs. Stuart managed to feed the priest after most of his visits, usually with a bit of soup or some baking she was doing, in between caring for her growing brood.

Of course the family regularly attended church on Sunday. Mrs. Stuart took to the Catholic Women's League which organized socials and fund raisers as well as any local bits of charity work that needed doing. Charles was peripherally engaged in these events, usually dragged into them against his will by Katherine, though he did take to regularly attending a mid-week mass.

Father David found himself constantly running into one of the Stuarts, either Billy or Charlie at school where he taught, or after mass, or at a social event. More and more he found himself drawn to their home. He was a favourite of the two elder boys, and he doted on the two and then three girls Helen, Charlotte and Mary.

When the elder Charles couldn't take the boys to see a barnstorming Yankee baseball team come through Toronto in 1931 it was Father David who took them. When Mrs. Stuart was called away on social work it was Father David who minded the children, playing games, and teaching them piano. As the children grew they all had a soft spot for the priest, considering him almost a member of the family - like a stray uncle.

Chapter Nine - 1933

Despite the economic downturn, most people believed it was a temporary setback. The ground had shifted on expectations but there was always a positive believe that relief was right around the corner.

In the Stuart household the early years of the Depression still held the promise of endless possibilities. It was the obsequiousness of youth that helped maintain spirits in an ever darkening economy.

As Mary started to grow and became less smelly. With the added responsibilities faced by Kate the priest seemed to be around more often to pitch in. The family construction business still managed to keep the Stuarts busy and employed though Toronto's boomtown days were gone.

Buildings that had gone up too fast to count were usually completed but new projects became topics of local conversation - especially the new Arena built by hockey entrepreneur Conn Smythe.

Smythe engaged the Stuart firm to do some of the finishing work on his hockey palace Maple Leaf Gardens. Hockey had been growing in popularity and Mr. Smythe cannily realized he could capitalize on its growth, knock out any competition coming from the Toronto St. Patrick's former ownership group, and make a tidy sum renting the Garden's colossal space for other events.

Even after that fateful day, October 29, 1929 when all the optimism of a developing continent crashed with the financial markets, Conn Smythe carried on building his monument within sight of his team's former home on Mutual Street, east of Yonge and north of Dundas.

The crash of the markets unnerved investors who held their money. Without spending on products, jobs were shed and then without workers earning money to buy more goods, the economy spiralled down further.

By 1931 the economy had bottomed out but showed no signs of picking back up. Charles and Katherine worried about their future but spent most of the time with the day to day tasks necessary in a family of five children. The family had not suffered particularly – there had been a few minor investments that turned sour but with the business of paying a mortgage and building a family there wasn't much money to invest. Charles' caution and his lack of resources had saved him from engaging in the speculation of the late 1920s.

As the economy contracted in the early 1930s there wasn't much work save on large government or institutional projects which were been built for a fraction of their pre-depression costs.

The family business turned in the direction of God. New churches were being built all over the Toronto region and the Stuart Construction Company fit in perfectly with the trend. Charles took his natural inclination to the spiritual to new heights at this time. He first attended mass to drum up business and often to speak to the priest to show his commitment to the faith, but soon he attended because he had the time to enjoy the peace an hour's service afforded him.

Father David only rarely celebrated the midday mass that Charles frequented due to his duties at the school. On occasion the two did cross paths and shared stories of the little Stuarts.

In these Depression years Katherine often used leftovers from the evening meal to fashion a soup or stew that she made available to daily workers who often showed up at the side door of the big old house. She did not know but Father David would send tramps, men with no prospects who had been turned out of their jobs, to the Stuart home which he had marked with a slash to the side of the main gate.

The transients insisted on performing some task to gain their meal and Katherine, having become used to their need for dignity saved outdoor tasks for just that purpose. Having split some logs and stacked the resulting firewood these men would gratefully partake in a hearty bowl or two of stew usually at a picnic table by the side of the house or even in the ramshackle kitchen when the weather was inhospitable.

The children were well aware of this but knew enough to never talk about it nor approach the men. Katharine was charitable but also cautious. She had heard tales of more than one of these transients unpredictably rising up in anger, shattered by years of living hand to mouth as their hope for the future trickled away. Sometimes the sight of children set them off, so gossip had indicated.

A soft knock, almost apologetic, at the side door was almost expected on a June evening.

"Ma'am?" said a man in a once sharp suit, now missing a button and noticeably worn by hard wear with tattered cuffs probably due to its first incarnation. He clutched his hat. "Understand you need some wood split?" he asked, hoping he hadn't been beaten to the work.

"Yes, I'm glad you are here – I'm always afraid of running out. There are several large logs just out back. Can you split three of them and stack them with the others at the side of the house, and if you'd like I'll have soup and sandwiches ready for you when you're done."

"Yes Ma'am, that would be good. I'd be most grateful," he said knowing not to inquire about other work that would be saved for the next in need who came by.

And so passed another evening at the Stuart household.

A few times a week Father David would happen by to check up on the men he had sent to the home. There he would often share a cup of tea with them before they got on their way where he would offer any news of jobs both short term and perhaps longer.

Some of these men were able to hook on to jobs lasting several weeks or even months during which they could save some money, even send it back to their families, or stash it away to get through the leaner winter months when labour jobs became scarce.

He would often check in on 10 year old Helen, eight year old Charlotte and a rapidly growing Mary. Helen would usually be engaged in chores around the home or be practicing piano while dreaming of dancing. Charlotte similarly played piano and would be playing with little Mary or showing her the basics of caring for neighbourhood babies.

Baby Fred was not yet a consideration. Of course when he was born he was more work than any of them, but as the baby they indulged him and he believed that their indulgence was his natural due.

In later years all the children could conjure up memories of the priest with Fred having only the vaguest memories as he was the youngest.

Memories of the priest were shared among all the siblings. Some were direct reminiscences and others built up from family stories of his doings, creating an impression of memory.

He was with the Stuarts often at big events and almost ubiquitous in the day to day. He often spent time with the younger children. As they got a bit older the two boys lost interest in the priest's visits, as he naturally gravitated to the two youngest children, though Father David might still engage with the older two boys to fix a machine or get a homework question answered.

64

Chapter Ten - 1940

One shared memory was a vivid recollection of the priest sitting at the large dining table for what must have been a large Sunday dinner. He was sitting beside and speaking to Charles Sr. when he turned to Kate and asked what she thought of this Hitler man in Germany.

The war had started but the Stuarts knew little about the reality of Germany and Europe. Helen, who was just finishing school, quickly offered her opinion saying she could not believe the stories of Mr. Hitler's cruelty but rather believed he was setting Germany on a proper path. Father David's kindly smile faded when Helen interjected.

"Evil is often dressed up in pretty clothes and speaks in soothing tones," he said. "Beware Helen, the facts are often not what they seem, and are often dressed up to give you a false impression of reality."

The subject changed and the shared moment receded into memories. Father David's comments were remembered as later events suggested his insight at the time was almost a prophecy. Father David was a gentle and steadying presence in the lives of the Stuart clan.

Charles Sr. was put out by the exchange and more than annoyed that Helen had interrupted her mother. He did nothing to mask his irritation and kept a sour look on his face, annoyed that a mere child would answer a question so obviously beyond her ability to comprehend. Helen was silent and hurt by his reaction.

Charles Sr. had a grudging respect for Father David. He would routinely engage the priest in deep discussions usually started at the Sunday dinner table and then carried on with a glass of port in the sitting room. Charles Sr. was a deeply reflective man and he used these discussions on religion, philosophy and even government and current events to descend deeper into the church – taking to mass more and more until it became a morning ritual after he retired from day-to-day involvement with Stuart Construction.

Father David seemed anxious to share in the fellowship of a large family. He was more often at the house in the after school hours for a tea and biscuit with Kate or Beth, the family's helping hand, who was one minute a nanny, next a serving girl and the next a washer women.

Father David helped Beth secure her employment with the family and soon she was all but a part of it like the priest himself. She was expected at Sunday dinner but spent most of it stirring, ladling or serving. At first this seemed normal however in later years it became evident she simply wasn't comfortable at the big formal table and would eat on the run only to join the family for sweets and tea after dinner.

The children were not privy to Beth's origins other than her connection to Father David. In later years Helen passed on what she knew as she and

Beth were about the same age.

Beth's parents had been members of the church but they had died in a car accident. They had been older when she was born and she had no other family. According to Helen, her mother wanted to adopt Beth but Charles said she was better suited to domestic duties and that some independence was better for her long term prospects than trying to fit into an unfamiliar family situation.

In the end Charles, who rarely put his foot down, insisted that Beth be taken in as a domestic servant while Kate treated her virtually as her own child. Charles did not object to the details of the arrangement and apparent compromise as Beth was too young at about 16 to be fully independent and too old to be adopted into a family as a full-fledged member.

By the time she joined the Stuart family both older boys William and Charles had gone off to war so there was space enough for her and with little Fred only just starting school, there was plenty for her to do.

After the war she met Thomas Herrington, a young man new to Toronto, who ended up there upon returning from Europe and finding his parents both dead during the interval.

Beth and Thomas set up house not far from the Stuart family home in 1947 and started their own family. As the years wore on Beth still came by the house three times a week to help Kate keep the house operational. As the Stuart children left home there was less and less to do but the routine stayed the same – Kate initially kept Beth's wages up to help her and her family along.

She paid her the same wages for 40 years until she died, even though for many years they had long since stopped doing much but changing the beds and sweeping out the kitchen. It seems the purchasing power of the dollar declined at pretty much the same rate as the workload in the Stuart household.

Chapter Eleven - 1940

William enlisted first. Bill was 20 years old, had the desire to match his father's service in the Great War, see the world and make his peace with it.

So off to war he went. First by train to Halifax where he boarded a giant troop ship leaving for Europe in the late winter of 1941. With his family background in construction he was assigned to a front line logistics and supply unit of engineers which built anything necessary and was tasked with being as mobile as possible.

They were supposed to join the front line troops once a position had been determined but practicality meant that they were with those troops to help select bivouac locations and consider their options for supply of materials. More than once in the early stages of the invasion of France problems arose as those without training decided to pick unsuitable locations for their base of operations. The unit travelled as front line troops. They were similarly armed and ready to pitch in - even if they were often placed by their commanders where fighting was unlikely to occur or be light.

Reality had these engineering units rigging up necessary bits to make commandeered buildings habitable. They rarely built on the go as the front seemed to move in fits and starts. Existing buildings were often abandoned and could be used, with a little work, for command quarters, hospitals and equipment locations.

Often the engineering units were used to scout out likely locations and report on the integrity of blast damaged buildings.

Basic training in Canada consisted of a little marching, a little shooting and a lot of learning to take orders. Bill melted in with his platoon mates and soon the group was thick together and ready to plunder all the experiences that occasional independence of leave and aging charm of Europe could offer.

Their unit was formed up in basic training as those with a similar background to Bill were tossed together. Ed Franklin and Francis Edwards were naturally suspicious of each other at first but soon became bookends of a group including Bill and a childhood acquaintance of his named Johnny Posser. Posser was lighthearted and took very little seriously. He did voices, mimicking his mates and the officers, as well as locals and anyone who crossed his path. He had attended St. Mike's in Toronto with Bill and worked summers with Bill for Stuart Construction.

Of course the boys' CO insisted on calling everyone by their last names so much to everyone's confusion Ed became Franklin, and Frank became Edwards, Bill became Stuart and Johnny Posser became Poser because nobody could take him seriously. Johnny would descend into a pose like Rodin's The Thinker, pretending to be deep in thought, whenever anyone referred to him as 'The Poser.'

To the officers the name meant he was not a model soldier and to his mates it referred to his lack of reverence for the seriousness of war. Everybody took their duties seriously and even Johnny, deep down knew when to kid and when to get serious so most of those in the unit appreciated his lighthearted nature.

Long after the war, stories abounded about these men and how confusion saved them from punishment for their hi-jinks or how they covered for each other on and off duty. In later years John Posser would still do a bang up impression of their CO while among friends at the Legion. He would occasionally do both Ed and Frank, but only at particular times as both of whom did not survive the war. Bill encouraged John to do their friends because, he would say with a wry and somewhat distant expression, it was all he had left of them.

Bill would stare into space for long periods when their names came up at family events, sometimes even excusing himself from the table quite upset at the memory of his great friends. It was not the traumatic stress suffered by his father, but a drifting reverie of very vivid memories called up by events. Bill always sat with John Posser in his visits to the Legion, and often could be seen in silent conversation with him between sips of salted beer.

Chapter Twelve - 1941

"Hitler has stopped the bombing of London," said Father David. "I wonder if they will start up again after Christmas?"

England had survived the blitz, but nobody knew it yet. Canada was at war and an uncertain air hung over every task as Canada mobilized.

Men were volunteering for service. Even a 36 year-old Father David expressed some interest in volunteering as a Chaplin. That, however was not to be.

Father David and another priest had both asked the Bishop to be considered for overseas duty. The other priest was a little younger, spoke three languages and seemed likely to get the post. Uncertainty hung in the air. The colour seemed to have gone out of everyday things.

"Very little seems to have changed," said Helen to her mother one early spring evening. "We are at war, but except for the talk, the metal and rubber drives, and the newsreels you would never know it."

Father David was waiting on his transfer request as the winter of 1941 was turning into spring. He still managed a busy life ministering to church members, organizing various drives, and school efforts.

He often ran little errands which gave him the opportunity to drop in on parishioners and engage them in lengthier conversations than a quick goodbye would yield after Sunday mass.

He volunteered to take a casserole which had been delivered to the church to a young family who had just had twins. The days were warming up and much of winter's accumulation of snow had melted but the nights remained cold. That evening a few flurries danced in the cold air.

He wheeled his car down a dark street looking for the address. The steaming casserole rested on the passenger seat beside him, wrapped in a blanket. Small homes ran down both sides of the street. A few houses further down, the street took a sharp left turn to pick up where more homes lay around the corner. After the turn there were no homes on the right hand side of the street where the land fell off into a ravine with a creek running along the bottom.

As he approached the turn at the end of the line of homes he finally spied an address and realized he was still some distance from his goal.

Frustrated at his inability to see the house numbers in the dark, he impatiently sped up to get around the corner to resume his search. As he entered the turn a small animal ran in front of his car. He jammed on the brakes.

Immediately he began to slide out of the turn. Before he could react his car had slid off the road and down an embankment into the ravine. What would soon be called 'black ice' had formed as the afternoon sun went down refreezing the sun melted remains of winter's snow but looking like a wet spot on the blacktop road on which it rested.

The car bounced once and dove down the steep hill. It careened off one tree and then hit a large oak head on.
The noise of the crash faded away and all that remained was the soft sound of the car's warm fluids leaking into the cold ground.

Nobody witnessed the crash, but some in their nearby homes looked out at the street after hearing the thump. A man living in the corner house looked out at the turn - at first seeing nothing amiss. Then he noticed the tire tracks leading off the street and disappearing. He quickly got his coat and ran. As he approached he could see the ghostly shimmer of steam rising through the bare trees.

Father David was dead.

Years later Fred called it "the most traumatic time of my life." The close connection the priest had to the family and the tragic circumstances mixed in with the uncertainty of war and its result, devastated the Stuart clan.

To the Stuarts, it felt that Father David was the first casualty of the war. Even though his death had nothing to do with war or its preparation, his death was the first of many that would change the world around.

Later that evening Charles Sr. rose to answer a knock at the door, muttering something about not expecting anyone and it being too late for deliveries.

Sitting at the piano, practising his scales in a nearby room, Fred could see him in profile standing at the door. Charles blanched momentarily and then grabbed onto the doorway for support. Fred turned on his bench, alarmed at his father's distress. Charles straightened himself up – murmured a few more questions and then thanked the messenger with a forced smile.

Fred looked at him as he made his way back to his favourite chair in the sitting room. He stared straight ahead and then held his head in his hands. Fred approached.

"What's the matter father? Was it terribly bad news?" Fred asked with no idea how bad it could be.

"Fetch your mother for me please."

Happy to have something to do Fred went to his mother who was playing cards with two of his sisters and told her that father wanted her to join him in the sitting room.

"A messenger just delivered him some bad news, but he wouldn't say, he just asked for you."

Fearing one of her parents had died, Kate steeled herself during the walk to the front of the house.

She entered the sitting room asking what news had arrived. My father asked her to sit down as he rose to close the door. There was silence.

The girls had followed their mother along, curious to the news, and stood with Fred down the hall waiting for an indication that they would be let into the secret. A few moments of silence were followed by a loud "Katherine!" and a soft thump.

The door opened to Charles doubled over, on hand on the door knob and the other still cradling Kate who lay partly crumpled on the floor. She had fainted without so much as a word, only a little squeak of surprise, a sound so faint that only Charles had heard it.

"Please get me a glass of water and help me with your mother."

Charlotte hurried back to the kitchen and Mary, Helen and Fred gingerly moved their mother onto the large chesterfield. That task done Fred asked his father for the news. He considered a moment, then realizing the children would have to know, told them as matter-of-factly as he had apparently told Kate.

It had a similar effect. Fred felt as if his six years immediately doubled, he was stoic. Helen froze and then began to weep. Mary, who was perhaps closest to the priest, fainted into the arms of Charles with the same squeak of surprise as her mother. Charles put her gently into his favourite chair.

With Helen crying and Kate and Mary unconscious, young Fred calmly asked his father for details. As Charles related them Helen began to sob.

The house was sombre for weeks.

In fact it never really recovered. Spring came and Kate only managed a cursory planting in her garden. Only later did everyone realize she had planted vegetables and spruced the perennial plants but added none of her customary annuals or other colour that so pleased her.

Slowly Kate took to spending more time with her own mother staying away for days at a time. Charles completed his retreat into the church. With the older boys away and the priest's visits gone, the Stuart home took on an almost ethereal quality; a sleepy, routine, glassy reflection as each day's necessary tasks were walked through to their completion.

The oldest brothers Bill and Charles had both laid plans for taking part in the coming war, the greatest adventure of their generation. And one they would not miss. Charles had unexpectedly taken their side when it came to enlisting.

The shock of the priest's death, the pure finality of it, fired Charles to pull every string he could to ensure his boys would serve their country with dignity and in relative safety.

Chapter Thirteen - 1942

Over the years Bill let out bits and pieces of his time during the war. Mostly for public consumption and enough to satisfy their curiosity so they would not press him. It was only years later that he related any of the daily dose of violence, almost as if Bill was cleansing himself of bad memories as he grew old and realized nothing would change them or soothe his pain.

At first he leaned heavily on the amusing anecdotes of life overseas, the Canadians as strangers in a not-so-odd land, one that was more like home than home was.

"Boy did we have fun. England was wonderful; ancient buildings, tradition and history on every street corner, money in our pockets and girls everywhere."

"Street corners were likely to have the same names as two streets that crossed in Toronto. It was magic. It was a slightly dodgier version of home but without the crosshairs of family and civil behavior holding us back."

"After six months of training our platoon was granted a week of leave. Ed, Frank, Johnny and I decided to see London."

"We took in most of the sites, Westminster Abbey, The Tower of London, Buckingham Palace, Trafalgar Square and the inside of many a pub."

"On our last day in London the boys and I were edgy. Not looking forward to heading back to our camp at Salisbury the next day we were determined to have a great, good and memorable time."

"After a little more site-seeing we made our way back to a pub just north of Leicester Square. The White Horse was just far enough off of Piccadilly to have gone to seed, but close enough to maintain an air of respectability for patrons who needed such reassurances."

"There was still a lot of bomb damage around but while buildings were abandoned and some were under repair, all of the debris had been cleaned up. People were concerned that the bombing could resume until the Jerrys took on the Russians, then that fear slipped away."

As the years lengthened Bill would tell his own family of some of the horrors he had seen - the heartbreak of jerry-rigged hospitals, wandering civilians with their homes destroyed and their lives rendered void by war, or orphans too young to even know to beg for help and too frightened to try. Bill would never elaborate other than to say someone in his unit would help these souls, but never with any detail of how.

He did not speak of battle, though it was mostly the immediate aftermath of engagements where he found himself. The brutal back and forth was taking place just out of his sight, just over the horizon, where the loud noises were masking the shrieks and cries for help. He had seen things he could not reconcile, could not shake from his conscious mind but he learned to divide his mind and hold them aside from his everyday, peacetime mental exercises and needs.

As he aged, Bill spoke to those who asked, of the shock of sudden death of an acquaintance. The soldiers rarely made friends other than those they made in their naiveté as they soon realized that too often they were separated from them either by orders, circumstance or death.

Chapter Fourteen - 1943

As fighting men, colonials and Canadians, Ed, Frank, Bill and Johnny, in their leave from duty, had found the right place. In fact they had been there a few days before and chatted up some of the local shop girls stopping with their friends for a quick drink before heading home for the evening.

Not having found a better place during their London sojourn the boys decided to head back to the White Horse on their last night. At least they had felt welcome before.

As soon as they got settled the barmaid remembered them and filled their glasses up a little beyond the publican's necessary legal limit. Frank offered to go to the bar and get their second round and struck up a conversation with her, which he continued after delivering the beer to his mates.

He found she came to London with her sister from Birmingham after the

Germans bombed much of that city. They came to live with their cousin who had inherited a small house west of the city, an area unlikely to be hit with German bombs, which were aimed at factories, dockyards and military bases.

As Frank continued his quest with the barmaid in snatches of conversation in between a very busy night serving thirsty Londoners, the others got caught up in a conversation at a nearby table between three shop girls who worked in stores in nearby Piccadilly.

The boys were due back at base the next morning and already they had sipped their way though several pints. Once the pub closed the barmaid joined Frank and the boys and their new acquaintances and marched off into the night.

They found a dance hall. The windows were covered so no light could escape, due to blackout regulations. A passable swing band played well-known numbers from Tommy Dorsey, Glenn Miller and Duke Ellington.

They settled at a table. Frank and Bill went to the bar to collect drinks. When they returned Bill saw a local at a nearby table make a rude gesture to his tablemates.

He asked what had happened but two of the girls downplayed the incident. Ed said some of the men seated near them had berated the girls for being in the company of the Canadians.

Seeing nothing nor catching anyone's eye at the next table the boys ignored the issue and carried on. The two girls returned to the table but looked very uncomfortable.

The band continued playing swing favorites and a cloud of cigarette smoke diffused the low light. Eventually the boys got up and asked the girls to dance.

"Come-on love, dance with me," said a voice from a nearby table. At first the girls ignored the invitation and then shook their heads quietly in hopes of being left alone.

"Is he bothering either of you?" asked Frank.

"He's a regular at the pub," said Brenda. "He's always had a thing about English girls talking to soldiers."

Brenda told Frank that the unwanted attention would blow over. They rose to dance again. As they danced Brenda told Frank about her life since the war began. She had been forced to move due to bomb damage. Several of her friends had been killed and injured during the blitz.

"The hardest ones are the children. They do not want to be separated from their mams but they are very vulnerable to the damage. That's why so many have been sent out of the city."

Frank was considering how much he liked Brenda when a head slipped in between them quickly hissing, "So this is your new boyfriend?" before turning to Frank and saying, "She's not the sweetest but she's a mite comfortable."

Frank was shocked. He stepped back still holding one of Brenda's hands. As he stepped he landed on the foot of the interloper who pushed the now off-balance Frank hard off him. Frank went down.

Seeing the commotion from the table Bill saw the instigator push Frank hard and the look of helplessness on Brenda's face. He broke off his conversation and waded into the crowd. Ed was right on his heels. Not having seen anything Johnny stood up at the sudden movement of his buddies.

Frank started to get back up, acknowledging that he tripped, when the local guy took advantage of his vulnerable position and kicked him in the ribs, followed by a swing into his face as Frank opened up from the kick.

There was a scream from Brenda who pushed the instigator. She had seen him often in the pub and had occasionally engaged in a bit of light banter with him. He had a silly grin on his face and said, "If that's how tough these bloody soldier boys are, phah. Hitler's gonna win. I better start working on my German."

"I am going to miss your attentions, though maybe I'll find me a nice fraulien once the nasty stuff clears." He started to turn away.

He turned into a hard right from Bill. Ed grabbed him by the shirt and when he turned to flee, Ed was pulled towards him. The force toppled them both with Ed landing on top. That stunned him and Ed began to pummel him getting in a half dozen shots before someone grabbed his arm.

Frank had managed to stand and was playing peacemaker in the melee. One of the local's friends had made his way towards the battle but he let himself get carried away by the crowd as it became apparent that the Canadians had the upper hand and nobody wanted any more violence.

Frank grabbed Bill and Ed and said they should get out of there fast. Brenda ran with Frank. Johnny corralled the other girls and they exited quickly. Management seemed quite content to simply be rid of the combatants. Once outside they heard the music start up again - a bit out of tune at first but quickly recovering the proper tempo.

The group went back to the flat that two of the girls shared. They had a quick bite to eat and cleaned up as best they could. It was very late. Brenda offered to drive them back to base several hours drive distant.

.

A ramshackle old car pulled up to the gates of the base and four disheveled soldiers spilled out. Brenda looked on from behind the wheel. The boys were just in time for reveille and roll call. They explained to the MP at the gate that they'd had difficulty getting a ride back to base after dark. A kindly old gentleman had offered to drive them but couldn't find his spectacles so he had conscripted his young niece to drive.

The MP looked over to the car and apprised Brenda. He was skeptical but nodded slowly before waving them into the gate. The boys called back their thanks and Frank stood and waved slowly and nodded before turning past the guard post.

The MP came out to the car as Brenda began to move off. He motioned for her to roll down the window.

"Been up all night eh?"

Brenda looked at him but said nothing. Her red eyes gave the MP all the confirmation he needed.

"I hope there was more than just you with them? Where does one go to find you lovelies?"

Brenda looked firmly ahead and drove off without a word, slowly at first to give the MP a chance to speak again or demand that she stop. He did neither.

Chapter Fifteen - 1944

The White Horse became the pub of choice for the boys. It's distance made visits infrequent. Frank knew he could find Brenda there most evenings and took to spending what spare time he could with her even if it meant a few hours of travel each way.

Training intensified. With the Russians engaged with the Germans a second front was required and inevitable. One day some troops simply up and left. Those remaining only later understood their mates had gone to North Africa and Italy. The bulk of the troops remained in England and it was obvious that eventually a major invasion would be launched on France.

Frank spent as much time as he could with Brenda. She explained that the man in the dance hall wasn't her boyfriend but she had been nice to him when he came in as he was from a local family and she knew his sister. His auto repair business had been destroyed in the blitz and he was bitter, blaming anyone in a uniform for his troubles. He was trying to cobble together his business again, but without proper tools, without many autos on the roads and without much success.

Somebody seemed to have warned him off as he disappeared from the pub. Brenda pointed out his sister a few times.

Life settled into a predictable round of duty, training and leaves. Frank and Brenda had taken a short trip together to Birmingham during one of his leaves where they met with Brenda's remaining family. They were distant but cordial.

Frank commented on it and Brenda explained that many girls who had taken up with foreign soldiers had been left disappointed and with their reputation in tatters.

Frank realized this was about as blunt as Brenda could be - however he couldn't take any plunge with the invasion of Europe hanging over their heads.

The threat of the invasion was inching nearer. Fear was in the air. Fear and expectation. Everyone knew the push was on. Orders had come that all men must return to their units. All leaves were cancelled.

Even the dimmest of COs knew the invasion of Europe was imminent. Word had filtered through the ranks that the next night without a moon was June 6 – two nights away.

Frank made a decision. He wrote a letter to Brenda explaining his fear of not returning and leaving Brenda's future crippled. He promised to return to her once the war was over and to write to her often.

Bill had become friendly with one of Brenda's friends. Karen worked in a shop near the White Horse and lived with her aging parents in the north of the city.

He would often double date with Frank and Brenda as they spent much of their spare time with the girls. Bill felt much the same as Frank and did not want to make a commitment to Karen that war might disqualify him from keeping. Karen understood that for them to have any future together they would have to weather the storm of war.

Bill slept soundly in his bed. He was anxious for action, sick of all the build up but he worried now about Karen. However there was nothing he could do on that score until the issues of war had been decided.

The camp was pretty somber the next day. Guys were engaged in a number of final preparations. Letters home were top among the list. Quite a few of the men wrote two letters. The first one they posted immediately, the second they held on to, with a whisper to a buddy or CO to look for it if necessary.

Sleep was difficult – however, the weather closed in and some guys, convinced the invasion could wait another night, fell asleep expecting nothing.

Then the call came. Shortly after midnight the camp was roused and fully laden troops taken to the seaside where they boarded troop carriers for the ride to France. The wind was up, but the night was clear enough. Dim shapes hovered over the surface of the water. Too many shapes to be boats, bobbed on the waves as the greatest seaborne invasion in history faced its most vulnerable hours.

Bill felt a sense of dread. He knew by the time he fell asleep after this day, nothing would again be the same. He barely had time to consider the butterflies in his stomach or wish for the end of the up and down bobbing of the boat, when he heard some scraping on the hull, he heard several gun shots and then the gates of hell opened up. A fire fight erupted around him, but with only a sliver of beach visible from the landing craft he could only hear it.

A line of bullets pinged off the side of the craft just as the bottom scrapped hard against the rocky shore and the craft ceased moving forward. Bill moved with the surge looking to reach the beach and whatever protection they could find. He found himself chest high in the surf and all too quickly emerging from the water wanting to leap on the beach but unable to move his feet quickly. He fell onto the strand.

Bill got his bearings and ran crouching to a little wall 40 feet up the beach. Again he and a few members of his platoon tried to get their bearings. Much of the battle was taking place further down the beach. In fact Bill surmised that they had gone largely unnoticed by the Germans. Ammo that had hit them was that which had gone wildly astray from major action on both sides of them. The platoon quickly gathered.

"They'll soon see our boat," said Bill. "We have to move. Where's the CO?"

Frank jerked his thumb toward the craft, "He was in the surf with us but I don't see him anywhere."

Bill reacted quickly. Frank, you and Ed go back to the strand to find him. Maybe he was hit. The rest of us will work our way up off the beach. Maybe we can catch the Jerry's before they even know we're here. If we wait too long they'll see the boat and we're done. Come on."

Bill wanted his friends safe and they all needed their CO's training. Once they separated Bill didn't think twice about them, he was concerned with getting off the beach quickly.

Crouching down he picked his way up the hill, pausing to look for any sign of the enemy. There was plenty of noise but it was all around them and not right on top of them like it had been in the minute before they landed on the beach.

As they worked their way up the beach Bill saw some sand that looked too smooth, like it was manmade - he figured it was a bunker or some defensive position. He motioned two of his mates to one side, another two to the other and showed them his complement of two grenades. They pulled theirs and moved quickly to the concrete emplacement. The sound of gunfire erupted from the bunker as the Germans appeared to have engaged the landing craft. The Canadians who had worked their way up the beach were close enough to be out of the line of sight.

"Find a target and get behind me, guns ready on three," he paused, nodded at his charges to see they were ready. "One, two, three."

He jumped forward, leaped a narrow trench and jammed a grenade in a pipe on top of the structure. He then reached over the edge of the trench to the side of the bunker, to another exhaust pipe near a doorway, which opened into the sunken trench. He jammed the second grenade in there and jumped and rolled to the back of the emplacement. One of his mates was already there and the other landed on top of him.

Then, several deep booms were heard from inside the hollow concrete shell, and then another louder one from the doorway near the trench. Smoke crept out of cracks in the concrete and through the remains of the pipe holes.

Bill grabbed his gun expecting Germans to come out but there was nothing. He heard a few muffled shots. Others moved toward the front of the emplacement and quickly swung their grenades through the openings before diving for cover. More explosions shook the ground and smoke poured out of the turrets.

As more Canadians reached them from off the beach - Bill motioned them to secure the bunker and explore the series of dunes that could be hiding more emplacements.

Bill took a few men and scrambled off the beach to a small house. Ascertaining nothing odd they burst inside. An old man emerged from the floor boards. "Merde," he said. "Americans. Then it has begun."

Bill pointed to his shoulder insignia but questioned the old man. Posser had been learning French and found that the Germans were mostly concentrated west of their position though a small convoy had moved east during the night.

The Germans had been expecting the invasion much as Allied troops had.

Just then he heard a familiar shout and the door burst open again, it was Ed and Frank with the CO hanging between them.

"Shit, how bad is he?"

"I'm hit in the leg but my brain still works, or it did before that trip up the beach," said Lieutenant Tom Barker.

Squat and solid as a rock, Lieutenant Barker was a regular guy. He was spit and polish enough for both the army and a bunch of non-coms. His father had been regular army after the Great War. Barker's experience in the reserves won him his commission.

"Just put me down on that chair," said the Lieutenant motioning to a nearby armchair at the head of a great wooden dining room table. Ed and Frank ushered him across the room and he eased into the chair and leaned back.

"Thank you for a little sanctuary," the Lieutenant said to the Frenchman, whose name was M. Bodellaise. Posser repeated the thank you in French. The Frenchman held open his arms with his palms up signaling a grudging welcome and a resignation to the invasion of his home, his beach and his country. Nothing would ever be the same again.

There were voices outside. Quickly Ed and Frank raised their side arms and in burst two more Canadians – who stopped immediately upon seeing the muzzles.

"Jeez, you guys are loud enough to wake the dead, which you might have been if we were a little more trigger happy," said Lieutenant Barker. "Ed, you and Frank take up posts outside and keep and eye on any movements of Jerry or us. Gather up any of our guys who come along. You two guys go with them. Password 'Lancashire' if you want back in without a gun in your face."

Soon the room was a bit less crowded. Barker caught up quickly with M. Bodellaise while Bill fashioned a tourniquet for his leg. He formed up his plans quickly.

"Bill, I'm stuck here until I get this under control, can't travel well. However, we can use this as a base to form up."

M. Bodellaise produced a sour look mixed with French resignation to his immediate fate.

"Get outside, find a good spot to watch the main road and set up for a German troop. If I have my bearings correct and our host can be trusted there is a small river east of us and a few bridges we need to take care of. Then get further inland and secure the bridge - it's about five miles up the river. We need some space to operate before the Germans counterattack."

"If the action is really west of here then expect some Jerrys to head that way along the road. If you have to, defend the bridge from the west bank of the river. Sniping isn't good enough, however, don't give away the position for a car or two unless you're really dug in and have some mustard with you. Once you're dug in come and get me. If you see O'Grady with the radio, send him here quick."

Bill left the house with a whispered "Lancashire" to whoever might be outside. A firm 'Lancashire' echoed back to him.

The main road was only about a hundred yards behind the house through a small copse of trees. About a quarter mile west there was a perfect little rise on the south side of the road giving a great view of any traffic, the house and even people coming off the beach, silhouetted against the morning sky as they crested the rise between the beach and the fields.

It wasn't long before a solid group of 20 and then almost 100 infantry were collected, the radio sent to the house and trenches were being dug on the hill. Distant booms to the west were constant as it appeared heavy fighting was still going on.

Bill sent two demolition teams to nearby bridges and a small group to reconnoiter the bridge a few miles up the river.

Lieutenant Barker joined the group with a makeshift crutch. "Divisional says Germans at Caen have mustered and moved west. We've got to stop them. The Americans are getting pounded and we can't afford to lose the whole flank. It's up to us boys. Looks like we might get some help though. The English are east of us and will likely take the brunt. We'll get anyone smart enough to try to flank them. Could be a few strays. Could be the whole bloody German army."

The CO issued a few orders and the company frantically prepared for a few minutes before word came that a small column was headed their way.

"We couldn't get the bridge wired in time, should we blow what we got, let them pass or challenge them? Our boys say it's mostly troop trucks and a few artillery pieces as well as several tanks leading the column."

Barker quickly formulated his plan. Six guys with rocket launchers and flame throwers made for the ditches and trees on each side of the road further west of the bridge. Other guys hid in the deep ditch on the south side while the main mortar fire was dug in just behind the crest of the hill. The rockets were their deadliest weapon at least for the time being.

The plan worked almost too well. As the column crossed the bridge each man waited for the signal shot from the hill to jump into the ambush. Much of the German counterattack had swung toward the beaches to the east as British troops were having at the Germans in their sector. Thus it was only five tanks, four artillery guns and 25 troop trucks that passed behind M. Bodellaise's farm as the sun rose behind the overcast sky that late spring morning.

Two or three rapid shots rang out from the direction of the farm house. The column immediately slowed as its attention was drawn unexpectedly north toward the beach. The second of delay caused by the unexpected shots gave Lieutenant Barker all he needed. He unleashed a volley at the escort to an artillery piece confusing the Jerrys more as his company sprang up and blasted the German column with everything they had. Two tanks were hit immediately. Three more began to reverse course but were stopped by their own artillery pieces so as they slowly moved their cannons around to fire they were hit by multiple rockets and flame. The tanks were all dead and the ground was littered with German bodies, piled at the foot of their troop trucks, killed as they tried to get out. Some were shot in the trucks where they sat and others ran toward the beach only to be met with a hail of gunfire from infantry positioned to cut off their escape.

As soon as it began it was over. As the gunfire died away, two Spitfires roared in low over the beach and began to pepper the remains of the column. But the burst was short as smoke trailing from the tanks attested to the Canadian victory.

Several Canadians were injured, some by friendly fire, and all were stunned at their first taste of combat. The carnage was almost total. Germans simply didn't have the time to give up and the Canadians were too afraid to have taken much notice if they had tried.

In the end they captured three artillery pieces and damaged or destroyed one artillery and five tanks as well as killing more than 350 Jerrys, badly injuring another 100 and knocking off any hope of quick German reinforcements for the western beaches.

After the action the engineers wired the bridge and blew it up. Word came that the other bridge was down and the most distant one was held by a small group joined by some stray British and American paratroopers. All was quiet in that area.

Radio traffic was heavy as Canadian units co-ordinated with their British counterparts to secure the areas around the landing beaches. The Canadians had penetrated inland further than any Allied troops. British troops rushed to the bridgehead the Canadians had secured.

Bill and his posse all came through without a scratch. However, The Poser was a little quieter than usual in the immediate aftermath of the ambush, his quick wit slowed by what he had seen.

Ed and Frank had been firing on one of the artillery escorts. Bill had been expecting to simply fire from his position but quite unexpectedly for him he left that job to those around him while he scanned for Jerry's eluding the attention of the assaulters. He shot two Jerrys in the front of one truck and killed another driver who was being ignored by the main group of snipers.

The longest day was not over. Divisional command sent more orders for the company to head for Basly or Beny-sur-Mer to secure the way to Caen.

Barker quickly got the troop together.

Resistance was light as the troop rolled southeast through the French countryside led by the few German trucks still operating after the ambush. They had painted over the Nazi symbols.

There were very few people to be seen at all. Occasionally people would peak out of barns of houses watching the convoy but for the most part the citizens wanted no part of the shooting. A small knot of men flagged down the lead truck which approached with caution.

It was a few members of the French underground, offering their support and local knowledge. Two jumped into the lead truck and the convoy lurched ahead again, still meeting no resistance.

The Frenchman explained their countrymen were afraid to be seen abetting the invaders in case they should have to answer for it later. The Nazi yoke had been very hard and every family had some horror tale to tell.

Just as Bill began to wonder if all Germans had abandoned Normandy, two Messerschmitt BF 109s streaked over them just above the trees. They happened across the road so quickly they didn't even have time to shoot. Both planes kept going low across the fields making for the Channel.

So there was action going on, likely hotter than theirs, thought Bill. As the convoy moved knots of paratroopers began to link up with them looking for their units. By now an engagement with the Nazis seemed imminent so the column slowed and fanned out as they moved closer to Caen. Just as they decided to dig in, so as not to get too far ahead of the rest of the invasion force, four German tanks broke through some trees on a rise at the end of a field. Shells immediately whistled with one bursting among a group of stray British soldiers killing two and severely injuring two more.

The troop hit the dirt and started shooting with little in significant armament or possible tactics to stop the tanks. Without the advantage of surprise their light arms were no match for the tanks. Orders to fall back were circulating just cannon shells exploded all over one tank and disabled another. Two Spitfires had swooped in from nowhere and as they disappeared two more came in low and laid bursts of heavy cannon fire all over the German tanks.

Two of the tanks were on fire, one smashed by explosions and another dead with smoke and crewmen pouring out and holding up their hands in surrender. The first German was shot before anyone knew they were surrendering.

The Canadians set up a perimeter on the rise using the trees as a camouflage and the height as a sentry. They spent an uneasy night collecting more and more men and occasionally a mortar.

Radio communications let them all in on the apparent early success of the invasion. The Americans were still fighting in the west but were winning the ground behind the beaches while the British had some trouble but were not far behind the Canadian's position. Reconnaissance suggested the Germans were still fighting in some of the small villages but were digging in at Caen, the biggest city in the region and one that appeared to be heavily defended.

A week later the situation had changed little as resistance was crushed and the temporary ports put into operation to ferry much needed heavy equipment and reinforcements into the area. The beach heads had been won but days of ferreting out Nazis remained. By this time the Allies had formulated their plan for Caen. Dump as much high explosive as possible before going in and routing out the Nazis street by street and house by house.

Battleships lobbed shells on Caen. Fighters kept the skies clear while bombers flattened the centre of town.

Bill, Ed, Frank and The Poser dug in for a long fight.

Chapter Sixteen - 1944

A large number of specific and varied operations were conducted to squeeze the Germans at Caen. Day by day their positions became less defensible as the Anglo- Canadians closed in. Eventually the Germans, fearing encirclement, left the city to regroup to the east.

Frank and Bill were assigned to a detail which was supposed to clean up the city center - ferret out any snipers, booby traps and unexploded ordinance. Johnny and Ed were also doing the same duty but with another small group.

There was little evidence of snipers, though every time there was a noise like a gunshot the boys hit the dirt. Soon they realized that many of these 'gunshots' were wires and other construction materials that were snapping under the strain of collapsed buildings and fallen masonry.

It wasn't long before they ignored the noises waiting for some more evidence of a shot as a signal to take cover. As the days went by they worked their way into the city centre, a large square surrounding a small dock facility, forming a little harbour off the river that ran through the city. Some smaller supply ships and local fishing vessels had been commandeered by the army to run supplies into the centre of Caen.

The clean-up operations were taking several weeks. There was much unexploded ordinance and even a few ammo dumps the boys found which had to be cleared carefully. They found a few abandoned German soldiers most of whom were either dead or near death.

Some of these bodies were booby trapped with a grenade underneath, set to explode if the body was moved. Occasionally these did explode leaving a lot fewer rats in Caen than one might have imagined, given the circumstances.

Army command was getting ready to move east but had left some resources in Caen to help locals get the city back on its feet.

Bill and Frank were going building to building along the east side of the central square about half a mile from the Cathedral and ancient Citadel. They would spray coloured signals on each building as they secured it indicating the state it was in and whether it should be bulldozed.

Most of the city centre was destroyed and there was little that could be saved.

"We should save some paint and only indicate which buildings should remain," said Bill. "There isn't much left to salvage."

Each day however there was a little less rubble in the streets and damages seemed a bit more organized. The French were scooping up materials they could use for their own reconstructions. Caen would have a lot more rubble walls covered over with whitewashed stucco in the years after the war.

As the detail moved off the square and east of the cathedral they encountered what had been a farmer's market before the destruction of the city. Bill headed into one three storey building as Frank headed into its neighbour. The usual practice was to look at each floor moving up and then search for any basement that might still be intact. Often times there was not much left of the upper floors to inspect.

Bill poked around and saw his building must have once housed a dress shop as there were mannequins and bolts of cloth strewn about the main floor. Upstairs there was some large tables and cloth cutting machines.

Some of the bolts of cloth were quite salvageable.

He heard a stirring from above. He pulled his revolver and backed into a space opposite the stairs. Soon a matronly woman descended the steps quite matter-of-factly as if determined to get some work done.

She looked around until she spied Bill in the low light. "Monsieur, can I help you find a dress?"

Though the woman was dazed by the destruction it only took Bill a few minutes to ascertain she had not lost her mind. She was trying to trade her wares for a promise the building would not be condemned.

"All of my material is here, all of my cutters," she said in passable English. "I have nowhere else to put them should you tear down my Shoppe."

Bill realized that as they got away from the city centre they would encounter more and more cases like this - where there was significant damage but even greater hardship should they tear down somewhat intact buildings.

He asked the woman a few questions about how she had intended to repair the upper storey. Satisfied he left with a promise that her situation would be reconsidered at an appropriate time.

Bill left the building and painted a large circle on the outside main floor. There was no indication of Frank, not even a sign painted on the outside wall so he figured that Frank must still be inside.

Bill skipped the building and entered the next one. It had been a bakery. Most of the ovens and tools were intact and again only the top floor, what appeared to be an apartment, was damaged. Bill did not encounter any people though there appeared to be some evidence of recent occupation.

He retraced his steps to the first building calling for the proprietress. She made her appearance as he moved up to the second floor. He got the feeling that he was entering a private home uninvited.

Bill enquired about the baker and was told that they were also trying to rebuild the business but had gone to the western suburbs to stay with relatives while spending the days rebuilding. Bill said he would allow the building to remain up but needed to speak with the baker to explain the situation.

He retreated again, still finding no sign of Frank. He was a bit worried, Frank should have completed his survey by now. This time he entered the building looking for Frank, and carefully picked his way along a darkened hallway. It appeared as if there was significant damage probably due to some hand to hand fighting and a direct hit from a shell. Despite the daytime inspection damages rendered this building very dark inside. He felt his way up with one hand on the stair rail and the other braced against the wall. He called for Frank.

Bill felt a stab of pain and a jolt as he put his hand on a live wire. The jolt made him jump against the stair rail but it had been broken and he fell through, grasping at the remains of the railing as his feet disappeared beneath him. As he fell he looked down and realized the floor was gone underneath him. He grabbed the broken rail with both hands to slow his fall only to have his own weight break off the railing in his hand. He flung himself by the hands away from the immediate hole he saw hoping to avoid a longer fall. His right foot caught the floor but his left found open space.

Bill pitched to his left and reached out to grab anything to arrest his fall. He managed to slow himself but dropped into the abyss. He landed on something which broke his fall, though he took a nasty whack on the head as he tumbled down.

Lying dazed for a few minutes - Bill tried to let his eyes get accustomed to the gloom but the rattle that his head had taken made it impossible to focus.

He passed out.

Bill awoke in a cot in a tent with only dim light. A medic noticed he'd come around.

"We got you - but you have a nasty bump on the head and some other cuts and bruises - you might even have some broken ribs and some other injuries - you're going to have to let us know what hurts."

Bill just looked at the medic, still not entirely comprehending his situation.

"Oh and your buddy . . . he didn't make it." The medic turned away and Bill exhaled heavily before passing out again.

After a few days they sent him back to England to convalesce. He had a very significant concussion, broken ribs, a broken arm, a broken pelvis, and cuts and bruises that would take months to fully heal.

Once he was able to move around Bill was determined to go to the White Horse. He did not know what he was going to say to Brenda. As summer waned he was finally strong enough to make it to the White Horse on his own. Brenda had not seen him come in, and was serving a table holding a tray full of beer. She swung away to move to the next table to deliver the last few pints. Taking in the battered Bill, still using crutches to steady himself, she caught sight of him and for a moment stood stunned before dropped her tray full of beer and fainting.

Ever after Bill wondered if he should have written to her first given the shock of her reaction. She told him the bluntness of him standing there without Frank was the quickest and most painless way for her to receive the news.

Chapter Seventeen - 1942

Charles Jr. who was called Chas by his close friends, looked so much like his father that two of the enlistment volunteers called him by his father's nickname when he signed up.

Chas went to war a year after Bill. Knowing his father's troubles after experiencing the front lines in the Great War he quickly demonstrated his abilities around engines and was given the job of mechanic and truck driver. Being just behind the thick of the fray suited his personality and he turned the war years into his own grand tour of the capitals of Europe. The only problem was once he reached these cities, there wasn't much left to tour.

Stationed just outside London he was a bit of a jack of all trades and ended up with an air force unit where he worked on planes, trucks and beer.

Charles's stories were legendary even among veterans long after the war.

He seemed to stretch protocol to the limit and could manage to wiggle out of the tightest jam with a quick joke, a wry smile, and a promise to procure a jeep for his interrogator whenever necessary.

Not that the jams were very bad, but he seemed always to be just a touch on the outside of protocol and military discipline.

"Now that is a right proper beer," said Chas Stuart, "whipping his mouth with his sleeve. So good, in fact, I'll have another."

Chas Stuart, Royal Canadian Air Force – or was it Army – he could hardly remember he'd been seconded back and forth so many times – it almost didn't matter. He was a whiz with an engine and loved tinkering with them.

The pub was crowded, but then it was always crowded, filled with smoke and locals desperately trying to down a few before last call.

Chas was the only uniform in the place, or at least he and his friend from the base, Thomas Clive Baird or TCB for short were the only two. That's because they snuck off the base after lights out for a quick one. Careful they were not to mention their circumstances nor draw attention to themselves by talking about doings on the base. They had been slipping out frequently and had not been caught.

That luck was about the change.

The door to the pub opened and two uniformed military police entered with white armbands to signify their special authority. Military police were not an unusual site but usually unwelcome. They appeared only when tipped off that something untoward was afoot.

The pubs windows were tightly sealed to maintain the evening blackout. Blackouts had been ordered since the autumn of 1940 and the aerial fighting that became known as the Battle of Britain. However, with no German bombing to speak of for more than a year, the regulations, once happily followed, were now grumbled at and occasionally ignored.

Chas and TCB slunk down in their seats. It wasn't the blackout the MPs were here to enforce. A quick glance around and it was obvious to Chas they had no avenue of escape. A few other pubs had back exits which the boys had scrupulously maintained for their first few months of their evenings on the town. However, their guard had slipped.

As the MPs made their way through the crowded pub, eyeing everyone in the place Chas figured he'd try to bamboozle his way out of any confrontation.

"Evening, there gents . . . I mean corporal and corporal," said one of the MPs as he made a show of looking at their military insignia. "Fine night for a bit o' bitter?"

Chas offered a quick salute. It was returned offhandedly.

"Hello guys. We haven't seen anything amiss in here tonight, have we Tom?" said Chas. "In fact I was just saying that the windows are covered especially well to maintain the blackout."

"It's not the windows that brings us here. It's you," said the second MP, obviously relishing the moment.

Chas looked confused. "We just got here," he said, pointing to their full pints. "We stopped in for a quick one on our way back to Bensinghurst – the Air Force motor pool just down the road." Chas pulled a stray set of keys out of his pocket and waved them like they were still hot from use.

The MPs looked confused.

Chas seized the opportunity. " Just delivered a jeep to brass in London so we travelled back together." Then he lowered his voice, "You guys are looking for someone, eh? You know there were two guys in here in uniform that left just a few moments after we arrived, eh Tom."

"Er, yeah," said Tom. "They were up at the bar I think."

The MPs looked surprised. "Well we had a report. How long ago did they leave?"

Chas embellished the story and sent the MPs on their way with a promise not to linger or cause concern for locals. He got their names too. Never know when knowing an MP will help out, he thought.

The boys finished their pints and quietly left the pub. They curtailed their evening activities for a while after that one.

Chas loved London. In fact he liked it almost as much as Edinburgh, where he had served with a special air training unit for several months in the summer and early autumn of 1942.

Edinburgh was magical. A city of ancient spires, renaissance buildings, cobbled medieval streets, broad planned avenues and formal gardens. And while Edinburgh Castle presided over all, it seemed that any small rise in the landscape was home to a monument, a memorial or some other special construct.

Edinburgh was compact and homey. It was unknowable and yet endearingly familiar.

Taking a jeep down Princess Street in the shadow of the Castle, Chas had again run afoul of military protocol.

This particular jeep had flags mounted on either side of the hood denoting a military VIP. Chas had been asked to pick up the jeep and give it a quick tune-up while the VIP was in a meeting.

Chas, not wanting to be accused of impersonating a VIP removed the flags from their mounts. He was listening intently to the engine and paying much of his attention to the handling of the jeep as he drove it a little erratically on his way back to his base. In the process he cut off a couple of other military vehicles and a few civilians and left a trail of irritated drivers in his wake.

He tuned the jeep. In fact, he found a serious defect in the wheel bearing and telephoned the VIPs adjutant, to ask if they were willing to wait the extra time necessary to fix the problem or if they simply wanted to requisition a new jeep.

The adjutant said his boss loved the jeep and had had it specially modified to carry important documents and additional personal affects for lengthy stays away from Army headquarters in London, so he wanted it fixed and returned.

Chas obliged. Having some extra time he polished up the jeep and replaced a defective piston, which was causing a serious engine knock. The jeep purred as he tooled through Edinburgh. Again he was very conscious of the engine sounds and handling. He was enjoying the little bit of freedom too much to notice a black car which had been trailing him for several miles. It smoothly glided up a little too close to his back bumper when he parked in front of a large stone building where the VIP was waiting for his car.

He got out of the car looking for the adjutant as three men got out of the black car.

"Hey, driving a little wild there eh, soldier boy?" said the driver.

"Huh, what?" said Chas, confused by the confrontation and still thinking about the wheel bearing he'd just fixed. "Oh, did I cut you off. I'm sorry. I was thinking about the jeep that's all."

"You should be thinking about the road, soldier boy," said another, rather large member, of the black car's crew.

"Sorry, I guess I should be more careful, but I was trying to listen to the wheel bearings," he said as he reached in to the jeep.

"You nearly hit us, we were forced up the curb and only Richard's driving kept us from a smash up," the big man added, moving toward the jeep door and standing where Chas would have to go around him to get back in. Chas got his back up.

"Hey buster, I said I was sorry, but I actually had something important to do and wasn't just along on a joyride, wasting the day away."

The driver had moved closer and was looking to pick a fight.

"I didn't hear your apology. All I heard was a lot of excuses for nearly running us off the road. In fact the rim may be damaged. What are you going to do about that soldier boy?"

"Well you drove it here, so it couldn't be too bad, smart guy," said Chas. "So it appears I'm not going to do anything." He turned to reach into the car for a second time to get the VIP flags,

The biggest of the three guys took advantage of Chas' inattention and pushed him into the car while kicking his legs out from under him. The third guy, until this time silent, jumped into the passenger seat to hold Chas' head down while the other's jumped in to pummel him.

Just as the first blow fell everybody stopped cold. A sharp rebuke, and those that could, looked up to see the adjutant and General Bernard Montgomery, inquiring without words for an explanation. Chas simply regained his feet and now having gained the flags moved to put them into the flag holders.

The three malefactors, caught red handed, were speechless. Montgomery was a surprise to even Chas who figured the car belonged to some military bureaucrat or paper pushing colonel.

"These 'gentlemen' didn't like the look of your car, nor were then impressed with my efforts to fix your wheel bearing and piston problems," said Chas, breaking the silence.

"Call the MPs," I believe they might have several questions for these 'gentlemen'. Corporal make yourself available to the MPs should they need a statement.

Montgomery motioned the three into their car and confiscated the keys. He got back in his jeep but refused to leave until the MPs had arrived and taken charge of the situation.

Chas never did find out what happened to the three men.

His transfer back to London was partly due to Monty himself, as he found out later. His expertise with engines and timely manner was noted by the adjutant who recommended Monty get him seconded to the motor pool at Bensinghurst, when a second needed repair to Monty's jeep had been botched at the London base.

It was there that he had the opportunity to tinker with some airplanes that were used as trainers and to ferry important documents around England when speed mattered.

At Bensinghurst word spread through the ranks about the disaster at Dieppe. Chas had immediately known something wasn't right. His unit was put on alert, and unknown to him was due to ship over within a few days of a successful beachhead being established. However, preparations for the move had come to an abrupt halt after several units had shipped out. They did not return.

Word leaked back to the grunts that the operation had been a failure but lessons had been learned for the next great landing. By that time the Americans had joined the effort and the next landing would be a more monumental undertaking.

Conversation among the soldiers questioned the whole operation as it appeared to be ill-conceived and poorly undertaken. The regular soldier did not want to believe that their leaders were so dismissive of their lives, so foolish in their approach of objectives. The idea that Dieppe was a practice run at an invasion did not sit well with the men who wondered if their lives would be forfeited for research purposes rather than a real battle.

While most of what transpired on the beach is well enough known, the military planning for the Dieppe operation is not as well known. Almost immediately after it happened brass took to calling it a raid rather than an invasion. There was probably some truth to that, as commando type raids did take place with some regularity. However, the troop commitment and back end planning resembled a small invasion with the expectation of establishing a beachhead.

If it was simply an exercise to find out what a true invasion would really require, that has never been completely established, though the facts would bear witness to the theory. There were never enough men to capture and hold a significant portion of France, and while some post landing strategy and equipment was in place it was woefully short of what was necessary. The question remains if military planners merely played the part to sell the operation or if they knew they were sending the young Canadians into a suicide mission to gather intelligence for the real invasion and to appease the Russians who wanted a significant second front.

Only many years later did evidence emerge to suggest that it had been a giant ruse engineered to allow army intelligence to steal a German enigma coding machine.

Chas knew there had been a real problem. Some of his mates served with the Royal Hamilton Light Infantry and the unit had been decimated and not returned to their former quarters.

Chas knew he would be in the first wave of support 24-48 hours after any successful crossing. His participation was a major indication that the initial phase of an invasion operation was successful.

When the big day finally came two years later it was almost a relief. Huge numbers of men mustered from their quarters a little after mid-night. Chas spent a sleepless night. If the invasion managed a foothold he and his fellows would move into high gear. Immediately upon rising the remaining units were told to rapidly prepare to move out.

Of course there was much running about getting things prepared and then much waiting as night fell and no word of moving out had been announced. The next morning the air was thick with airplanes which were still operating out of their English bases but having a nearly unopposed opportunity to support the infantry. Muffled booms syncopated across the Channel as battleships poured their shells into France.

Then the units were herded into a ship and were moving with the swells across the Channel – never knowing if the whistling sounds they heard were seeking them out.

Huddled in the troopship one kept his head down. Then the big front gate dropped down and the first truck rolled off the makeshift ramp and onto a huge pontoon dock. Materiel was being unloaded from a dozen ships with a dozen more pulling anchor and a dozen more waiting for space.

Men were running around hauling, pulling, and yelling, all with their heads jammed down unnaturally deep between their shoulders. And yet there appeared to be no resistance coming from behind the beach.

Chas drove a truck filled with high explosives bang down the ramp and across the pontoon bridge swaying in moderately heavy seas. He managed to get out on the beach and was directed to a little road cut between two hills which led to higher ground.

There was little evidence of German occupation. Chas was told he'd be on the move at any time as soon as those troops who swarmed inland started to meet resistance.

His immediate responsibilities taken care of he sat down at mess with a couple of infantrymen.

"Well I nearly shit my drawers when the gate opened up and there was a 100 yards of surf to wade through, good thing it wasn't too deep," said one when Chas asked how things had gone for them. "We met some resistance but it seemed to melt away. Anyhow when it was hot, it was hot."

"I still haven't found Eddie or Hounslow. They were with me at the start but I lost track of them as I worked up the beach. It's all a mess, they could be anywhere," he said, trailing off and catching a knowing look in Chas' eye. "Aye but not there. I checked this morning and I checked the wounded."

Just then a big bloke with a shock of blond hair and a sling holding his arm to his chest whacked the infantryman on the back of the head. "Hey lardass, I guess it pays to be slow. Hounslow and me take all the heat and you saunter up behind."

The infantryman brightened considerably – "hey where'd you get too when it got hot?"

"Oh just taking out a Tommy nest up on the rise, good thing a grenade landed right amongst them just when they spotted us – it must have come from a way back – but nobody I know can throw that far."

"And Hounslow?"

He caught some shrapnel and they evac'ed him back to England this morning – he's going to have a nasty scar" he said indicating a line snaking around his forehead and right eye. "But he can see and he can walk and that's a damned sight better than many others. Elmsly lost a leg and Chelmsforth was carted off after leaving a little bit of his innards behind on the beach – s'pose the medic figured he didn't need them."

Chas sat listening to all this quietly. Then Eddie noticed him. He explained that he had just arrived a few hours before driving an ammo truck and that resistance seemed light.

"Maybe now boy-o but not yesterday," said Eddie. "Mind you once we got the beach and took out a couple of their machine guns nests they seemed to disappear. I'm guessing it wasn't too heavily defended here and they'll regroup somewhere inland.

As this conversation continued the boom-hoom of distant guns sounded to the west. "It appears the Yanks are having a rather harder time of it."

Just then a corporal stopped at their table with orders for everyone to report to their CO and be ready to move out. The Canadians were being deployed to stop any reinforcements from reaching the western beaches and the English were being sent east towards Caen – the biggest city in the area.

Chas was set to tinkering. Deep in thought he didn't even jump when the hand landed on his shoulder. He knocked himself out of his reverie on pistons and plugs and turned to see who hit him.

"Why Chas you still alive?" boomed the voice of Flight Lieutenant Gordon McAuly. Chas had worked on McAuly's Spitfire VZ-B back in England. In fact McAuly had more than once complimented him saying the engine ran really well after Chas had worked on it and sought him out when it didn't.

"Chas old bud, can you take a gander at The Bee when you're done. She's not purring like she does for you?"

Chas smiled, "Sure Gordo, let me finish here first."

True to his word Chas found his way over to McAuly's plane and started tinkering. He found a few minor imperfections and some minor damage to a fuel line which he repaired.

When McAuly wandered back from the mess Chas told him what he'd done and said the fuel line repair was only temporary as they waited for parts.

"If you say it's a go, then it's a go, Chas."

McAuly jumped in. He turned over the engine and immediately broke into a huge grin before giving Chas the double thumbs up.

As McAuly taxied down the chain link runway Chas was approached by his CO.

"Chas I need a mechanic to get down to Ver Sur Mer to help repair a few damaged jeeps. Seems the boys were doing a bit of hard driving but they haven't met a lot of resistance yet. Grab your gear and go with Fredericks, he's waiting for you."

Chas bounced along a few miles of country roads until they could see the spire of St. Emille peaking over the next rise. The road smoothed out and as they approached the edge of town where the Canadians had made their camp. Chas set to work.

He fixed a few jeeps and made jerry-rigged repairs on a few German troop carriers that had been captured. He painted over the German insignia so they wouldn't take any friendly fire. He still didn't even know where he was to bunk down - probably right on his spot. He asked a couple of non-coms where he could get something to eat.

As dusk was approaching Chas was getting ready to stop for supper when a commotion struck up to the west of town, about 400 metres from camp and around the bend in the river. Shots whistled by as a line of German soldiers emerged from the woods and started into town across a bridge over the river.

Believing the town as secure as anything they had had for years, townspeople had let down their guard and were now scurrying to get out of the path of the swarming Germans. Chas realized he was about the last to know and the Canadians were mounting a sporadic return of fire, trying to pin down the Germans until reinforcements could come.

As he was standing among the jeeps on a bit of higher ground along the river about 200 yards from the bridge, a burst of machine gun fire cut across one jeep. It pinged off the metal, then raked across the chest of the motor pool chief dropping him with a surprised look on his face and a bullet hole in each breast pocket before ringing off some engine parts beside Chas.

He hit the ground.

After a moment he began to crawl behind a jeep and watched the battle unfold. The Canadians had stopped the Germans from advancing on the camp but they still poured out of the trees and swept across the small bridge into town.

A few Spitfire's had appeared, but at the end of their patrols they were unarmed and only able to swoop down on the German advance in the hope of slowing it down. Once in the town in numbers the Germans would be difficult to dislodge. The Spitfires could only fly during the day and with night fast approaching they only had a small window to act. Chas figured other planes had better be already in the sky or this battle would be bloody.

Gunfire raked the Canadians from behind as they tried to get into defensive positions behind buildings near the bridge. Chas tried to figure out where it was coming from and then saw the telltale airburst of a machine gun nest in the church steeple. The church was at the end of the road from the bridge in the center of town. It appeared that this counter attack had been planned even before the Germans abandoned the town to the advancing Canadians.

Then Chas saw it. A glint in the sinking sun and VZ-B swooped in over the camp and headed directly at the advancing Germans. McAuly fired a burst at the troops traversing the open area at the town end of the bridge then he hopped up over the trees and barrel rolled around and up before looping over and swinging back on the same line. He swooped down out of sight and Chas heard another burst and then a thick column of smoke rose behind McAuly's plane which reappeared above the tree line, this time with a German Messerschmitt on its tail.

Chas seized his opportunity. With McAuly heading right at him he leaped up on a table into McAuly's sight and raised his hands touching his fingers together.

The plane wooshed over his head and turned east toward the Channel and then sharply banked west swinging around on a direct line into the center of town. Smoke still trailed the Spitfire.

Looking at the steeple as indicated by Chas on the ground, McAuly saw the telltale puffs of gunfire coming from openings in the bell tower and aimed at the Canadian camp. He closed on a different vector and before the machine gunners knew he was there he squeezed off a three second burst of the Spitfire's powerful cannons which tore through the church's bell tower, spraying shrapnel and bits of sharp stone fragments through the and steeple. The gun was silenced.

As he flew south of town ready to swing around to head for a landing in the gloom, he flew straight into the path of a Messerschmitt which was waiting for him to come back to the river crossing. The German pilot stayed above the likely vector of McAuly's attack and dove down on the plane and put a burst into the purring engine. McAuly's plane exploded and broke up before cart-wheeling into the river south west of town.

Canadians on the ground seemed to have mastered their weapons and with the threat from their rear neutralized they charged into town across the north bridge near their camp. A company ran straight into town two blocks before turning right to meet any Germans who had come via the west bridge. A few bursts of fire surprised the leading Germans. The others dived for cover into buildings and doorways.

A Canadian tank rumbled down the street scaring up a number of Nazis and driving them to slaughter or surrender. Canadian reinforcements went door to door clearing out any stragglers and encountered only a little resistance. The Germans had little in the way of a battle plan once their surprise had been exhausted having expected to drive the Canadians off before they could form up a defence. They were surprised instead that the Canadians held their ground.

Chas had cheered as McAuly fired his burst into the steeple and turned to see if anyone else in the camp had seen the brilliant flyer and the decisive shot. There was nobody around. The motor pool chief still looked surprised and everyone else had run for battle stations.

In the days after the battle townspeople kept stopping patrolling soldiers to praise the brave flyer who had knocked out two tanks approaching the town from the west through the trees and who had then put the machine gun nest in the steeple out of commission.

Though the river was searched and parts of the plane were found, the Canadian searchers didn't find McAuly's body.

Townspeople only knew the plane and had seen the wreckage pulled from the river. Without any ceremony someone erected a crude wooden sign celebrating McAuly's effort. The sign read Rue VZB and was placed on two corners of the main street of town.

Soon the Canadians were on the move south and east as they swept through Basly, Mattieu and Epron while Ver sur Mer was left behind to heal the wounds of war.

Chas received a Distinguished Service Order for his efforts directing McAuly toward the steeple. A few of the logistics support platoon had seen him stand on the table and make the steeple gesture. They commented on his bravery given the damage and death the Germans had inflicted on the motor pool.

Several months later Chas followed the invading army into Holland. After years of living like slaves to the occupying Germans the Dutch would almost faint at the sight of the Canadians.

Early one morning while Chas was working alone on a particularly vexing throttle issue he heard a scrape behind him. He spun around to see a little girl, perhaps seven or eight, trying to steal a plate of breakfast he had brought along for himself while he worked.

The girl was caught red handed and scampered away but Chas was too quick and blocked her escape. He offered her the plate. After a moment's hesitation she reached for a bun and ate it quickly. She then made to put the rest of the food in a little satchel she carried.

Chas understood. He motioned to the little girl that he would get her more food if she would wait.

When he returned she was gone and his heart sunk. The little girl reminded him of his little sister Mary. Just as he was about to return the basket of food to the mess, the little girl emerged from a pile of jeeps and auto supplies and urgently pulled Chas to come with her.

He followed her willingly to a small farmhouse about half a mile away where he was taken inside. Two older adults started when they saw the uniform but quickly realized it was not German. Chas held out the basket and the older woman haltingly took it with a bow and a few Dutch accented mercis.

An older girl, came into the room and hugged the young one tightly. She stayed as far away from Chas as she could but held on to the young girl and alternated praise for her with thank-yous to Chas in a heavily accented English - French mix.

He nodded and realized they were uncomfortable with both his uniform and the charity. He withdrew and walked back to camp.

He arrived before reveille when only a few sentries and stray men were up and about. As he re-entered his motor pool work shop, the little girl was already sitting there. She had a big smile on her face and was holding four German belts with the army issued buckles still attached.

Chas' eyes went wide. This little girl was offering him a few souvenir trophies of battle she had collected in return for his deed.

Chas waved them off, but the little girl insisted, so Chas took one of the buckles and tucked it in his pocket. He marvelled at the resiliency of people. Possession of the buckles would mean certain death if caught with them by Germans. And yet they were the only currency in which the starved and beaten Dutch could trade.

Chas's unit remained near the little girl's home for several months as late summer battles raged to the east and the stalemate extended through the cold of winter. The Allies had reached too far into German held territory but the Germans could not entirely repulse the Allied offensive. Both were hampered by weather, a major German counter offensive to the south and the terrain.

Chas made several visits to the ramshackle farmhouse with food and medicine. Each time they tried to pay him with a belt buckle but he had routinely refused telling them to use the currency in other transactions they could make.

Several weeks later Chas saw the adjutant he had dealt with in Edinburgh. He asked him to fix a problem with Monty's car.

Investigation revealed the problem which he fixed but also uncovered a coin sized hole in the front kickplate, likely from running over some metal debris. Left the way it was it would quickly rust the interior of the frame and destroy the vehicle.

Chas needed some metal to solder into the hole. Dreading the difficulty in finding the necessary curved piece of metal he remembered the buckle with its convex face. He knew regular soldiers were unhappy with Montgomery as it was his rush for territory which had overstepped its reach and caused much of the delay in advancing.

Chas used the central emblem on the belt buckle as his repair piece and soldered it to the inside frame of the general's personalized jeep. It had the same convex profile as the pipe. Nobody would ever see it, and he would feel better, a silent protest at Monty's grandiose over reach. And silence was better in the army.

He cut the slightly convex center out with a blow torch and placed the resulting curved circle on the curved kick plate to cover the hole, securing it by melted the metal together. The remaining section of the buckle, now a three sided clasp might come in handy in some other repair, so he tossed it into his tool box among the other stray bits of material left over from other jobs.

For several weeks Chas took to making a daily visit to the farm house to drop off extra food from the mess. Soon the little girl Gertie would break into a big smile when he approached and scamper off to alert the house of his arrival. The older girl Lise was always ready with something to eat for him when he got there. As the Dutch campaign was being pulled together and the Germans forced to fall back the army moved on. Chas made sure the little family received a bit of money or a visit from a travelling friend to ensure they were alright.

Once the tide of battle had swept past them they were free to rebuilt their little farm. However the two adults appeared significantly older, were very frail and not much help. Though they never said anything Chas figured they were the grandparents of the two younger girls - nobody ever volunteered any details, and while Chas moved on, his concern for the little girl and her family remained.

Chapter Eighteen - 1943

Helen Stuart spent much of the war working in communications.

She started as a bank stenographer and quickly graduated to delivering communications services for the bank between brokers, agents and the bank's institutional clients.

Early morning of one very cold late spring day in 1943, Helen was sitting at her desk sorting through the previous day's detris, when Mr. Auden-Smith, the aging manager of the communications department called across the open floor of desks and waved her over to his office.

Usually a reserved old gentleman, more comfortable with the fashions of the previous century, on this day he was more than a bit flushed and animated.

Helen took a moment to organize her mess a little as she made ready to leave her desk, using the moments to consider what the meeting might be about. However, caught up in Mr. Auden-Smith's agitation and the futility of dawdling over her jumble, she threw the papers down and started towards the line of offices.

"Hurry Miss Stuart, hurry. Come to my office now," he said with an impatient wave of his hand as she approached. He managed a nervous look over his shoulder back into his office.

Mr. Auden-Smith moved to meet her and quickly whispered that bank president W. H. McKindley was in his office wanting to speak to her. He looked terrified.

Helen was immediately curious. Certainly she wondered if some wayward waybill or purchase order had inadvertently altered the bank's future, but knew it must be something else.

Mr. Auden-Smith reached the office door first and gallantly directed her inside while attempting to manage his composure. As they entered Mr. McKindley stood and greeted Helen almost as if they were acquainted.

"Miss Stuart, I am pleased to see you. Has Mr. Auden-Smith told you why I am here?"

"No, sir," she stammered, "he has not."

"Well, last night I received a most unusual phone call. As Mr. Auden-Smith knows we are here for a meeting. What he doesn't know is that there will be two other people joining us."

There was a knock on the door and two men in business suits and overcoats stepped into the office, through the door Helen could see there was a third man, similarly dressed, standing in the corridor. The small office was getting crowded.

"Mr. Day and Mr. Goode?" asked Mr. McKindley.

The two nodded in the affirmative and seeking out Helen, asked her to sit down.

"Ms. Stuart, thanks to your punctuality and habitual early arrival, we have asked Mr. McKindley to arrange to meet you here, where we would attract little attention."

He went on, hesitating only a moment. "Mr. Day and I understand you are familiar with all types of modern communication through your job here at the bank."

Helen nodded.

"We are also of the understanding that you are a member of the Stuart Construction family and are thus somewhat intimate with that business?"

"I helped my father with their books, and worked two summers helping my uncle as a purchasing agent," said Helen, a little defensively.

Mr. Goode nodded. "I don't think her age will be a barrier," said Mr. Goode to Mr. Day. Mr. Day nodded slightly. Mr. Goode plunged on.

"We are with the government engaged on military business and need a communications specialist who is familiar with building and construction. Are you interested in helping your country in a time of war?"

Helen hesitated.

"Yes, of course I am," she answered slowly. "But I am young."

"Miss Stuart, youth is not a deterrent, many people are taking on responsibilities at very young ages in these extraordinary times. Nor should you worry needlessly about being taken from your family. Our location is just outside the city and we can arrange daily transportation."

Helen smiled, as the government men had so easily ferreted out her concern.

Mr. Day quickly dismissed the two bank officials thanking them for their help. Mr. Auden-Smith knew he was going to be trying to fill an opening and Mr. McKindley's curiosity overwhelmed his anger at being swept out of the office of one of his own subordinates.

The third man in a great coat and suit, nodded at the two ejected bankers and cast his glance down the hall with a smile. The bankers moved down the corridor.

Closing the door behind him the third man spoke.

"Miss Stuart, what I'm about to tell you is strictly confidential – in fact, it is classified beyond merely Top Secret. If you communicate any knowledge of what I'm about to tell you, whether you take the position I offer or not, you are subject to strict sanctions from the Crown."

"Would you like me to proceed?"

Helen nodded her understanding. Curiosity had overwhelmed her.

Mr. Day explained that there was a top secret military intelligence installation just east of Toronto located on some remote farm land on the shore of Lake Ontario. The base required wireless communications experts, who could send and receive complex, coded messages with various allied command centres around the world. This person needed to have some experience in the building trades because much of the messaging concerned factories, munitions, and logistics movements.

Helen was intrigued by the ability to be on the cutting edge of technology and the war effort. She immediately agreed and was told she would be picked up by a car each morning at the bank from a secure basement parking lot and taken to the base. If the car was not there she was to wait at Bay and Temperance for alternate pick up. There was a daily password and password response.

Camp X was situated on Lake Ontario about 35 miles east of Toronto. It was isolated. A jumble of long low buildings kept down local curiosity. It looked like a farm operation, which is what it was prior to the war. The military often ran tractors on perimeter roads or through the fields to keep up the illusion with locals.

Only a very tall antenna tower punctuated the skyline. Locals were told little and outsiders were quickly engaged by subtle but ubiquitous security. For all intents and purposes it was a farm. Albeit one owned by a particularly private farmer.

Personnel who were shuttled in an out of Camp X usually travelled at night. Some came by land others by boat. The Lake, an abandoned gravel pit, wooded areas and wide farm lands were used for training exercises for agents who were sent behind enemy lines, most often to organize or supply partisan underground resistance groups. Sometimes they trained for specific missions which included demolition.

Helen quickly found her place. She trained the would-be agents on wireless and code. She learned much about the hardware of radio and telegraph and saw new machines including one which transmitted drawings or plans from one piece of paper to another piece of paper in another city. At first such marvels seemed like magic but she quickly grew used to them, speculating on their design but never getting any more information than was necessary for her to perform her duties.

There were several horses that were kept on site, used mostly by those training for overseas duty to ensure they could ride at need. Helen, who had had almost no contact with the beasts as a city dweller, came to the stables often to see the horses. Soon she was spending much of her lunch hour helping to feed and care for them. She even learned to ride as the horses required regular exercise that was not always available as part of their duties.

Helen noticed an unusual amount of activity in the early spring of 1944. She had worked at Camp X for a year and only two incidents had broken the monotony of arriving at her assigned pick up location at 7:45 a.m. each day. She often wondered if the car came to get her or was waiting there until she arrived. Molly Marie, another former employee of the bank, was driven in the same car and occasionally other people joined them.

Several months after taking the job, Helen attended a party hosted by a friend of an old friend from school. Helen was introduced to a young Frenchman, who said he was from Trois Rivieres in Quebec. Helen thought his accent a bit odd, but having little experience with French Canadians or French in general she paid little heed.

Stranger perhaps was his apparent working class background and current job in finance and apparent familiarity with some of her acquaintances at the bank. Strangest of all was the way he simply did not look comfortable in casual clothes.

Helen ran into Jean-Pierre on several occasions and enjoyed their conversations. He asked her more and more about herself and what she was doing with the Bank. She fell back quite easily on her cover story that she was on assignment for the bank. His questions were always open ended and he was quick to change topics whenever she appeared uncomfortable.

Just as she began to look forward to his appearance at various social occasions he disappeared. After making several inquiries she was taken aside one morning by Mr. Goode, who she occasionally saw at Camp X, and was told that for the duration she should be particularly circumspect with regards to her social activities.

Jean-Pierre was never mentioned. In fact he simply faded away as so many people did during the war. It wasn't until many years later that she even thought of him again and realized he might well have been a foreign agent.

Work at Camp X became intense that after St. Patrick's Day 1944. Many of the workers at Camp X were asked to remain on site, staying in a barracks that had been constructed for their use. The Camp moved from having overnight duty into a full 24 hour operation. Specific instructions were never issued, but the work load became so large that those being swamped with assignments simply took advantage of the opportunity.

One evening in late April, with many of the workers on site and asleep, a huge commotion broke out. Loud speakers told the workers to remain in their rooms.

Trucks rumbled past, lights glared across the compound. Dogs barked. Quiet descended on the Camp. Then two explosions, a hail of gunfire and a few deep explosive concussions. Running feet and then silence. An announcement over the public address system told Camp X residents that the training drill was over and they could return to their beds.

The next day there were some deep ruts in the road and a noticeable presence of enhanced security. A closer look showed some fire damage to a storage building. Word circulated that the training drill was actually a co-ordinated attack on the camp. But that rumour was never substantiated nor was the incident ever mentioned again.

As April 1944 moved into late May, traffic through the training center suddenly ceased. Communication traffic doubled, then tripled with managers and supervisors routinely jumping in to cover the extra work.

No one said anything. It was obviously the frenzy of preparations for the long-awaited Allied invasion of Europe. After early June passed the work slowed a bit and took on a more routine hue. Much of the communications work had been moved to England. While not privy to actual intelligence data Helen could quickly discern from armament orders and troop movements if the Allies were have a good day or a bad one. She took comfort in the fact that there were many more good days than bad ones.

Helen celebrated the ending of the war like everyone else. After VE Day, work at the Camp noticeably slowed and people who had been there for months and years suddenly vanished.

Chapter Nineteen - 1946

The house was festooned. Glitter, banners, flowers and every decoration Kate Stuart could muster was on display.

Fred was 11 and his brothers were returning home from war.

Kate went down to meet the train.

Both Charlotte and Helen wanted to go but Kate forbade them, remembering the end of the Great War celebrations and insisting the station would be crowded. Besides, the big party would take place at the house, where the girls were needed to make sure all the last minute touches were complete and to welcome the guests.

Both Bill and Chas had stayed on with the army in Europe to help with post war operations. They had spent time as members of the occupying force staying for almost a year before returning home. Bill was engaged in the logistics of rebuilding much of Europe and Charles was needed to restore vehicles and identify parts and requirements.

Charles Sr. showed little emotion at the end of hostilities. However early on the morning of the party Fred did come down to see him kneeling beside his easy chair.

"Drop something?" Fred asked without thinking.

"Ugh yeah," said Charles Sr. torn from his reverie. He grabbed the chair to haul himself up, then made to reach down between himself and the chair. "There it is." And he climbed easily into the chair while blessing himself quickly with the sign of the cross.

Fred dismissed the incident at the time but years later realized in the quiet of the morning he had been praying his thanks that his sons had returned in one piece.

That morning Charles said he had to run an errand as Kate readied herself to meet her boys. He left saying he would pick up his own mother on his way and bring her back to the celebration which would be attended by relatives and close friends.

Union Station had seen many troops returning so the melee that occurred as young families and parents mingled in a very small space was not unexpected.

Kate Stuart worked her way onto the platform and managed to get a spot waiting beside the only notch in the otherwise long flat wall that flanked the main track line. She waited making faces at a small child hanging over the shoulder of a young woman. The little girl was dressed in her Sunday best, obviously waiting for her father, who she had probably only seen in grainy photographs.

Then the east end of the platform became noisy and within seconds a large engine was in view entering the station. It pulled in past the throngs; almost everyone straining to see loved ones hanging out the windows. Those who saw someone started to move through the mass of humanity towards the still moving cars. The layer of excitement and focus on the train kept any anger at the jostling to a minimum.

The train stopped and made a final short heave before the doors were thrust open. The first soldier on the step stopped momentarily to survey the crowd for a familiar face before the surge behind him forced him to step down and into the crowd.

Kate held back as the crowd surged. All of a sudden there was some space around her and she felt Bill and Charles had a better chance of spotting her if she stayed put – and besides this is where, she said in her letters, she would be, at the notch in the wall.

As boy after man disembarked from the train and joyous reunions took place in front of her she remained steadfast in her place despite some jostling. She was patient but more than a little anxious. Those boys knew she'd be standing right here at the wall notch, near where the fifth car would stop.

Wounded veterans were making their way off the train. A lost arm there, a lost leg, an eye patch, badly burned skin. These soldiers had been recovering in Europe on light administrative duty while they underwent treatment for their injuries. Some were disfigured but most were simply self-conscious of their injuries for the first time in months. They had come to terms with their fate but their loved ones were seeing for the first time what had been described to them in letters.

The father of the little girl near her had arrived. And after a three way hug with his family tried to coax the little girl to lift her head from her mother's shoulder and look at him. Both mother and father failed to get the little girl to break her shyness until they put her down and she fell into her father's arms and nuzzled up to his shoulder the same as she had her mother's.

Kate smiled. That ice seemed melted, she thought.

As the scenes of joy, reunion, wonder and fear of the unknown took place all around, Katharine started to worry. As her fear rose in her throat, she felt a tap on the shoulder. It was Bill, with Chas lurking just behind.

"Hi Mother, we were just helping a friend to get off the train – he lost his leg and three fingers, making walking and carrying his kit a little tough. We made sure he found his family."

Katharine was speechless. Bill had grown an inch taller and was filled out, no longer the skinny boy he was when he left. Katharine dissolved. She grabbed him around the neck as her five year wall of strength crumbled in an instant. She reached for Chas who smiled at his mother's silly joy.

"Well it's nice to be remembered," he chided, as she reeled him in.

"I'm so glad you are both home and safe," said Katharine. "I don't think I realized until just this minute how much I worried."

"Where is father?" asked Charles. "I thought he'd come too, and Charlotte and, and Helen and Fred."

"They are home preparing the party. Your father had to pick up your grandmother."

A solitary figure, hiding in the shadows near a doorway, who had been watching Katherine and the two boys, reached up to brush away his tears, disappeared into the station determined to get his mother to the house before a taxi could deposit the returning heroes there.

Charles hadn't even been aware of his tears. They merely filled his eyes with water which he couldn't dry. He thought it was the spring sun that was in his eyes for the first time after months of gloom.

He jumped into his old Packard and rumbled to his family home where Kate had knocked all those years before to find his mother waiting. She chided him for being late and for not meeting the boys at the station.

"I had to get you Mother," he said, "and besides, the platform would be very crowded."

"You could have taken me to the house earlier, and then I could have helped with the preparations."

They arrived back at the Stuart family home just in time to remove their coats before the signal came that a taxi had arrived in front of the house. Charles Sr. stood in the kitchen as the crowd of guests moved to the front door. Charlotte couldn't contain herself and she ran out of the house with a shriek across the wet front lawn in stocking feet.

The elder Stuart gazed out the back window into the woods behind the house. He glimpsed the once grand treehouse now in disrepair. It seemed significant somehow but he couldn't put his finger on why. Perhaps, he thought, he should let the local boys fix it up and use it now that his boys would be around to make sure mischief was kept to a minimum.

It took an hour to get into the house and calm everybody down. Bill realized he should make a little speech, saving him the job of telling his story a hundred times.

He stood in front of the fire and climbed up on a handy ottoman.

"Hello everybody, hello," his voice rose to get everyone's attention. "Hello. Chas and I are very happy to finally be home." The room erupted in cheers and an impromptu version of "For They are Jolly Good Fellows."

"We did our bit, saw a bit of the world and I for one am interested in a bit of R and R before joining Stuart Construction. I've been able to spend my time with my brother Chas on the crossing and heard in detail the amazing story of his war, especially the incident at Ver sur Mer just after D-Day after which he was awarded the DSO - a high honour indeed. But I better let him tell it."

Charles stepped up to the ottoman and smiled at the cheers.

"I too am grateful to God and to you for your prayers at getting through the donnybrook over there. While my close calls were never that close – they were constant, and mostly due to my lack of attention on French roads," he said to a pent up laugh that rippled through the room.

Chas and Bill had joined the great unspoken conspiracy among servicemen to never speak of the horrors of what they had witnessed and taken part in, sometimes with relish.

Charles told the highlights of the story at Ver Sur Mer and McAuly's heroic defence of the town and of his little bit in it. He wore his DSO with pride. Yet he made no mention of it but did say he would like to take a trip to Gordon McAuly's home town of Winnipeg and speak to his family. McAuly had been awarded the Victoria Cross for his valour on that day.

Their duties done the boys mingled among their relatives and friends deep into the night. With the party far from done Helen introduced

Charles and Bill to her friend Molly Marie Spenser.

Helen and Molly had met during Helen's wartime service - sworn to secrecy regarding their activities - they said they were on assignment with the Bank, when asked, working out new accounting strategies and methods. Even with the war over for nearly a year the bond of secrecy remained. Helen had returned to the Bank after the war and then been recruited into Canada's diplomatic service. Molly had returned to the Bank and moved into training and administration.

Some of the guests gathered around the piano where Katharine started out with some old favourites to get the singers started. By the time she broke into war tunes the singers clamoured for more.

Bill joined in after a bit and turned to see Molly Marie had joined him. She smiled at him while exuberantly singing the second verse of The Streets of London. He smiled back.

Bill had left Karen in England. They had spent some time together but Bill's duties and desire to return to Canada conflicted with Karen's responsibilities to her family and her unwillingness to leave England. Bill had remained in England willingly after the war to be with Karen. In the end they decided he would return to Canada and they would decide about their future by the Christmas of 1946.

With the singers going strong Chas saw his mother move into the kitchen. He took the opportunity to have a private word with her.

"Mother, I appreciate you shepherding every young woman my way, but you know I'm married now," said Chas. "Anne will be moving here in a few weeks, once I have arranged a place to live and she can conclude her affairs in England. I thought we would take a short holiday before I start work."

"It's all so sudden. I thought maybe it wasn't real."

"Mother, you will love her. I certainly do. Her family is respectable, her . . . "

"Then how could they let you marry her," Katharine blurted out. "Oh Charles, I don't mean it that way, but I would have a very hard time letting one of my children run off with some foreigner and move thousands of miles away."

"You know Mother, England isn't really that far away. Sure it seems like a very distant place but that is just the difficulty of travel. Heck in a snow storm grandpa's house in Burlington is a very distant place. With the war over travel will get easier. And England is very familiar to us here. So is Burlington for that matter. Things have the same names, streets are the same, though they don't have any roads that go straight. Anne will fit in here very well. I know she has written letters to you and my sisters. Did she give you any cause for concern?"

"No of course not, but she could have carefully crafted her words - you probably coached her on what to say and ask about."

"Of course I did as I wanted the communication to flow right from the start. There will be things for Anne to get used to, most of which have probably eluded me. It will be more difficult for her than us - we are all together."

At that Katharine relented. No matter what influence Anne had on Charles, he would be near to home while Anne was leaping into the void.

"Mother I've never heard you once worry out loud."

"That's because you only listen, you don't see. I have worried about you

144

and your brothers and sisters forever."

"You don't have to worry about us anymore. We are all grown up."

" Not a day goes by where I haven't worried about you or for you. It is a very large strain, a heavy burden actually, but one I have taken on gladly and could never give up. It's a part of me. Now your father, he handles it better, he refuses to let it weigh on him. He only takes on what he feels responsible to bear."

"Well, father has other responsibilities beyond our day to day general welfare. He has a company to run. He has always fulfilled his responsibilities to everyone. I only hope that Anne and I manage as well as you and Dad, when we are faced with the same burdens."

"You will Charles. You look exactly like your father did at your age. He was a bit more serious and you seem a bit more spirited - but you are a Stuart through and through."

"I will be joining the firm in a few weeks. I need to find a place for us to live and I'd like a bit of a holiday first."

"You'd better tell your father."

"About Anne? Surely you didn't keep that from him?"

"No, no. Tell him about when you want to start. He wanted to take you to an initial construction planning meeting he has on Monday."

"I have things to do. Well, I guess I could go, just so I'm familiar with the project when I do start in."

Chapter Twenty - 1948

When the war ended Helen went back to the Bank but was shortly approached by the federal government and took a job trying to resettle soldiers and provide goods to ravaged European economies. After that she took a position in communications systems though she was soon approached by the Canadian diplomatic corps.

Helen gained some experience before jumping at the chance to move to London and work for the Canadian High Commission. She took the job in the spring of 1948 but decided to travel Europe before beginning the job that autumn.

Helen left for Europe in May determined to see for herself those places that became famous during the war and those that were famous before it. She also wanted to tour some of the locations that Bill and Charles talked about. She had arranged a trip to Arnheim in Holland and Caen in France.

She mentioned her plans to the High Commissioner. Several days later the High Commissioner approached her with a plan – she could travel Europe on a fact finding mission for Canada.

They wanted to know what areas were recovering, what industries were regrouping and which were still devastated, and have a general report on possible immigration requests to Canada. The request fit her plans, in fact it actually shaped her plans while giving her the flexibility to go where she wanted.

The trip would take several months so she arranged to break it up into several smaller excursions. That way the High Commission would get small, more timely reports rather than one huge survey that was months out of date.

Helen began her European trek in the United Kingdom. She spent a week at Canada House, and the offices of the High Commissioner getting familiar with the country, geography, history, war facilities and assets.

Helen began by taking short trips around London. Quickly she fell into being a tourist but used her diplomatic credentials to get behind the doors closed to the public to see the reality of the situation. London was still scarred from the Battle of Britain. She toured airfields and abandoned army camps – and asked what plans were in place for the future use of the facilities.

On one of her trips Helen happened upon the Royal Mews in London and spontaneously flashed her credentials and asked to speak to the Horse Master about his charges. Her interest in horses had stuck with her even after she left Camp X. A strange look appeared on the face of the stable master.

"N-n-now who's this that is i-i-interested in sp-sp-speaking to m-me?" said a voice from a small office in the stable.

Helen was just about to bluster something about the Canadian High Commission when King George VI emerged from the office in full riding gear. He was frail but smiling as the stable master stood aside and the King confronted Helen Stuart. Her diplomatic training helped her handle the surprise.

"Your Majesty, I was unaware you were also Horse Master here, though perhaps I should have guessed," said Helen. "I'm from the Canadian High Commission and I'm just doing a bit of looking about before I take up my official duties in a few months time. I have a soft spot for the horses."

"Well I do love Canada," said the King. "The Queen is particularly taken with the place. Which part are you from?"

"I am from Toronto, Your Majesty."

The King turned to the Stable Master, "Ian, I am expecting a riding companion for today. When she arrives please ask her to show this young lady around."

He turned to Helen, "Do you ride Miss, Miss ….?"

"Helen Stuart, and I have ridden some, but not often, and not recently, I'm a city girl, sir."

"Pity, but perhaps I should have expected that, being from Toronto and all."

The King's companion arrived. She was only a few years younger than

Helen and quickly agreed to show the Canadian around.

"I so would like to visit your country some day," she said. "I'm told it is wonderful."

The two girls quickly fell in together, talking first about the horses then about Canada and then about their war time experiences. So fearful of the potential sanctions about speaking of her wartime work, Helen remained fairly circumspect about her experience with her new acquaintance.

"I worry about the Horse Master. He seems to be wearing out. I think the war took a heavy toll on him."

"He seems fine to me but of course I've just met him. A bit of time should set him right now that the strain of the war has lifted."

"All the time in the world will not set right some of the wounds this city has suffered," said the young woman.

She approached a chestnut colt. The horse threw back its head, happy at first to see her and equally stand-offish. She hadn't been round the stables in more than a week.

She reached out her hand to show him and then rubbed his nose, whispering in his ear while reaching for some dried apple slices in her pocket. She continued rubbing the colt's nose with one hand while offering apple bits with the other, all the while speaking a stream of quiet nonsense into the horse's ear. He nodded vigorously and took the offerings.

She moved alongside the colt.

"His name is Seelon – an island off India that my uncle is partial to, and the Cockney version of Sea Lion."

"The code name of the Normandy invasion," spouted Helen with a smile of pleasure at the word play.

The young woman looked at Helen quizzically but only for a fraction of a moment.

She continued working the horse, picking up a brush and then tying on a saddle.

"There, Seelon is a little demanding. He's got a bit of spirit so I'll take him. Let's get Canterbury ready for you, he's a little more sedate. A better choice if you don't ride often."

The two horses ready, the young woman called to the Horse Master that they were about to go and were told to get started and that he'd join them presently.

The two girls started off, through the Mews and into the western grounds at Buckingham Palace. The young woman was a very able rider but she had to fight to keep Seelon on the straight and narrow. Pretty soon they were trotting along at a good pace worrying mostly about keeping Helen on the saddle and Seelon from rocketing ahead.

As promised King George soon hove into view, cutting across an open field to catch the girls on their second turn.

"You're having to work a little there," said the King, referring to the young woman's mastery of the feisty colt. He smiled. "I thought you'd like that horse as soon as I saw him at Balmoral."

"The Scots horses all seem to have more than their share of spark," she said.

"Well, I'm quite happy with Canterbury," said Helen. "He won't let me make a mistake."

"But a Stuart - you must have a Scots background. Half of Canada seems to be Scots, " said the King.

The three rode a few turns around the grounds until Seelon's rider said, "Once more with feeling," and took off at full gallop.

Helen looked at the King.

"We'll never catch her on these horses," he said, "but Canterbury could use a run all the same if you want to let him go a bit. I'm turning back to the Mews – I have some business this afternoon."

"Thank you Your Majesty, this has been an unexpected pleasure."

After the King turned away, Helen kicked up Canterbury, who was able to notch it up to a speedy canter but no more.

As Seelon came round behind Helen the horse slowed to a trot to fall in with Helen's mount. The girls chatted amiably, with Helen explaining she was in London for several more weeks before she made her way to the Continent for several months on behalf of the High Commission and her own curiosity.

"Please write me and tell me all about it," said her acquaintance with a warm smile. "I should so love to go and not be watched all the time. As you might imagine it is difficult for me to poke around places. I like visiting but it's always so staged. I do so enjoy it when the staging comes apart, falls down or is otherwise compromised. The poor people are mortified but I get to see a little bit of real life – a bit of colourful language, a bit of fright and even panic."

Helen bade goodbye, thanking her for the talk, and the ride and wondering if she would ever see her again.

Helen left London for a few days to see Stratford, Oxford, Coventry, Warwick and the Cotswold Hills as well as Wiltshire, Stonehenge and Salisbury.

The trip left her very tired. Rounds of cultural monuments, war time bases and factories which were being converted into post-war production, and conversations with bureaucrats and government bean counters took their toll.

Helen saw the restoration of Warwick Castle, the complete ruin of the once imposing Kenilworth Castle, and the ancient battlements of Sarum, the Iron Age hill fort north of Salisbury.

In Salisbury Helen met with a Canadian diplomat who was negotiating to have some of the Cathedral's treasures sent to Canada as part of a cultural tour and exchange.

Kenneth Whitting was a former Major in the Canadian Army who had come back to Britain two years after the war at the behest of the government. He had family connections in the Portsmouth and Winchester areas, had been on the path to being a diplomat prior to the war, a war in which he distinguished himself earning a couple of medals for bravery, skilled preparation in anticipation of events, and the notice of army and government officials. In fact he had turned down a late in-theatre promotion to colonel because he felt that higher rank would hinder his post war career in the diplomatic service.

Helen was very impressed by Mr. Whitting who seemed worldly beyond even the most skilled diplomat. Perhaps most impressively, he knew where he was, how to get where he was going and who to talk to – even if that meant the greaseman at the local garage or the Lord Mayor of Salisbury.

Whitting, while kind to her, paid her no more heed than was necessary a fellow Canadian, and young trainee into the world of diplomacy.

"Needless to say, watch your tongue with these men of God," said Mr. Whitting as they were preparing for a meeting with the Bishop of Salisbury. "They are quick to offense and essentially are looking for a reason to deny Whitehall's request that some national treasures be toured about to shore up this Commonwealth idea."

Helen nodded. She was not one for outbursts, yet the warning seemed perfectly responsible. She would barely open her mouth.

The cathedral was magnificent. Tucked in a close in the middle of the ancient city of Salisbury it sported a tall spire – noticeably off center, and a copy of the Magna Carta, the Great Charter of legal rights signed by King John in 1215. It was the document that ended the notion of a divine right of kings, and laid the foundation of common law and the responsibility of parliamentary government.

The notable spire could not be displayed across Canada but the Great Charter could and that's what Mr. Whitting was trying to convince the bishop of Salisbury to allow.

Whitting was coy, not mentioning the charter at all until he had secured a few other artefacts and treasures of the cathedral to be part of the traveling show. He gently mentioned the desire of Westminster to gain access to one of the four existing copies of Magna Carta as part of the exhibit. He explained the need for Canadians to be drawn into the Crown and Commonwealth especially in the face of overwhelming influence from the great republic to its south.

As the two Canadians took their leave of the bishop and emerged from the cool stone edifice into the cathedral close, Mr. Whitting turned his face to the warming sun.

"That went well. I know we didn't secure the document, Miss Stuart, but neither were we rejected outright. The bishops are protective of their treasure but, well I can't help but think Whitehall has softened them up a bit. When we make the pitch formally and we tell them all the security measures we will take, I think we will get it."

"It would be lovely to show the Charter and all the other bits and pieces in a big travelling show. How many cities do you think will be involved?"

"Not my area Miss Stuart. I get the agreements. Someone from the High Commission and Foreign Affairs will make the detailed arrangements – I should think at least three or four cities across the country but the bishops might want less travelling once they've let the document go."

The pair had nearly crossed the grassy yard. Helen took her leave of Mr. Whitting intending to scout the area around Salisbury. He ceded the car and driver to her for the afternoon saying he had business with London and paperwork to complete before an informal diplomatic dinner that evening, which she was expected to attend.

Helen took a motor tour of the town and marvelled at its ancient alleyways. As the car climbed the rise north of the city the wet, cold ground began to give up its mist in the warm sunshine. It was in that rising mist that she toured the iron age hill fort and ancient city site of Old Sarum.

There were a few people wandering about the hill top where the foundations of old stone buildings suggested a much grander past.

"Really not much to see," Helen said aloud, unaware of anyone nearby.

"But lots to imagine," said a man as he stepped fully into view. "Most of the stones were taken from here to build the city down there," he said, waving through the mist to the virtually unseen city to the south.

"It's strange how the mist hides the city, but above it, from this height, you can almost see the sea," said Helen.

"You are a Canadian," said the man. "Daniel, Daniel McFarlane."

"I am Canadian Mr. McFarlane. How might you know that?"

"It's your accent and manner," he smiled. "More refined than an American, more American than an Australian, and more curious than an Englishwoman. That and I grew up in Canada and only recently have returned to the land of my birth. Strangely the accent comes back but not quite as strong."

"Nice to make your acquaintance Mr. McFarlane."

"Oh, no please call me Dan," he said with a smile, "as my Canadian friends do. Here, I'm usually Daniel. While that is formal enough for business and English tastes, I do like to exercise my colonial egalitarianism."

"You are in business?"

"Yes, I am an agent of a number of Canadian companies looking for new business here or looking to partner with English companies interested in export. It keeps me busy. However, I always stop at Old Sarum when I'm in the neighbourhood. It's just something about the place that seems so monumental even in its decay. The vagaries of fate and all that, I suppose."

"Do you know that when they decided this site was too small, they shot an arrow southwards to determine the location of the new cathedral and ultimately the town that would grow up around it?" he said.

"Yes, I've heard that story," said Helen. "That cathedral is quite distant. Quite a powerful bowshot. This is an interesting place, but a little sad, sort of has an Ozymandias feel to it – you know 'Of that colossal wreck, boundless and bare, The lone and level sands stretch far away.' At least the downs do anyway. Shelley, I think or Byron maybe."

"Well then you need to see it on a clear day when its progeny, Salisbury, is spread o'er yonder plain," Dan said. "It's perhaps less spare then, and you can see how this spot of time gave birth to that one."

Helen smiled, "Perhaps you are right, Dan, there is value in seeing things from different perspectives."

"Would you like to join me for dinner tonight? I have a business related dinner engagement but I can bring a date. Our business talk will be light and short. In fact you might find it interesting. That is, if you are not leaving the area today."

"Unfortunately no, Dan, I already have a dinner arranged for tonight, and will be leaving Salisbury in the morning."

Helen took her leave and found her driver under the curious eye of Daniel McFarlane. She made a few more stops and thought about how pleasant it had been to speak to someone on her travels. Mr. Whitting and other Commission officials treated her like a piece of necessary baggage – certainly acutely aware of her but rather uninterested in anything but her presence.

Helen returned to her hotel with enough time for a quick cup of tea and an opportunity to ready herself for a semi-formal dinner with Mr. Whitting and a few Commission staffers he had business with.

Eventually she heard a tap on her door and a muffled voice of the bellhop with the message that she should join her group in the dining room.

The hotel was trying to pull itself up from its post-war drabness. Still in need of major attention for upkeep that had gone undone during the war it was festooned with cosmetic touches in an attempt to tart it up. Once a grand hotel it now looked like an aging lady, trying desperately with paint and fabric to look young and fashionable once again.

Helen entered the dining room and was escorted to a table with four men and two women already in attendance. She was introduced around by Mr. Whitting. She nodded at the two men and one woman who were attached to the Commission who joined their party. They were engaged in Winchester and Portsmouth trying to get artifacts for the Commonwealth tour.

In addition, Helen made the acquaintance of Geoff and Mary Wilson, a Canadian businessman and his wife who were eager to get the High Commission to help bring machinists from Britain to their factory in Canada. She noticed there was an empty place at the table – as one guest had not arrived.

Helen sat down and listened as the conversation resumed.

Almost immediately Mr. Whitting jumped up, "There's our stray guest," he said with deference. "I hope you didn't get lost in Salisbury?"

"No I spend a lovely hour at Old Sarum," said the man, with a glance at Helen, "and met an extraordinary Canadian there who quoted Shelley and seemed quite lost in thought."

Daniel McFarlane was introduced around the table and the dinner commenced. Helen ascertained from the conversation that Daniel was well acquainted with Mr. Whitting and the Commission staff and that he had quite a number of business dealings on both sides of the Atlantic.

Dan disengaged himself from the general conversation as soon as pending inquiries were completed and future contacts established.

"Miss Stuart did you get round to Old Sarum on your travels today?" asked Mr. Whitting.

"Indeed I did and I was ambushed by a loitering local historian full of all sorts of tidbits about the place. Not at all the sort of conversation that bears repeating."

"Stuart? I'm guessing you're from Toronto," said McFarlane.

"Yes, my family is in construction there," said Helen with a smile. "I am working with the High Commission here in London. My first assignment is gaining some knowledge of local conditions in England, France, Germany, Holland, Italy and Switzerland now that the post-war reconstruction is well underway."

"Stuart Construction, I know them, is it your brother Chas? I have done a little business with him. We served together briefly in France."

"You know Chas? He never mentioned a McFarlane in this war stories."

"That's because I spent much of the war chasing him out of pubs. He was an extraordinary mechanic - impressed Monty and a whole bunch of brass. It probably helped him out of more than one scrap."

Dinner conversation turned to more immediate business and government matters. Mr. Whitting did manage to get Mr. McFarlane to agree to help sponsor the artifact tour.

"Perhaps we can take a sarsen stone trilithon from Stonehenge on tour," said Helen with a smile. "I was planning on touring there tomorrow."

"They are a bit large for travel," said McFarlane. "However I'd be happy to show you in person as I too was planning a trip there in the morning."

"Thank you Mr. McFarlane, I will join you, though I do not see any potential commercial aspects of Stonehenge."

"I don't always go places just for commercial purposes. Some things are just worth exploring."

Chapter Twenty-One - 1948

Helen picked her way through the Dutch countryside. There was very little to distinguish one place from another in these rural areas. The land was very flat with little still standing after the war had swept it clear.

Dykes bordered the fields and roadways ran on top raised above the fields. Only a few windmills broke the horizon. In the cloudy low light, Helen would have no idea where to go, without the signs at each crossroads.

After a bit of back and forth and a few necessary inquiries Helen found the little house she sought and knocked. She was expected. There was a great commotion inside and soon the door was opened by a girl of about nine years old with another girl Helen guessed was in her late teens, standing behind her.

Chas had made all the arrangements and asked Helen to use her connections to make his plans come together.

There were two aging adults in the home as well. Chas had thought they were the two girls grandparents but explained to Helen that he wasn't sure and perhaps the little group had banded together during the war. Helen was ushered into their home. They were nervous and uncomfortable. The asked after Chas. The question confirmed she was in the right place. Chas had given her a detailed description of the home and the two younger girls but a little additional corroboration made Helen feel a bit better.

Helen had used her connections to speed the girls immigration papers through channels. Chas had signed on as a guarantor and had made arrangements for the girls to work and board with a farm family north of Toronto. More often Dutch immigrants were asked to take on difficult labour intensive jobs upon arrival. The girls felt lucky.

Many Dutch who emigrated to Canada after the war were expected to put in several years in lumber camps or on marginal agricultural properties to provide the labour to help expand the Canadian economy. The arrangements they endured were often only a step better than indentured servitude. Often the sponsors took advantage of the immigrants and treated them not much better than slaves. However, that was not the rule as many of those who took in immigrants could related to their situations having been in similar circumstances themselves and looked to treat them fairly.

Helen sipped her tea and looked around the small farm house. It was obvious the family had managed significant improvements in their living arrangements since Chas had last been here. There was evidence of a larder. Tea was offered quickly and included buns and butter. The family was clothed in old, worn but ultimately neat and clean cloths - a far cry from the near rags that Chas had described.

Helen handed Lise and Gert their papers for entry into Canada. Helen watched as the grandparents smiled and wept - happy for the opportunity for the girls to start a new life and unable to contain their sadness at losing them.

Chapter Twenty-Two - 1952

The 1950's were go time.

Bill had married Molly Marie. He had spent some time with her as she was often at the Stuart home in the months immediately after the war and his return home. She was very good friends with Helen and was always invited to events at the house. In fact she was more familiar with the house and various goings on than he was when he returned from Europe.

Helen plotted her rise up the corporate and bureaucratic ranks and Molly Marie settled back in at the bank. Both remained very tight-lipped about their war time activities. Mr. Goode had put the fear of God into their oath of silence.

Chas had brought Anne from England shortly after the war. During the time he spent in London immediately after the war and his time in Berlin during the initial occupation, he had met and courted Anne. She was working for the government helping to get England off its war footing and back to a domestic economy. She would tour military bases and was sent to armaments facilities and factories to assess the best way to step back from the wartime activity. Chas had been assigned to drive her and the team she was with between facilities.

Chas had stayed in England for several more months than required by army command as he was smitten with Anne and wanted the time with her. In the end it took very little convincing to have Anne drop her career in the government and join him in Canada.

Helen could never quite get the dashing David McFarlane out of her mind, or out of her life as he kept popping up at unexpected times. He did it so often that at first Helen had been annoyed and then annoyed at herself when he wouldn't surface in some remote location and she found herself wishing he had.

Eventually they formalized the inevitable and moved to Ottawa where David could operate his consulting business and she pursued her diplomatic career. They often visited England, first using the same hotel on their trips and then purchasing a small cottage north-west of London to use as a business base and occasional holiday home.

Charlotte had married Frank Delisle. Mary had married Bernie.

Stuart Construction was building, building and building some more. Bill, Chas and their two cousins Michael and Lawrence, who Bill and Chas referred to as the Avenging Angels, had begun to take over much of the day to day administration of the company though Charles Sr. had not relinquished the last word. His older brothers, who co-founded the company with him were retired but maintained a consulting role through their children.

Charles Sr. did let the boys make decisions but only after a thorough review of the specs, finances and opportunity cost of each project. He referred to his oversight as his additional two cents being added to the estimates. He was particularly mindful about how one project would lead to another. As long as he got his say, he was confident the boys could handle the business.

"We do commercial and institutional buildings boys," he said. "If we get into tract housing we will become a tract housing company. Serious building projects will not come our way."

"Dad, the Avenging Angels say Uncle George, your own brother, thinks the tract housing market is too lucrative to ignore. They have a plan. They want to form a new company to engage in building tract housing."

A big smile spread across Charles Sr. face. "That is coming right from George. He's been pushing for that for years but always forgot that two companies is twice as much administrative work. However, with the next generation coming on board, I guess it makes sense. What is the name of this new company."

Angel Homes started business right in the offices of Stuart Construction but they were careful to separate the businesses and after a few months the new company took offices of its own.

Bill found himself using the purchasing power of Stuart Construction in buying supplies and materials for the new company. They would carefully resell them to Angel Homes but it allowed the new company significant financial leeway. They began to get a lot of new contracts to build huge numbers of houses in Toronto's new suburbs.

Chapter Twenty-Three - 1953

It was beautiful. A piece of furniture really. Polished wood, brass inlay, about four feet tall with a modern Art Deco face and matching dials.

Everyone had a radio in their living room. Not everyone had one this nice.

Bernie turned it on. The sound resonated through the room - rich, full and wonderful.
He listened for a few moments, spun the dial to CFRB and turned it off.

As he heard Mary walking down the hall from the kitchen he turned it back on.

"Welcome hockey fans across Canada - the second period is about to start with the Toronto Maple Leafs holding a 2-1 lead on the Detroit Red Wings," announced Foster Hewitt, the voice of hockey in Canada.

Bernie settled into his armchair. Mary entered the room and sat expectantly waiting for Bernie to turn the station. She didn't often listen to the hockey game.

"Happy anniversary dear," said Bernie. "I just wanted to hear the start of the game. You can choose anything you want to listen to."

Mary looked up and saw the new radio. She moved in for a closer look and studied the dials. A couple of neighbours had been talking about an Abbot and Costello comedy special being broadcast that night but Mary wanted to hear music. She turned the dial to her favorite station which broadcast live music, often from whatever important band was in town - tonight it was Benny Goodman. The familiar strains of 'I May Be Wrong' flowed into the room. Both Bernie and Mary marveled at the depth of sound the radio provided. Mary liked the rich look of the wood casing.

As applause followed the last strains of music the band immediately launched into 'Dancing in the Dark.'

"Oh, I love this one."

"Me too," said Bernie.

He jumped up and grabbed Mary and began to dance around the room. She giggled. The curtains were open and she didn't care who saw them. Bernie steered them over to the doorway and deftly flicked off the light with his elbow.

"It's been a good year, hasn't hon?"

She smiled at the tiny waver of trepidation in his voice. He wasn't sure what her response would be.

She hesitated just long enough, "Yes, dear, it has been a good year. It takes a lot of work to get a family started."

"I wanted us to have something we use every day for our anniversary. Something that will last," he said as they continued to waltz around the room, avoiding furniture and potential trips on the rug.

"Now I know what they mean by 'cutting the rug'," said Bernie sardonically. Mary laughed.

I always thought they meant dancing so much that you wore the rug down to two pieces, never did I think they meant cutting it off so you don't trip on it."

The song ended and they broke their embrace. Mary usually sat in one of the high back chairs near the back door so she could hear anything cooking on the stove. Today she sat on the chesterfield.

"Why are you sitting there?" Bernie looked back helplessly at the radio as another song started to play over the applause coming from the radio.

Oh, let's dance to this one too, then we can rest."

Mary took his hand and they moved slowly to 'Autumn Nocturne.'

"Because my chair isn't big enough for two," she said.

"What's not big enough for two?"

"The chair."

Bernie continued to dance but Mary could feel his uncertainty. "I'll need more room to handle the baby."

Bernie kept the slow dance up. "Is your sister coming over tonight. Mark isn't a baby anymore."

He let that sink in. Then he pulled out of the embrace and held Mary by the forearms and a big smile creased his face.

"When is this baby due?"

"February."

"We are going to have a baby in February?"

Mary nodded, it was her turn to be a little unsure.

"That's wonderful," said Bernie. "Now what do we do?"

"We already did it."

Mary explained she had suspected and been to the doctor to confirm. The doctor said she was about two months pregnant. They decided not to tell anyone for another six weeks until the family reunion, held every Labour Day weekend.

Then the musical spell was broken.

"News . . . . Flash . . . . Korea . . . . the War Department announced a few minutes ago that the war in Korea is over. An armistice has been signed at Panmunjom near Seoul. Combat operations have been halted on both sides while negotiators work out the details of prisoner release and the location of a Demilitarized Zone between United Nations Forces and the Chinese backed - North Koreans. It is hoped that these details can be handled quickly. We now return you to your regularly scheduled broadcast."

"Wow, the war is over and we are having a baby," said Bernie as Autumn Nocturne returned to the room. "Things are looking up."

Bernie and Mary talked for the rest of the evening about their future - which room to turn into a nursery, if they should find a bigger home, when Mary should stop working and on and on.

Bernie's job as a hydro lineman was secure and Mary would work as long as she could or at least until Christmas at her job at the local library.

Plans were being formulated even if they did not know the gender of the baby. Mary said she could probably borrow much of the necessary baby things, a crib, a stroller, blankets and baby clothes from her sister Charlotte and her sisters-in-law.

Bernie kicked himself for the extravagance of the new radio, but he figured that they would be spending many hours with the baby listening to music, radio plays and regular drama and comedy show as well as the news and of course hockey games.

Bernie had heard about television, in fact he had seen one only a few months before, as the Canadian Broadcasting Company had launched a channel not long before. He was intrigued by the ability to see pictures and sound like a movie but the set he had seen provided a very murky picture and poor sound compared to a good radio. In his heart he figured television would grow but it would have a long way to go before it could compete with radio - not only on the technical side but also in terms of interest of people who would have to buy the expensive machines.

Radio was here to stay and he now owned a very nice one.

Chapter Twenty-Four - 1955

Lise trundled back home from work in the fields. She was used to the hard labour of harvesting fields and collecting up the produce.

With Chas Stuart as their sponsor Lise had come to Canada after the war with Gert and had settled into a farming community north of Toronto particularly favoured by the Dutch. Charles had secured them a good position with a well known local Dutch family who were eager to help their own and make a connection through Chas into Toronto's business community. It proved a good match.

The deep loamy soil was similar to many agricultural areas of Holland. The Dutch were able to buy up the marshy land that had daunted others and turn it into a wonderland of carrots, onions and other field crops.

Gert was in high school nearby and she helped Lise in the fields when she could. Lise's smarts and effort had built trust with her Dutch benefactors and she not only worked the fields when necessary but she acted as a part time nanny, part time farm hand and part time logistics manager on the farm.

It was Lise who supervised much of the vehicle maintenance and organized the annual jam making operations - a lucrative addition to the farm's cash crop.

Lise new she was lucky as the family she was employed with treated her and Gert much as their own; like distant cousins perhaps, not entirely on the same level as the immediate family, but with fairness, dignity and closeness reserved for family.

She had heard stories of others who were not so fortunate with their sponsors or employers and who had to endure privations and hardships only a notch better than what they had left in Europe.

At first Lise suspected that Chas's occasional visits to the farm kept everything in place as his presence alone was enough to ensure fair conduct by the farm owners. However as time passed she had seen dealings that suggested she was employed by a rare and fair man, who prized quality, effort and equity above profit or advantage. With little in the way of leverage she had always been a bit reserved and wary though both she and Gert were very well placed. Her strong no-nonsense managerial skills were highly prized.

Lise realized that she would soon have to move forward with her life as she was her youth was running out and her options narrowing. However, she was torn between her worry for Gert and for her uncertain understanding of the future.

Already several young men had flirted with her and made their interest known. That was sure to intensify during the coming winter months as other work on the farm slowed.

She wondered if she should seek out Chas for some advice. He was the closest to family she had in Canada and while distant, he had always been kind.

Lise wrote him a long letter seeking his advice, careful to allude to her concern for Gert and Gert's future as she was only barely a teenager.

Chas wrote back saying her future was in her own hands and that she should be concerned about her position after any marriage. Gert was helpful on the farm and would still have her place there, especially if Lise anticipated continuing her employment at the farm. He offered to act as a go between with any family and with her sponsors should her situation change through marriage.

Chas' letter fell from her hand. She was grateful for Chas' help but . . . . Lise wondered if she should just move forward and leave well enough alone - she had made her situation and now must live with it.

Lise wrote Chas and asked to meet with him to have a formal conversation about her future. Chas agreed and on the appointed day, Lise arrived in Toronto at the offices of Stuart Construction.

"Nice to see you Lise. I trust Gert is well and things on the farm are going well? asked Chas.

"Yes, the farm almost runs itself now as everyone has seen the advantages of the way we organize things. We have had a bumper crop of fruit this year so our jam making operations are going full tilt."

Chas called Lise into his office and motioned for her to sit.

"You have something or someone on your mind, Lise. Do you want me to speak to the family for you? Who is it?"

"No, that is not my reason for being here. I need more than that. More than advice, more than reassurance. I am so sorry to burden you but I have nowhere else to turn."

"I will help if I can Lise but remember what I told you when you first came to Canada. I can only help within the bounds of my abilities, though I will help where and when I can."

"Mr. Stuart, Charles, I am fearful for my future. I am no longer a young woman and must determine my future course."

"Yes, you need to decide if you will marry or remain ... as you are. As for Gert, she must know that at some point in your life you will need to make this decision. I trust you've prepared her for any transition?"

"I have. I have tried. However I am torn in two. I have my desire to build a long term life, and my responsibility to Gert."

"You have been approached to marry?"

"Yes, I have been, and I have sensed other opportunities that may materialize should I encourage them, but I sense that the window for that decision is small."

"You want me to help you decide. Please be frank with me. I know many of the families in the area. Who has approached you."

"That is not the issue. Well, I guess it is .... oh, Charles, I don't know what to do," she took a deep breath, almost sucking in air to suppress a sob.

"I have no one else to talk to and I don't know what to do."

"Please let's discuss this rationally. I will hold your confidence. Who has approached you and what promises have been made. Oh, God, you aren't pregnant are you?"

"No, no. It's nothing like that," she said gathering herself. "It's Gert. I cannot bear to leave her, to abandon her."

"She knows you have to move ahead. Sisters are always close and in time she will marry too and hopefully remain close to you."

"That's not it," Lise braced again. "Gert is not my sister. She is my daughter."

Chas was unable to speak. He began to shake, first from his hands, then into his shoulders as he tried to comprehend the implications and contain the horror of what the revelation revealed.

"You are so young, how can that be?" Even as he said it he realized the awful truth. Gert was the product of war and invasion. Of course, Lise could not bear to be estranged from her but the truth cast a pall on Lise's future.

Chapter Twenty-Five - 1957

It was going to be an unusual day.

Several years ago Helen had written to her riding companion after their chance encounter at Buckingham Palace. They had struck up a friendship of sorts - mostly through correspondence punctuated with occasional visits when Helen was in London.

Her friend had married but with the death of King George in 1952 she had taken on more significant duties. Helen had maintained contact and often spent time with her.

She was invited to Buckingham Palace for a private tea several times each year - in fact her friend insisted upon Helen's basic itinerary when she and her husband Daniel McFarlane were in London so time could be found to at least share a cup of tea. Diplomatic concerns and Daniel's business interests often brought them there from their permanent home in Ottawa.

Helen struggled with exactly how much information to provide her diplomatic colleagues regarding her inside connection to the Palace. At times she felt like a double agent as she did not want her diplomatic duties and responsibilities to infringe on her friendship. Daniel as informed that Helen often met an old friend when she visited London and he was sharp enough to figure out the connection and the reason for remaining quiet about it. He respectfully stayed clear.

However today was different. Helen's friend was in Ottawa. While only in the country for four days there were endless rounds of duties and various ceremonies that must be attended.

Despite the lack of time available Helen's English friend insisted upon visiting Helen in her home. The visit was conducted in the strictest secrecy and allegedly spontaneously with one knowing save Helen herself.

A small black limousine pulled up the driveway of the substantial McFarlane home in central Ottawa. The house was on a beautiful quiet winding street filled with large homes, where professors, diplomats and successful businessmen and their families lived.

Leaves were at the height of their autumn colours as the car, followed by a single large sedan pulled up at the McFarlane home.

The visitor quickly exited the car and went into the home. After a bit more than 90 minutes she left, with a cheery wave and was whisked back to her other duties.

Chapter Twenty-Six — 1958

Charlotte yelled up the stairs for Thom to come down.

"You're going to be late."

A few minutes later she realized Thom still hadn't come down for breakfast nor were there any of the usual noises coming from upstairs.

He hadn't been feeling well for several days, sporting a mild fever and some aches and pains. She had put it down to over-exertion on Labour Day weekend when the boys tried to cram in as much summer fun as they could into the 72 hours before school started.

"He's fallen asleep again," she said to herself, more than a little angrily.

She ran up the stairs and looked in his room. Thom was lying on his back eyes wide open and scared.

"I can't move, mom. I've been trying for 15 minutes. I can't move hardly at all, only my arms a bit."

It was polio.

Weeks of hospitals and doctors and fear would follow and eventually Thom graduated from a wheelchair to a cane. He would eventually recover from everything to a small limp, but his life was changed forever.

Those first few weeks put tremendous pressure on the family. Frank could not cope and simply left everything to Charlotte. Frank buried himself in office work and stayed long hours working on multiple projects some of them invented to fill the hours.

Charlotte was able to spend much of her time in the hospital with Thom. For weeks she would be there most of the day, the two of them working on Thom's school work. Charlotte would leave only late in the afternoon to be home for Mark and to get the evening meal prepared for her older son and husband.

Often times Frank would call saying he was stuck at work. He made a habit of stopping by the hospital on his way home in the deep evening. Thom came to love those instances - looking forward to his father's visits. But the nurses would hustle him out and he would allow himself to be pushed.

One evening Frank stopped by the hospital very late. The annoyed duty nurse, let him slip into Thom's room with only a nasty look. Thom was asleep. Frank sat by Thom's bed and looked at his son. Thom was improving and could walk a bit with support. Doctors said he was on his way to the necessary improvements that would get him home. Frank wanted to scoop him up and take him home right then. He had never grown used to having a hole in his family with Thom in the hospital.

Thom stirred. He realized his father was there but was closer to sleep than wakefulness. He managed a contented sigh. He was comforted that his Dad was nearby - something that Frank never knew as Thom would cheerfully wave goodbye when Frank had to leave. He said goodbye with a smile because he hated to be a burden on this father or his family.

Frank sat there for 15 minutes with Thom mumbling but never able to come fully conscious. He looked at his watch and realized it was very late. He had trouble leaving his son alone every night. He was toying with the idea of staying the night as the nurse seemed to have forgotten him. He stood and gave Thom's arm a squeeze and asked Thom if he wanted him to stay.

"No it's okay dad - you can go," said Thom quite clearly, though he remained partly asleep.

Frank shrugged. Looked at his watch again, said goodbye and left.

A few seconds went by for Thom who heard the door open and shut. In his sleepiness he wasn't sure what had happened. Then with a flash he understood that he had told his father to leave when all he really wanted was to have him there - and that Frank was pleading for a reason to stay.

Thom sat bolt upright in bed. He swung is torso over the edge and grabbed the walker beside his bed. He had been practising with it for days but always had a therapist at his side as walking any distance was difficult.

Thom manoeuvred himself to the door and flung it open. He managed to get out into the hall and yelled. The door at the end of the corridor was just about closed.

"Dad, dad, don't go. Come back."

He knew that his father was somewhere beyond that door and he moved as quickly as he could down the hall. But he couldn't manage it and fell. He climbed up the walker and fell again. He was too late - he couldn't catch his father nor could he tell him how much he wanted him to stay.

Thom drove himself to improve his walking. The prognosis was good. Nobody mentioned that night. The nurses had scolded him and complained that they had much sicker people to deal with and didn't need to be picking him up off the floor.

However, Frank began to get home earlier and be there even in time for dinner with Charlotte and Mark. He still had trouble with the absence of Thom from the house even if he knew Thom was only a few miles away in the good care of nurses.

His inability to make things right and his feelings of powerlessness in the face of the disease sucked the will out of him. He no longer felt like the master of his own fate.

Frank figured once Thom was home the feeling of helplessness would fade. However he feared having to face another crisis. He was unhappy with his inability to cope, with his weakness and his apparent lack of strength that Thom's sickness had revealed.

Chapter Twenty-Seven - 1967

'One, two, three, four, five Canadians' and many more gathered to greet Queen Elizabeth during her long tour of Canada in its Centennial Year.

Helen had entertained her friend again for tea and had been invited to accompany her friend on several of the Royal tours, remaining in the background as an extra set of eyes and ears. The Queen was apparently looking for native insight on several matters including the rise of French separatism in Quebec and the feeling of Canadians toward the Commonwealth and the United Kingdom.

In the six weeks the Queen toured Canada Helen had many opportunities to speak to her long time friend. Helen remained circumspect regarding her connection to the Palace, and always wondered what the reaction would be from her diplomatic colleagues who she thought would feel it was her duty to divulge the connection. Helen had long ago decided that her friendship was sacrosanct and she would never use it for personal or professional advantage.

The two women chatted amiably over their tea. Much as two neighbours might spend a few minutes catching up on family events and various goings on. Of course there were serious issues to be discussed, but they were never treated as anything more than curious topics.

"I have been away from home for a long time. This trip is quite lengthy and I miss my children," said Helen's guest. "It is too bad that I haven't been able to arrange for any riding here. I so long to go for a trot somewhere with a lively mount. Next time I am here I am going to insist that we arrange that opportunity."

"I haven't been riding in a while either," said Helen. "Living in the city and travelling so much doesn't lend itself to such pursuits. There is a riding farm a few miles south of here that . . . . "

Her guest visibly perked up, but after a moment's thought sighed in resignation. "No, it would never work. There just isn't time."

"I've never gotten my oldest boy interested particularly. Oh, of course he'll ride sometimes but I don't think he really likes it. My daughter on the other hand loves it, especially the jumping - she rode in Montreal last year. I guess all those lessons paid off," she said cheerily, punctuated with a sip of tea.

Helen was a seasoned diplomat and often was called in for special assignments in difficult places around the world. When introduced in London events the two women had to suppress knowing grins and follow through with protocol and decorum lest they tip off their much closer friendship.

"Is there anything about this French-Canadian situation that you can tell me?"

"In our circles most seem to want to avoid the topic. The French have always been very sensitive to their English counterparts - feeling oppressed by the majority, as it were. It seems to me that by allowing so many minority rights in Quebec we have simply opened the door to endless demands for more. So much so that I believe separatism will burst into the mainstream in the next few years. I'm not sure we can do anything about it at this point."

"That is all together too bad. I only wish I could convey my affection for those things French. Speaking the language alone does not seem to have much effect. I think the only way to get any traction in Quebec would be to denounce a 1,000 years of English history."

"I will keep my ears open during the tour of Expo in Montreal. Perhaps there will be some insight I can provide you."

"I'm very pleased you can come. Please pass the milk. I'd going to have another cup. These . . . you call them 'butter tarts' . . . . are absolutely delicious."

Chapter Twenty-Eight - 1969

It came from the television, clear as day, though slightly delayed among the technical tones and clicks, "That's one small step for man, and one giant leap for mankind."

"What an odd thing to say," said Andy out loud. Andy was nine, a curious and focused child, he took after his father Bernie.

"What would you have said?" Bernie asked.

Andy's sort-of friend, Jeff, was sitting in front of the television on a thick, shaggy, rust coloured carpet. He was the first to answer.

"What would I say? Probably, 'Hello. Anybody home?' Yeah, 'Hello, moon -men, take me to your leader!" said Jeff warming up to his latest act. "Or maybe, 'Who put the TV camera down here if I'm supposed to be the first man on the moon?' "

"It's attached to the leg of the LEM," explained Andy, who was sitting beside him and who had read all about the moon landing. "Lunar Excursion Module," said Andy, answering Jeff's question before it was asked.

"Anyway, it's an odd thing to say, but boy is it neat-o," said Andy. "Maybe I'd have said, 'Watch out for that last step, it's a big one'."

"That's what he said," Jeff blurted out, "It's a giant leap."

Andy was at Jeff's house because they had colour TV. Even though the moon landing was broadcast in black and white, at least shots of Mission Control and Walter Cronkite were in colour. Viewers couldn't be quite sure as the moon appeared to be a rather monochromatic place either way.

The two boys had their conversation amidst the general hubbub of voices gathered around the set. Several families had been invited to watch the historic moment and people were sitting on a chesterfield and in a couple of easy chairs. There were even people perched on the arms of chairs, sitting on the fireplace hearth and in chairs brought into the room. Everyone else was standing. A room which normally held 5-6 people was filled with 25.

"Now what?" said Jeff's father, a big burly auto mechanic. "So far it looks like a lot of nothing up there. Where's the cheese?"

"I understand they are going to collect rock samples and look around a bit. Armstrong is a geologist. Maybe there will be a lot of valuable minerals," said Bernie, before looking at his son. "It sure is a big deal though. Imagine what Granddad would have thought."

Bernie's father had died shortly after New Years and had been very excited about the potential moon landing. He had spent his life working on communications systems - mostly telephone switching equipment and something new called computers.

"I don't know why he was so interested but technological stuff fascinated him all his life," said Bernie. "He would have had more questions even than you Andy."

"Cronkite looks different, a little colour in his cheeks makes him look odd," one of the mom's said with a smile. "Pretty soon everyone will have a colour TV."

"Oh, I'll be waiting until the old set gives up the ghost," said Bernie, "No point in having two televisions."

There were a few sage nods acknowledging Bernie's contention. People started to drift away from the television set though Andy stayed, fascinated by the pictures and the modern language and terminology used by the commentators.

"Maybe I'll be an astronaut and fly to Mars or Venus," thought Andy.

Chapter Twenty-Nine - 1969

Charlotte's family also watched. Andy's cousin Mark wasn't with his family he was in the garage, making strange sounds on a guitar. Mark was 19, had long hair and wore blue jeans every day. It was the 'in' thing. When Charlotte told Mark and Thom what the 'in' fashions had been when she was in high school, the boys just cringed - how could anyone think that stuff was 'in' they thought.

Thom in particular seemed surprised that the 'in' thing was not a constant, but constantly changing. What value does being cool have, if there is no hard and fast definition of what cool is?

Mark had just finished high school and was deciding what to do next. Most of his friends were thinking about university and some, especially those with family connections had gone into a trade or job. He knew his parents would be looking to see what his decision was in a couple of weeks as summer wound down.

He couldn't help but wonder what the value of university was if everyone went? but that thought just brought down the litany of sober advice that made it all seem like the only thing to do - it opened doors, it set you on a career path, it kept you away from unpleasant manual labour and repetitive factory jobs, yadda, yadda. Something about choosing that life just didn't feel right to Mark, but he couldn't escape the logic of the mainstream.

He and his friends spent considerable time each day creating a cacophony - but they stopped early enough that the neighbours had not yet complained - except for Mrs. Haldiman two doors down, who had a new baby.

The boys had agreed to stop making their music when the baby's bedroom blinds were pulled. Mrs. Haldiman had played fair so far, but it had crossed her mind to leave the blinds pulled a bit longer than necessary.

As Mark tweaked the tuning of his guitar a couple more boys showed up. Kay had some news about a gig.

"Can we leave our stuff there?" asked Mark.

"Yeah, Mr. Schuy said we can use the upstairs for a month to practice as long as we play on the main floor for two weeks - two sets a night. Now we've got to work up enough material."

Kay was always working for the band - trying to get them gigs - deals on equipment and exposure on the radio. He was the keyboard player and chief peacemaker in the group and the main reason their song "Up With the Sun (Brand New Me)" had become a minor local hit. CHUM played it and they had managed a few gigs on the strength of the song.

The boys were completely different from each other to those who knew them, but to casual passersby, or those of an older generation, they were all interchangeable hippies, dungaree-wearing, long-haired, disrespectful of authority and not very interested in civil society. Even the most respectful young man was judged by the length of his hair as it made him look unkempt to the older generation. Lengthy hair made anyone sporting it immediately suspect rather than simply fashionable.

It was a statement of rebellion against the bland, straight and narrow, conformity obsessed older generation. Of course there were those who used the elements of rebellion as a sword in their desire for huge change in society. There were others who followed the lead of the counter culture as a way of support to their generation and there were still others who conformed to their own generation's manners and styles, and failed to see the irony in their actions.

The band members generally fell into the middle group as far as rebellion went. They were not radicals, nor where they calling for any huge change in society. Rather they were comfortable with the new status quo of style and symbolism imposed by the elder members of the baby boom. They supported change and forward thinking, even if they didn't really think about the future too much.

Kay had relentlessly promoted their song and the band for eight weeks trying to get airplay on local radio stations. He plastered posters anywhere he could promoting their gigs at two church dances and as the warm up act at a high school dance. He shamelessly talked about the song everywhere he went - even to cashiers in local stores. It paid off; he'd even seen a girl that he recognized from the A & P at one of the church dances.

Now they had a chance to be a real band - even if it was only for a few weeks.

"We gotta get our stuff downtown - then we can tune up a few covers and a couple of our own songs. We need two 90 minute sets - we go on at 8 and then again at 10:30 and I'm guessing we could have a couple of repeat tunes if we wanted to," said Kay with a slight grimace. He ran a line on the keyboard and punched in a chord for emphasis. "That's about 30 songs, maybe 40 depending how much talking we do between songs."

"Is he going to put us on the posters?" asked Gino.

"Yeah, I told you already," said Kay. "Not sure who the headliner is but the posters go up a week ahead . 'With the Sun' got us a bit of leverage - that and the fact that we are playing for free. It got us the rehearsal space. We have time to work on a few new songs and hopefully get us another single or two. Maybe that leads to an album. No screwing around though, right Pete? We need to work hard and be professional if we are going to do this."

Pete sat on a wooden work bench fiddling with his base guitar pretending he hadn't heard. He simply ran a riff, the best one he knew, but ignored the comment.

Pete's father owned an electronics repair shop where Pete worked on and off - a sore spot for his father, who groused about the time he was away from work, but a good arrangement for the band as Pete could wander off with the band as long as he told his father a few days in advance. More often than not the elder Pete would simply cover for his son himself. Pete knew his dad had a soft spot for his son's music and wouldn't object as long as he didn't push too hard.

The job and access to his dad's electronics parts and experience gave Pete a ready supply of electronics to work with and modify. Already he had built a little effects pad for his bass and was trying to figure out how to expand it. The rest of the band mildly resented Pete for his divided loyalties though they appreciated it was a trade off for his extra material contributions to the group.

"We gotta get our stuff down there tomorrow night and we can rehearse starting Monday - to be ready two Thursday's later when we start our gigs. Then it's . . . 'The Driftwoods" downstairs at the El Macambo'.

"With luck we'll be ready to record a few new songs by the middle of August and we can hit the school circuit after Labour Day - I'm working on getting us a few gigs," said Kay.

"This is a great opportunity'" said Mark. We gotta work hard though, the window isn't open for long."

He knew that most of the group were getting pressure from parents to go to university or college and that pressure would mount up with each passing week. This needed to work or the band's options would be limited - they might die on the vine and go their separate ways as without an alternative, education would become a priority and parental pressure too much to bear.

The Driftwoods borrowed a small delivery truck from Pete's dad, who despite his gruff complaining seemed to accommodate the group whenever they needed help. They moved their equipment and even some living stuff into the top floor of the El Mocambo, an old drinking and music hall in downtown Toronto.

They found a good sized room on the top floor, put a few light mattresses against the walls to baffle the noise - and hooked up their guitars and amplifiers and began to put their sound together.

First Pete hammered out a stattaco bass line, interspersed with a little rhythm line every 20 bars. Then Gino joined in with a steady drum pattern to match the bass line. They smiled at each other, this is how they always jammed. The grins got bigger as the sound got more complex. Sometimes the bass and drum would be in a familiar line and other times Pete's bass would take the lead.

Usually Kay would jump in with the piano and Mark would join in with a lead guitar line, meandering in different directions until he heard something that sounded good. Once in a while they would descend into a familiar song and simply play most of Honky Tonk Women, or Fortunate Son, or even Hey Joe.

When they were serious they would work out the progressions around a bit they had written and Mark or sometimes Pete would moan out a few nonsensical lines to get a voice line into the piece. The approach had worked well for 'Up With The Sun' and they hoped it would work again.

After a few hours work the room got a bit warm as the sun was high and the boys had been grinding away on their instruments. Mark introduced a few bars he had put together himself and asked the others to join in. Then Gino did the same thing and pretty soon they were grinning widely at each other as The Driftwoods had put together the musical backbone of a couple of new songs. They were elated.

Chapter Thirty - 1969

Kay and Mark were heading west to check out a possible gig at the Islington House, an old tavern-style drinking hole that had recently been booking local bands for Saturday nights.

Heading west on Bloor they were in Pete's dad's delivery van which the band had been using more frequently; enough that Kay thought they should firm up a deal for its use - like actually paying for some gas. Kay turned on the radio which warmed to the newsy voice of Wally Crouter at 1010 CFRB, the station of choice for the older set.

There was no FM array available on the old radio. The boys favoured FM stations which had begun to play album tracks and lesser known bands to counter the top 40 formats of most AM stations. Kay turned the knob slightly to get 1050 CHUM. Immediately he heard Mark twice - first yelling "That's us," followed by the sound of his singing voice crackling through the speaker.

The boys rolled down their windows and cranked the volume, impervious to the police car behind them. The siren sounded just as the last strains of the moody, bass-driven 'Time of Change' faded into the disk jockey's voice saying , "That was the latest song by Toronto band The Driftwoods - they are playing at the Islington House this Friday and Saturday night."

Mark, felt his elation turn to fear as the siren sounded, and Kay instinctively hit the brakes. Then he was confounded twice as the police car swerved around them and headed off on some call, while it struck him that they were going to beg for a gig at the 'I', when it was already apparently a done deal.

"I thought we were going to the 'I' to convince them to let us play?" said Mark as Kay eased the van into the parking lane.

"So did I, but now we are in a much better negotiating position; don't you think?"

After an interesting talk with the manager of the I, the Driftwoods were contracted for three consecutive weekends on both Friday and Saturday nights. They even managed to get a bit of food and drink thrown in to the deal.

As the manager excused himself Kay reached for the vinegar and sprinkled it over his French fries, then followed on with a liberal dash or two of salt.

"Well, things are looking up - I didn't even have to play my cards other than the reference to hearing the song on CHUM, he gave us everything we wanted, in fact a bit more," said Kay, gesturing to the fries. "I would like to know how the bar knew about our song being played on the radio and how they knew we'd fall into line. I won't be surprised if we see posters plastered around by this afternoon."

"Obviously they got tipped off. They must like our song if they are willing to take a chance on us," said Mark, stealing a fry from Kay's plate. "Can't wait to let Gino and Pete know - this is better than we'd hoped."

The boys discussed a few additional songs they should work up to add to their set. The first few gigs at the El Mo had gone well but it was a bit embarrassing to repeat songs even if it was from one set to the other - enough people stayed downstairs each night to hear them, rather than head up stairs for the opening set of the headliner. Pete had seen people get up and head upstairs once the band played a song a second time.

"We're down to three songs we play twice, we should get it down to one or none," said Pete, surrounded by old mattresses and cardboard boxes they'd lugged upstairs to act as sound baffles. "Mr. Schuy gave me a look in the last gig when we did Twist and Shout in the second set."

The band's equipment was actually in three different rooms. The largest room was their meeting space and where they placed the drums. Pete played bass in the hall while Mark and Kay were hooked up across the hall. The sound all came together in the hall so they had set up a borrowed reel-to-reel tape recorder to catch their sound at its best - sometimes the result was quite different to the band members from what they thought they could hear while they played.

"Any ideas for covers? We could throw in an extended jam - if we do it right, it's almost like working up a new tune and it covers off a bit of time. Maybe we could end "I Can't Explain" with an extended guitar and drum bit using my new bass pedal and then work it into "Pinball Wizard. I really like the bass line in that and there's some great drum fills too."

"You want to do a base pedal solo?" asked an incredulous Gino with more than a hint of a smile. "Cripes, people want to hear songs that are three minutes long, they don't want long solos on rhythm instruments, maybe a guitar bit or something," he tapped out a bit of drum fill on his snare.

"I think that's changing Geen," said Mark. "Think of that King Crimson album we heard the other day - some long stuff on there. And what about the end of Abbey Road?"

"No, that's just a bunch of odd bits stuck together," said Pete.

"Maybe, but its effective."

"What about that new band Heavy Zeppelin or something? They may not go off into tangents but their songs are longer than three minutes. And I heard a guy on the radio say in concerts they play 20 minute versions of some five minute album cuts."

"Well, a little experiment can't hurt I suppose, let's try it, but first let's figure out how we will transition from Can't Explain into the jam and then finish going into Pinball. After that maybe we should try to pick up a Zeppelin tune."

The Driftwoods professionalism evolved very quickly with their time at the El Mo and their gigs at the 'I'. The band was focused and worked long hours culminating in three hours of stage time each night. Kay managed to find them other events, here and there and they were soon faced with a choice.

The summer was ending and the band was confident in their direction. Each member was contemplating how to break it to their parents that they would delay post-secondary school to try music. They knew they had to continue to ride the effort they had put in and the success they had managed.

"Toronto is too small for us," Kay told the assembled members of the band. "If we want to keep our momentum up we have to start looking at the surrounding area and even further afield - I had a call from a guy in Oshawa and another from a couple of guys who are putting together a little road show, Hamilton, St. Catharines, Niagara Falls and maybe Kitchener. They saw us at the 'I'. They want us to open."

"Who's the headliner?"

"No, not The Who, they're a little too big for us. Guess?"

"The Guess Who? Wow."

"Yes, that's it, the biggest band in the country is playing a string of bars in St. Catharines," deadpanned Kay.

Then Mark and Pete got going.

"Yes?"

"I've heard of them. They're kinda new though. What do they sound like."

"More complicated that most - they do a great cover of America, you know, the Simon and Garfunkel song. 'It took me four days to hitchhike from St. Catharines' . . . 'I've gone to look for Niagara Falls'," he sang.

Everybody smiled.

"I wonder if we shouldn't work up a medley bit of funny lyrics to well known songs?"

"We're a serious band, not a comedy troupe," said Kay. "Though, if the tour falls flat, who knows."

He couldn't help himself. "She said the babushka in the balaclava was a spy. I said, 'Be careful her Faberge Egg is really a camera'. "

This time Gino laughed out loud. "Stop, stop."

Kay cleared his throat, even though he was grinning broadly, "In the mean time we need to work up more material - I have had a discussion with a couple of guys from Capitol Records - they want to buy our contract out from Queen Street Sound."

The rest of the Driftwood's stirred restlessly. "Man, this all seems pretty exciting said Gino, but I don't know . . . " he trailed off.

"Geen, what's not to know . . . . we should encourage the big boys, I think we can come up with some more stuff. Do they want an album?" asked Pete hopefully.

"Truth is guys, I think it's time to go big or go home, and that means hiring a manager and working out a contract with Capitol or someone else," said Kay. "It's getting beyond my ability to handle the office stuff and the music."

"Paul down at Queen Street said he'd be happy to let the contract go - he aims to make a good bit of money and he told me he can't handle the financial outlay of an album or even a single with a wider distribution than we've had so far."

Kay sprinkled some more vinegar on his fries, followed by two dashes of salt. He was letting the information sink in with his band mates. Everyone had to reassess their commitment to the band which had become more than just a lark over the summer.

"Why do you always put the salt on second? asked Mark.

"So it will stick to the vinegar and not end up all at the bottom of the pile of fries," explained Kay.

Mark looked at Kay with a newfound understanding.

"Thinking," he said with a smile, "thinking all the time are you?"

Kay nodded sagely. He hadn't every really thought about it - not consciously at least.

Gino burst the silence, "I don't know how I can do it. My parents want me in school, I've already paid the fees and it's hard enough juggling school with the band now."

"I've got the same pressure. I think we can work around that," said Kay. "At least until Christmas."

"My dad won't be happy but I'm in," said Pete. "If I tell him we're only committed until Christmas, he shouldn't be too upset."

"Yeah, I'm in too," said Mark. "Let's at least try this. Who knows, maybe we'll make a bit of money and have some fun doing it. As long a Gino's in until Christmas we can make it work."

"Geen, most of the work is Thursday to early Sunday morning, we'll rehearse Monday to Wednesday - so you will have that open. It's only for three months and it's all pretty local. You'll be pretty busy, but then we'll know," said Kay.

Geen nodded slowly taking it in. Kay took that as a yes. "Okay, its settled, I'll talk to the guy from Capitol as soon as I can - anyone want to come with me?"

Chapter Thirty-One - 1969

The road tour was pretty tough but incredibly productive. Days were taken up with song writing. The new management guys took care of the logistics, equipment, hotels, and travel arrangements, but Kay couldn't completely let it go. That meant the band often worked without their keyboards or drums - however with guitar and bass they were able to knock out a number of new tunes. They may have lacked in polish but they were definitely more musically sophisticated. At the same time they were plugged into the popular music scene anxious to hear what other bands were doing.

Kay layered on keyboard frills and riffs in live shows trying to find the right groove, the one that connected with the audience. Pete had an array of effects he could add to their sound and Mark was trying to pick up various new guitar techniques or string tunings that produced unusual sounds.

The Driftwoods released another single in November, the second song they had worked up during their time at the El Mo - but with quite a bit of instrumentation and effects added to the original arrangement. They were getting very good at layering on complimentary sounds that filled in a pop song's basic arrangement and made it much more interesting.

The single - Quick Time - was a rocking song with a memorable guitar hook and a fast beat. It featured a killer combination of protest, urgency and yearning in its lyrics, which was matched nicely with the hook and the melody. The song quickly gained attention locally and with Capitol's intervention caught the ear of radio stations in the States, bringing inquiries about the band from concert promoters in New York and even California.

The band's manager, Ernie Arch, assigned to them by Capitol, came in shaking his head.

"It seems The Driftwoods name sounds like a West Coast band. And, there is already a California band with that name. Capitol wants us to change it."

"How can we do that after all of the work we've done to promote our name?" asked Mark.

"We could just tweak it a bit," said Kay. "Like, The Amazing Driftwood's - well, not that . . . but something along those lines, you know."

The band gathered at a diner on College Street to discuss their name change. The place felt old and run down, it still had individual juke boxes at each Formica table with chrome accents on the back of the booth seating. It was a throwback but not unusual. Many older diners and restaurants still had one or more of these elements - they just didn't have all three.

Mark always thought of waitresses in roller skates when he came here, because his mother once told him that they used to serve customers that way once upon a time, in those ancient times perhaps half a generation before.

These days they walked and most waitresses had a bit of a surly disposition, especially with young people out on their own.

"If we change it, we have to keep it recognizable to our fans."

"Thank you Mr. Obvious!"

"Hey, it's not obvious. Look at Led Zeppelin, they were the New Yardbirds, and the Who were The Detours and the Beatles were Johnny and the Moondogs."

"Pete and the Moondogs - it has a bit of a ring to it."

They argued and suggested and ultimately got sidetracked - Mark, by a pretty girl two booths away and Kay by a poster under the cash register for a band he'd heard of but never seen.

Kay made it his business to check out their competition and keep tabs on the rapidly changing local music scene. Almost every day brought news of a new venue, a change to an existing one or news of local bands and players.

A few days later they were back together, this time getting ready for the second show as the opening act in a small tour Kay had arranged with help from Ernie.

The band sat around a motel room in Niagara Falls. They had just had a lunch together and were now gathered to try to tweak their name.

"How about Drift and the Woods?" asked Mark. "Okay, don't say it, that's stupid."

"Maybe. No, maybe it's stupid but we can't hold back - just spit them out and I'll write them down," said Ernie. "Trying to keep some element of the original name is a good idea."

"The Inventive Driftwoods?"

"The Elemental Driftwoods?"

"Get the Driftwoods? Get My Driftwoods!"

"That could be an album title."

"You mean like - 'With the Driftwoods."

"What about something completely different? We'll just go into our gigs with 'Our New Name' formerly The Driftwoods. After a while it will stick."

"We can't do that - not after all the effort we made so far - we are too tied up in the name."

"Tidal Driftwoods?"

"How about The Flotsam? Or the Jetsam - it's got that space-age vibe."

"The Jetson's? Jet-drift? Space-drift? The Drift? Mark, Kay, Gino and Pete?"

"Hey, that's not bad."

"Mark, Kay . . . ."

"No, no! The other one, The Drift. I like it," said Kay. "I'm circling that. Got any more?"

"Well, how about the D-Woods? The Woodies?"

"I don't think so," said Kay dismissively.

"I still like Pete, Gino, Kay and Mark," said Pete with a grin. They all laughed.

Pete gestured toward the motel window, where the electrical van was parked in full view. "Or even Peter And His Travelling Side Show."

"Now that's really funny," said Mark, "I was just thinking I should do an extended solo while you guys took a break. Oh, we already do that."

Kay, gave Mark a twisted grin, "Yeah, an extended solo in our 45 minute set."

"How about Electricity?"

"Yeah, I've always liked electricity. Power is good, keeps the fridge running and my guitar amped up."

Kay shot him a look. "How about Generator? Current? Current Generator? The Wire? Shock? I don't know. Help me out here."

"Well we don't have to decide today - we have until tomorrow morning."

Pete sighed. "Okay, I can live with The Drift. Anybody else?"

A week later their posters in Kitchener said they were The Drift, formerly The Driftwoods, playing their song 'Quick Time'.

Kay was usually first up in the morning with some business concern on his mind. But even he didn't rise until late morning while the others usually got up in time for a late lunch and a few hours jamming while doing the sound check at whatever club or bar they happened to be in. Ernie had arranged a fairly solid tour with most gigs being Thursday and Friday in one location and a Saturday night in a bigger place nearby.

The strategy worked as they were often able to build on their early week performances by drawing some of the same people to a bigger venue on Saturday, often with a bunch of friends in tow. Even the change in scenery seemed to encourage people to see them again.

The band soon recognized a few regulars who seemed to come to their shows often. Mark had made an effort to get to know some of these fans - at least the female ones.

The buzz around The Drift gradually grew and their set became much tighter and more professional.

Now they opened with their first local hit 'Up With The Sun (Brand New Me)'. An upbeat tune, it fired up the crowd and put them in a good mood. Then they played a couple of rousing covers.

They threw in a few bars of polka music to lighten the mood during their time in Kitchener during Oktoberfest. They swung into their own hit, the more thoughtful "Time of Change". Back to a few covers, interspersed with a few of their own songs usually not fully complete musically or lyrically and then capped off with the huge hit "Quick Time."

Their 45 minute set usually extended past an hour and appeared to annoy the headliners who were struggling to keep up the energy The Drift generated. Ernie knew the band would have to become headliners at the end of this short tour as they easily had two hours of material with some extended jamming and they were inevitably called back for the obligatory encore.

The boys always finished their encore with Pinball Wizard morphing into Summertime Blues.

They sometimes recruited a local drummer to fill in for their occasional Wednesday and regular Thursday gigs as Gino spent those days at school, joining them for the weekend. The hard life was showing on Gino and the band as they stayed up late, experimented with anything they could and rarely took a break from their adopted lifestyle.

As Christmas approached they began to consider the future again as their self-imposed deadline grew near.

"I'm in guys," said Gino. "I think I can do this commuting stuff until the end of next term and then I'll get a deferment on my degree."

"Capitol wants us to start a wider tour, New York, New Jersey, Massachusetts, Virginia and if that goes well, California," said Kay. "They want us to start right away, in fact a couple of dates have already been arranged in Boston - there's a number of universities there."

Gino looked crestfallen. "Where are we going to be at Christmas? I told my Ma I'd be home for a while."

"Capitol says the Christmas season's important because everyone is in a party mood and is looking for entertainment. That means we have to work. But they promise a break after that as the post holiday doldrums kill the concert scene. They want us for three weeks until New Year's Day and then they will arrange a tour of smaller cities down the east coast beginning in late January. In the mean time they want us to record an album. That means new material."

Mark and Pete looked at each other. Pete's eyes went wide. A record was exciting and new material not too tall an order in that type of crucible - they had done it before in their time at the El Mocambo.

Gino's head was down. He started to shake his head slowly.

"I . . . I can . . . I can't do this," he squeaked. He looked up at his band mates, they were all staring hard at him.

"I can't do this. I can't do both." Tears welled in his eyes. He pleaded, "I want to stay in the band and I want to finish school."

Nobody said anything. Kay had anticipated the choice Gino would have to make. He already had a few possible replacements in mind, but he didn't say anything. He wanted Geen to stay but he wanted a committed drummer more.

Mark and Pete were silent, each working out the possible choices and their desires. Crunch time had finally hit The Drift, formerly The Driftwoods.

"When do you have to know?" Gino asked Kay.

"After this week's shows at Western we are scheduled to go to Boston. We get a couple of days in between. We probably need an answer yesterday."

"Can I stay with you guys until New Year's? I'll try to let you know before that."

"A good compromise," said an upbeat Kay, with only a hint of the forced smile he pasted on. "It's your choice Geen. Obviously we want you with us - it wouldn't be the same. But we need you on board - completely.

216

Things are getting bigger, faster and crazier. According to Ernie there is even talk of a TV appearance - probably one of the afternoon variety shows."

Chapter Thirty-Two - 1970

Boston was a triumph. Their Christmas shows were sold out. They were getting great responses to a couple of their new tracks and bookings started to pour in from other schools up and down the Eastern seaboard.

Gino decided to stay with the band - he rationalized that it might only be for another few months and he wanted the experience with his friends. He was enjoying his choice - carrying on late into the night almost to make up for lost time when he had been forced into responsibility to carry his classes the previous fall. He had arranged for a couple of courses to be conducted by correspondence which had satisfied his parents and his own commitment to school. However, those studies had been pushed aside for the wilder times on the road.

After New Years the band took a week off and reconvened in New York City to record their debut album. It featured all three of their hits and two new songs that Capitol promised to push, "New Direction" a slow bluesy guitar laden tune with a nice hook and a mild protest lyric, and "Here We

Go (Again)" a bright, poppy song with a quick beat but drenched in guitar tricks, wah-wah and atmospheric echo.

Both had come out of their in concert jam sessions and had been tightened up in sound check practices.

"Capitol liked the initial track of "Here We Go" but they want a cleaner version," said Ernie.

Kay agreed, but they'd had this discussion before. Mark and Pete loved the guitar and bass tricks and wanted to keep them, in fact they were writing more songs in the same vein.

They had reached a compromise. The album would feature the heavily produced version of 'Here We Go' with all the guitar tricks while they would release the cleaner version as a single only. Pete and Mark had reluctantly agreed.

They set down to work on the poppy version so it could be released to radio stations to promote the album. Mark couldn't help himself and he insisted on putting a bit of echo on some of the guitar fills. Pete had helped there as he began to sit with the recording engineer and learn how to work some studio magic on the music as it was being recorded.

Soon the control room was Pete's second home as he sat with the engineer asking questions, making suggestions and generally immersing himself in the electronic wonderland that a modern 16 track studio could be. The walls of buttons and knobs, the gyrating sound level meters and the sliding volume controls presented an almost endless opportunity to manipulate the music. Pete was in heaven.

At night, or while recording equipment was being tested and rearranged, the band jammed. They managed a couple of new tracks, one that Kay particularly liked and another with a cool rhythm but nothing that Ernie said would be pushed to radio stations.

Kay secretly made plans to push his favorite on the new album oriented FM radio stations that almost preferred to play less well known album tracks.

At the end of the process they had a very tight album. It featured three previous hits, two potential new ones, a cover of Summertime Blues, a band and concert favorite that started out light and finished with heavy power chords and thundering drums.

The album also had three other original songs that they had played for several months in concert. Mark and Pete had always insisted they play them because they got a solid response from their audiences and because they were interesting to play as they featured some difficult chords and interesting changes while offering some room to jam.

Ernie had grabbed the band and taken them to Cape Cod one afternoon during their Christmas shows in Boston. They had taken a number of promotional shots of them standing in various locations. Capitol didn't want them in any place that was identifiable as they didn't want to tie them to one music scene or one area of the country.

They especially did not want their Canadian roots to be generally known. The band settled on a beach scene with the band angled down to the crashing surf. A little ice and a large piece of driftwood gave the picture a stark quality that nobody would confuse with the California scene - in fact north-easterners could instantly tie the photo to New England, given the style of building in the background of the shot. Capitol loved it, and The Drift didn't even know it had been chosen until they saw the finished product. No one had even thought to ask what the record would look like.

"Hey, nice touch with the driftwood in there," said Kay. "That's really good. The shot is a bit bleak for our type of music but it's serious and I like the vibe."

"Too bad it wasn't lit exclusively from the left," laughed Pete referring to the well-known Beatles cover photo. "Or maybe from the right, as the sun comes up."

Then came the inevitable listen, so they could hear what their fans would hear. Ernie prepared for the explosion.

The album had the pop version of "Here We Go' on it. Pete and Mark and even Kay were furious.

"What the crap is that," yelled Mark as he rose from his chair and began stomping around. "You guys promised. I hope this is just a demo copy."

They had worked for hours and days on the complex recording of the heavy version of this song. Mark had considered it his finest work. Pete had stayed up for days playing with the mix and adding background to broaden the sound and create a subtle interplay behind the melody. He thought it was a masterpiece.

"What the hell. You guys promised," screamed Mark. Even Kay was upset as he had relayed the record company promises and now looked complicit.

"I swear, it was a mistake," said Ernie. "When they took the final mixes they screwed it up. They were told to go with the heavier version and use the first version for the record - the single record."

"Look we can still use it - we can release it on another album. In fact Capitol is compiling an album to be released to radio stations promoting several of our up and coming acts - we could put the track on that album - it should get some serious air play. Okay?"

Nobody said anything. Mark fumed, Kay looked at his band mates and Pete and Gino simply looked resigned - Gino shrugged.

"Sooooo, I have your hotel arrangements for the college tour. We hit the road in three days, and play the University of Virginia on Friday and Saturday. Then we're in North Carolina, West Virginia, Pennsylvania, DC and Philadelphia. There are a few club gigs in there as well. The tour ends in May. If everything goes well, we'll be off to California in the summer."

The spring campus tour was a big hit with sold out shows and huge airplay - Capitol Records did what they promised and The Drift was looking like a well-oiled machine. The band still believed in the music and ignored some of the commercial issues to fulfill their dream of making music, recording it and playing shows to support it.

Every time the pop version of Here We Go was heard on the radio, Mark exploded. And it was on the radio in heavy rotation. He simply couldn't let go of the mistake. Each listen reinforced his belief that the switch had been intentional.

Mark fumed and never failed to take a shot at Ernie, though never when he was present. It was obvious the business end of the business got his blood boiling.

After the spring tour they took a break then got back together for a short session to work out some new material that they decided to preview in concert. The strains of the business were there for everyone even if the music flowed as quickly and confidently as ever.

223

Gino was having a hard time putting any time to his studies even though he had cut back on correspondence courses. Kay seemed more and more engrossed in the business of music, Pete was spending his free time on technical issues and Mark was doing some session work on the side and mixing it up on the local party scene. His late nights, supported most often by Gino were becoming an issue, though the others engaged in the lifestyle often enough that they had little to say.

The band's summer tour of California started in Denver in June and finished in Chicago in early December as more and more dates were added to accommodate their growing popularity and reputation for lengthy, entertaining, and increasing elaborate shows.

They played colleges but quickly graduated to medium sized venues, concert halls, festivals and outdoor summer events before finishing with a pair of arena shows at 18,000 seat Chicago Stadium.

They were spent and insisted on several months off the road to write more material and to get their lives back in order. The band spent Christmas apart. However at Capitol's insistence they did a few shows in the Toronto area and two in Boston.

The harder version of 'Here We Go' had received some radio play and was well received at college concerts but at the larger shows it did not get the type of enthusiastic response that Mark had hoped.

"It's just a bit beyond the mainstream Marky," said Ernie, intending to take the sting out of its reception. "I'm thinking when you guys go back to the studio, and by the by, we're looking at some studio time in February in London, that you consciously record some heavy stuff and some lighter stuff to satisfy all your fans."

"It's pretty hard to sing la-la-la when you see guys getting blown up every night on the news," said Mark, who then rolled his fingertips in a bit of air -guitar, "Deeper music is what's here."

"Yeah, I got this great bit where boy meets girl, boy gets girl, boy loses girl in napalm attack. It starts out light and fun and then I rip the strings off the guitar, musically of course, but with the distortion turned up full," said Pete. "It's got top 10 written all over it."

"What's it called?" asked Mark with a twisted grin.

"Light my Fire was taken already, so I have the working title, 'Happy Together', no shoot, that's been taken too. How about 'I'm on fire for you, baby' or maybe 'Senseless War Broke My Heart', or is that too political?"

The Drift came back together in February for a week in New York where they played a couple of shows to get back in the groove and talk to Ernie and their management team at Capitol.

"Okay boys, some good news. The heavy version of 'Here We Go' is number one in Europe, seems a few disk jockeys there got a hold of our promotional record and have been playing it in heavy rotation. So Capitol wants a tour split up by a few weeks recording. They've lined up some time in London, Paris and Stockholm."

Mark looked at Pete and Kay with a big grin. They took it in together with Mark even burping out a little giggle. "Stockholm eh, we must be popular. Are we playing any gigs there?"

Gino was fiddling with some paper, not really listening. "The beat goes on," he said.

The tour was a success though only a few extra dates were added giving the band significant time in the studio and in hotels to write the basic melodies for their upcoming album.

Europe was eye-opening to the boys, as it seemed cool, interesting and run-down compared to North America. They did a bit of sight-seeing and inevitably the experiences found their way into their songs. Musically they added a bit of banter and lyrically they started on some unfamiliar areas fighting between meaning and fun, a light touch and strong, serious themes. It was a difficult thing to pull off and The Drift were having trouble with their own identity as they wrote, rehearsed and played some of this new material.

Of course the new music was foremost in their minds but their fans wanted to hear the five hit songs and were just happy to be entertained. Mark was good at it, but even he started to get angry with the fans who only wanted the poppy, singable songs on which they had made their reputation.

The Drift recorded their second album 'Get It' which was packaged with a front cover photo of a stark London street scene, featuring a concert poster for the band. On the back was a pastiche of concert ticket stubs and smaller photos of each member in action. Mark was holding a microphone on a small stage and reaching out to some fans who were reaching back to him. Kay was stationed behind his keyboard, hands in position, looking very serious. Pete was bending some strings on his bass and leaning backwards looking like the instrument was extremely heavy and was causing him great pain. Gino was behind his drum kit with a big grin on his face and considerable sweat on his forehead, despite a headband to control it.

" I know where that was taken," he said, laughing all over. "That was our second night in Lyon when Mark fell over Pete's bass wire while trying to dodge all the underwear coming from the audience. Worst part was I couldn't see it until it was airborne."

"Just how heavy is that bass, Pete? We could get you a lighter one if you need it."

"Hey, I'm into it, man," said Pete. "I love the sound of that riff - it goes great with the drum in that one."

"You know what song that is?"

"Oh, yeah, I can tell from my expression," Pete laughed.

Mark looked at Ernie. "We called this 'Get It'. Why didn't we just keep it simple and call it 'Buy It'? It's more direct that way."

"The big boys liked the concert tie ins on the back," explained Ernie. "They want to keep you guys popular in the concert tours, that's where the money is."

"About that," said Kay. "I think we need a bit more clarity on where the money goes."

The recording process had been difficult as the recording was spread across several months in several different locations, with changes in equipment and difficulties integrating their own instruments into foreign electrical grids.

Despite the troubles or maybe because of them, the album featured a couple of big hits, the ballad "This Time" and a peppier tune with a lot of guitar effects and overdubbing, called "Chamonix." That little ski-town had impressed the boys who were taken with its charm, its setting and all the happy people a vacation village attracted.

'Get It' hit the stores in May 1971 and was an immediate success fuelled in part by a large new tour of North America and Europe finishing a year later.

They finished their tour in New York where they played a couple of concerts and did a number of the variety shows including a memorable stint on The Mike Douglas Show.

"You know, Mr. Douglas looked about as conventional as a Wall Street business guy, but man, I think he really got it," said Mark. "He asked about the music, the arrangements, about touring and about the good and the bad."

"Well, he was a travelling singer before he got into TV," said Ernie. "I'm sure he understands."

"There needs to be a word for it in the English language," said Mark. "I couldn't really answer his questions because we don't have a word for that almost mystical feeling that you get when the bent guitar note melts perfectly into the melody and the lyric. Even that doesn't do it justice as there is more to it than that. And it happens in other instances too, like sport, or a movie moment."

"You're right, there is no word for that feeling of perfection - it's the thing you remember about a great song or a bit of acting in a movie - where it all comes together perfectly."

"Can there even be a word? asked Geen. "It seems as though, while all these things are similar in nature, they're not the same and would need different words to accurately describe them."

"The Germans would have a crazy word for it - like 'perftonbendunstringaschadle' or something," Kay said.

"We need an English word, something a bit easier," said Mark. "Like 'soulbless' or something."

"Sounds like soulless, and that's not what you are trying to describe."

"There needs to be a word. Get on that," said Mark, letting the moment slip away.

The band was beat. They needed a break. Capitol wanted another album and the group agreed to get together after the summer. Having spent most of the last 30 months together, they went their separate ways for a time.

Chapter Thirty-Three - 1972

"Everybody says 'What is Canada, what's our identity?' "

"Oh Bernie, there you go again," said his exasperated wife Mary. "Hockey, hockey, hockey, that's all he ever talks about. I used to think he was interested because Andy likes it, now I think he likes it and Andy just got pulled along by the wake."

Bernie and Mary were at their neighbours home to watch the opening game of the Canada- Russia hockey series, an eight game affair played in September just before the NHL season was going to get underway. Players expected to win easily, make some money for their Player's Association and to play themselves into shape for the upcoming season.

There was a lot of anticipation as it was the first time Canada had been able to pit its professional players against the Russians, winners of several World and Olympic Championships. Russian players were officially serving in the Red Army, but were really full time professional hockey players using their army service to protect the guise of amateurism so they could enter international championships and Olympic contests which prohibited professionals.

Most Canadians believed the scouting reports that suggested the Russians were slow, overly methodical and did not have quality goaltending.

That assessment turned out to be inaccurate.

Canada had put together a team of professionals, but by no means the best possible team. Some players opted out, others were never asked, and Canada's best player, Boston Bruins defenseman Bobby Orr, was injured and could not take part.

Bernie was an assistant coach on his 12 year old son Andy's team. Andy was one of the best players on the team as he had taken very early to skating. He had played for several years on an outdoor rink before being old enough at age 8 to play organized hockey in a local league.

Bernie had already been approached by a few local hockey guys who had expressed an interest in Andy playing on a more advanced team in the Greater Toronto Hockey League, where local teams of all-stars played similar teams from around the city.

Bernie found the idea very attractive but he simply could not afford the very high price demanded by these teams which could be hundreds of dollars a season. That money covered coaching, more ice time for games and practices and several tournaments. Bernie preferred to pay the $50 annual fee for the local league and he liked helping out as a coach on the ice with Andy and the other boys.

Bernie sometimes caught himself trying to figure out how he could pay for the GTHL spot but also realized in his heart that while Andy was really good, he was one of a couple of players who might reasonably be called the best on the team. He wondered if the other fathers had fielded similar offers for their sons to play.

Bernie watched the Canada - Russia game start and wondered what it would be like if Andy was playing. Then Canada scored early in the game and broke his reverie.

"There. That was easy. We are going kill them," a voice chimed out.

"I don't know how easy it's going to be. Look at how they control the puck."

Then another goal went in for Canada. Bernie began to wonder if the scouting reports were correct.

"Okay, it's just a matter of how many times we get the puck on our sticks," said one of the other men. "Playing keep-away isn't hockey, you gotta shoot to score and that means giving up the puck."

The Russians tied it up before the end of the first period and then managed to completely control the game using their speed and long passes to frustrate the Canadians. Though everyone thought Canada would rout the Russians, they got routed.

"We have to adjust to their game. We have to grind them down," said Bernie.

The next day on the job, the game was all anyone wanted to talk about. The next game was in Toronto.

The Canadians adjusted their line-up and came away with a hard fought 4 -1 win.

The third game in Winnipeg ended in a 4-4 tie.

The fourth game was back and forth with the Canadians unable to keep pace and losing 5-3 while looking bad doing it. They were booed in Vancouver as they left the ice.

"It's frustration," said Bernie. "We can't seem to get on top of these Russkies, they adjust their tactics every time we figure out what to do. Now we gotta go to Moscow - I just hope we can keep it respectable. You know the Russians are playing like demons - if they fail they'll end up in Siberia or something. Our guys get to go back to their jobs getting paid to play - win or lose."

The Russians won Game Five in Moscow 5-4 to take a 3-1 series lead with a tie and three games to play. They had come back from a 4-1 deficit as Canada tried to nurse their big lead. The excuse machine went into overdrive.

"If we could just knock them around a bit more but the refs won't allow it."

"We gotta shoot more."

"We should have come to the camp in better shape. These Russian guys practice all year round."

"We were taking it as a lark, they had something to prove. It was a no-win situation for us."

"It's not over yet," said Bernie to anyone who would listen.

Canada won Game Six 3-2. Toronto Maple Leaf winger Paul Henderson scored the winner on a slap shot as the Canadians adjusted their play. They stopped the dump and chase tactics and played a possession style like the Russians. There were 31 minutes of penalties to Canada and only 4 to the Russians.

"Those refs are killing us - it's all that East German guy," said Bernie. "The commies are ganging up. They want to win this badly."

Canada won the seventh game 4-3. Again the game was close and again Paul Henderson scored the winner late on a breakaway. The series was unexpectedly tied 3-3-1.

Anticipation for Game Eight was electric. Canada had played their way back into the series. Everyone knew now that the Russians were a formidable hockey team.

September 28th, 1972 - the whole of Canada was on edge. Schools made plans to show the game on televisions in gymnasiums and classrooms. Businesses shut down - the entire country was tense.

The first period ended 2-2. Russia took control of the second period and jumped ahead 5-3 after two. Then Canada scored one. Quick skating Montreal Canadien Yvan Cournoyer scored to even it up around 10 minute mark. Canada was in the grip of hockey. There were battles in the stands, Russian soldiers were leaning on Canadian officials.

As the game wound down Russian officials made it known that they would claim victory in the event of a tie as they had scored more goals than the Canadians during the course of the tournament.

The last minute ticked away the puck ended up against the back boards behind the Russian net. Phil Esposito brushed it toward the front of the net, Cournoyer took a whack and Henderson, recovering from a fall near the back boards swung out in front of the net and scored for Canada, shoveling the puck under a sprawling Vladislav Tretiak.

With 34 seconds to go , Canada led in the series for the first time since the opening period of the first game. Jubilation on the ice was no match for the jubilation in schools, offices and on the street in Canada. The maple leaf has never shone brighter.

It was not until that moment that Canada was defined by hockey. A country searching for an identity - found it that day.

It's a British country with a significant French influence and a fierce American-style independence, forged in a faraway place under harsh conditions. A country that stood by its friends and family - its teammates - in two world wars. Canada was tempered by the caution and drive of pioneers and immigrants and forged by an inhuman determination to prove its worth on the battlefields of Europe. Efforts, that due to its small population, were lost among the bigger battles and bigger propaganda machines of its allies.

But they were not lost among Canadians who quietly nod at their allies achievements all the while knowing that with a grit and determination forged in a harsh environment they know their own measure and will persevere.

Even long after The Goal, most people in Canada would not admit that it was hockey that tied them together, that best showed what they were made of. Hockey did not mould Canada but through hockey, Canadians could clearly show the unparalleled determination to succeed that exemplified their nature and their character to the world.

However it was in that moment when in utter jubilation Canadians tossed aside their rational resignation of national expectations and realized the fearsome power of belief and determination. They had seen glimpses of it in war but here it was clearly displayed by an unlikely hero in the crucible of sport.

When The Goal was scored every Canadian had been holding their collective breath. Together as one, the beast of victory rose in their mouths and was made real.

Andy just yelled. He and most other Canadians couldn't articulate their joy - they just yelled. A fearsome cheer of determined victory. There was something else there in that moment, something else lay with that puck in the back of the Russian net.

In later years Canadians would win and lose similar series, they would come to prize international victories even more than Stanley Cups. The Cup was something you dreamed of winning with your friends while a Canada Cup or Olympic gold was a more serious thing. It became the peacetime equivalent of war, life or death.

While Canadians cheered their athletes in all sports, they often celebrated second best, or even a darn good, unexpected result. Not so with their national hockey team. It was often said, only half jokingly, a national team loss in a major hockey tournament meant the players were no longer welcome back to Canada. Their passports were revoked and the scorn and shame of the country was heaped on them - well, at least until the Stanley Cup finals.

Canada would never enter another international tournament without significant preparation and the clear expectation of victory. In a country where second best is regarded as a quality achievement it was a remarkable thing that hockey alone defied this notion.

The sheen of victory against the Russian team quickly gave way to a long look inward, as Canadians wondered how they could have underestimated the Russians and their skill.

Chapter Thirty-Four - 1973

Oil. It was the bearing grease of the modern world. In late 1973 the Organization of Petroleum Exporting Countries determined to use their market power to shape foreign policy.

The price of oil, which fueled cars, heated homes and was factored into the price of virtually all goods and services, skyrocketed. The ensuing shock rattled markets, grinded economies and started the world down a new economic and geo-political path.

Barely developed desert nations realized their economic power. They were awash in oil and were determined to convert that oil into other forms of wealth.

In the wake of the Iranian Revolution a few years later it all happened again. Fear of supply and geopolitical concerns forced the price up again.

These concerns were never really been resolved as the availability of oil from backward and intolerant places in the world has resulted in instability of the world's most important commodity.

Oil issues have the ability to affect our economy in so many ways that it was very difficult to predict how changes would occur and manifest themselves. The last quarter of the 20th century saw many pendulum swings in oil policy and outcomes.

Chapter Thirty-Five - 1973

It was June, 1973 and the Drift had come back together. A bit older, wiser and more careful after their wild three year run, the boys stepped back into the group gingerly at first. Except for Gino.

Mark had been doing a lot of session work. He married one of the back-up singers he first met while playing guitar on a record for Jethro Tull. He had sat in on sessions with Joni Mitchell, Neil Young and David Bowie. Some of it ended up on record, some didn't and none of it was credited - though he was well paid.

A few months later he saw her again when they ended up together at a wrap party with all the technical people and musicians after a David Bowie recording session. They had talked deep into the night and had not been separated since. A quick wedding in St. Albans a few months later was attended by Gino who happened to be in England on a holiday with his mother and sister.

Pete had been busy in the studio. With Capitol's blessing and financial backing, Pete had cobbled together a small recording studio and had produced several singles and an album by a promising Capitol Records band, The Seconds.

Pete had taken his knowledge of the recording process The Drift had used, and incorporated many new effects, instruments and techniques - some of which he had picked up in Europe. It produced a clean but eclectic sound that had many people in the industry talking. They began to seek Pete out as a producer.

Pete had returned to The Drift with the understanding that he would fulfill promises to produce two records at the end of the year. It was all he could talk about.

Kay came back to the group with contracts to be signed. He took them aside and explained how they were being paid by Capitol and what they had to do to gain control of their destiny and get a larger part of the profits.

"First we have to assign composing credits accurately, as our contracts have the money going to composers and the publishers." He explained that Capitol had been gaining most of the profits from the publishing and taking huge management fees from their concert tours.

The boys started to grumble but Kay stopped them quick. "They went by the contract. They have acknowledged it's time for an update. Ernie went to bat for us. Now we have a new contract - I've been working this out for a few months now. They acknowledge they have been well compensated for their efforts on our behalf and will continue to benefit from our success. However, we will benefit more. That's why we need another big tour and a few more records. I'm afraid we are in for a lengthy slog - but it will be worth it."

He handed them each a sheaf of papers to sign.

"I've formed a publishing company for our songs. That's the first couple of pages," said Kay. "We write our music together so we all get composing credits. Mark and Pete usually do the lyrics so they get a bit more, an extra credit for the lyrics that they split, or split with anyone who contributes. It's an incentive to compose. That's the second bunch of pages.

Our tours are split with Capitol as they organize them and promote them. All the details are in there. In fact I was able to secure most of the future rights to previously published music - Capitol thinks there is no future market for old songs so I picked them up for nothing and you never know. There is some money in background music for films and television. I encourage you guys to read it all. We pay them a management fee, a reduced percentage on future music and a lower percentage of the concert profits."

Pete, started to read the papers. Mark began to shuffle through them, more to ascertain how many there were and how impenetrable the language might be.

"Look guys, read them later today. I'll answer any questions. Ernie can answer too - he is being paid by us now, not Capitol. He works for us. Give the papers back to me in a day or two so I, we, can seal the deal with Capitol. We are going to make a lot more money under this new arrangement."

Gino was there as he had agreed to remain in the band while they looked for a replacement drummer. He had thought long and hard about his future and realized the touring lifestyle was not his first choice. He enjoyed all parts of the music business except for the tours, as he could not consistently refuse the parties, late nights and other inducements.

His parents had seen it when he returned from the tour. He denied the problem but found the longer he stayed away the better he felt. He had enrolled in college again, and had had a great year, refueling his academic interests.

He talked to Kay about staying with the band but not touring. Kay had been skeptical but wanted Gino to stay in the group so he had approached Capitol. They refused outright. They wanted a professional approach and said to Kay that Gino was not integral to the band's success, he did not compose and was not a particularly noted drummer. In fact, Ernie as one of his last acts as a Capitol employee told Kay that sometimes Gino's backing tracks had been re-recorded by a session man after principle recording had been completed.

At first Kay had been angry. Then he was resigned and sad that his friend would not continue with them or get the advantages of the new contract. He made sure that significant residual income from work already done would flow to Gino.

The band started rehearsing and bringing in new drummers through the process.

Eventually they had crafted the basic tracks for a new album though they used a session drummer for the recording.

Pete was the lead producer on the album which they called 'Side Streets' and he was the principle engineer. The album sold well in release but did not reach the sales of their previous albums.

Ernie put together a tour but found that having been off the road for almost a year, the band was almost forgotten, as they had had no new songs for many months. At the same time the music was changing. Longer songs, more complex arrangements, more instruments and the use of non

-standard recording techniques and new technology made the music more interesting but ultimately less joyful.

They toured but it all seemed like work. However the tours were paying off in terms of airplay and recognition.

"All this art-rock stuff is taking off," said Mark. "We can do that too you know. At least we can do it like us, but with more depth and a wider range."

Kay and Pete were skeptical but willing to try to help Mark with new material in this vein. The problem cropped up when the music became very complex as none of The Drift had a musical background in the classics or even through the Royal Conservatory of Music.

Pete's studio genius was at the forefront of the art they were employing but the rest of them were not really there. Their first attempts at art-rock came off poorly - once Pete laughed out loud at a bit Mark had recorded on his own, thinking it was a parody of the orchestral rock movement.

It was not. And Pete had to do some fancy explaining to get out of the hole his laughter had dug.

Mark gave up all his efforts for a couple of weeks as he stewed about it.

"I'm not sure how to go about this," he said. "Perhaps we should just jam like we always do and see what comes of it."

So The Drift jammed. They had managed a couple of working bits and some promising melodies when they opted for a few weeks in studio. Pete's tiny, cramped Brandel Street Studio was transformed into a camp shack for three weeks as the band argued and refined their art-rock approach.

"All it needs is a bit more harpsichord," said Kay. "No, double track the harpsichord and then run a slightly different progression half a note off track. That will make the sound fuller and sound like there's more depth to it."

Pete turned away and rolled his eyes. A few weeks creating music that was mostly alien to them and trying to record it using all the studio tricks, had gone badly off the rails, Pete thought. By now he knew he couldn't say it out loud without risking a huge blow out from Kay and Mark. Both believed in the project and had worked hard - but the result was something different than they had imagined. The Drift's heavy pop sound simply did not translate well into art rock.

The resulting album 'Orpheus, Thunderous and Melody' was a modest hit, scooped up by their fans and getting under the lip of the art-rock scene. Those interested in the more complex music simply didn't take them seriously.

The dramatic cover, a shot of Winged Victory with lightening flashing out of impossibly dark clouds behind her, was a major departure from the style that they had been using since their high school days.

Touring was solid but they moved into doing more shows in smaller venues. They couldn't manage their more elaborate shows on these smaller stages but they did manage to entertain and kept their costs down by moving to new venues twice a week rather than every day.

The band did not articulate their disappointment in the results, nor did anyone mention the significantly louder applause for their previous songs and even the occasional 'It's about bloody time' coming from the audience when then moved into more familiar musical styles.

'Orpheus, Thunderous and Melody' featured only five songs, all in the new art rock style. The songs did not catch on radio and The Drift was left adrift, abandoned by the Capitol promotional machine. The worst news came four months later when Ernie told them that Capitol released a live album to fulfill their five album contract. Capitol had not mentioned any plans for resigning The Drift to the label.

"You know, I really like this bit," said Mark as he noodled through a guitar intro to one of their new songs. "I'm not sure but maybe we should have taken more time with the arty stuff to let it mature and to work on the arrangements."

He fingered a few chords. "I just love this intro bit, especially the descending chords just before the ascending melody kicks in. It's just magic," he closed his eyes and played it through slowly.

Starting to play again he had a brainwave and motioned Pete to pick up his bass. "Hey Pete, follow me. He went through the intro again, this time much slower than usual.

"There when I hit the second go through, come in with the same progression, but play it behind me, then speed it up a bit until you are in front of me - yeah, like that," he said listening intently. "Now a bit quicker."

They ran through it again. "Kay, come in with the melody at the end of the second progression and double it up with the synth. No drums until we've gone through it again - but the fourth time we have to be speeding it up a quarter. We want it to be noticeable but not so we sound like chipmunks."

Mark was getting excited. "This sounds better than the record. We have to do this tonight."

"Let's play it through. When we hit the final verse start to slow it back down, and reverse the instrumentation - drums out on the last chorus, piano out on the repeat and guitar out one roll after the melody goes."

They played it through. Then again as the middle section had to be changed slightly. The sound check was done but they ran it through again.

"Man, I think you have a bit of producer in you Mark. That sounds great. Really great," said Pete. "We should play it that way all the time now."

The boys shut down and went out for a bite to eat before the show. All the acrimony was gone and they were all thinking how they could improve their new tunes. Pete was thinking about all the old ones too.

A new contract could wait. The Drift had a show to do and a renewed passion for their music and how to make it.

Kay dashed vinegar on his fries and followed up with two passes of salt. "You know, that new arrangement sounds good but you don't want to overdo it. Maybe some songs can use a fresh approach but others maybe just need a bit of tweaking - a bit more guitar here, moving the bass higher in the mix there. Some of your bass lines are lost in the mix Pete, and frankly some of them are really strong - really the melodic backbone of the tune."

Mark stole a French fry with a grin. "Where are we going tomorrow? In fact, where are we today?"

"You know where we are? Don't you?" asked Kay.

Then the radio station playing behind the diner counter started playing "Here We Go (Again)" with the DJ reminding listeners that The Drift was playing two shows and there were still a few tickets unsold.

Mark played air guitar to the song. Kay tapped along to the beat. They all had goofy grins on their faces when the waitress brought over their sandwiches.

"You guys like this song? she asked. "I remember it from high school," she smiled wistfully. "Enjoy your lunch."

Chapter Thirty - Six - 1973

"Hurry - we, you, are supposed to be there in 10 minutes and its a 10 minute drive," said Bernie.

As they arrived they greeted the other members of the team. Andy walked into the Room. Bernie followed.

Bernie liked to say hello to all the boys that were there and assess their game shape. He wanted to let them know a coach was present and it was time to get serious. He also wanted to scout out who was there and who came late.

When the boys were younger the dressing room was filled with players, equipment, fathers and mothers hovering over their boys to tie skates, help get sweaters on over shoulder pads and generally make sure all the equipment was in the right place and securely fastened.

The previous year some of the boys were able to get themselves dressed with minimal help. This year there were only a few kids who struggled with stuff - usually they couldn't tie their skates as tight as they wanted.

Bernie and the head coach Marc LaPointe had begun to give the kids the Room as they independently realized their role as coaches was fundamentally changing. The team had been directed by them in the past but now was only guided by them - the law of competition had begun to find its way into the Room as the team dynamic took hold.

Jim had been a head coach in Montreal before moving to Toronto a couple of years before. He had taken the opportunity to transfer out of Quebec after the FLQ crisis as he sensed the situation in Quebec was only going to get worse, either as separatists gained a deeper foothold on the public or as the government battled extremist elements.

Most of his friends had ridiculed the move calling Toronto a drab, colourless place, but Jim knew that he was tired of language being an issue every day and tired of the us against them mentality on both sides. Since he had left more people he knew had trickled out - mostly English speakers but also some immigrants who felt a French chill in everyday life.

Many had settled in Toronto's western suburbs near the lake, citing the similarity with Montreal's riverside suburbs of Point Claire and Dorval. In some cases people who had known each other in Montreal found they unexpectedly picked up their friendships in Ontario.

As the ice was being cleaned in preparation for their game Jim and Bernie entered the Room.

Bernie talked to the team about tactics, their opponents and reviewed what they had been working on in practice. He set the line combinations which he changed often to see if he could find some compatibility between players or just to shake them up so they didn't get too complacent with their role on the team. Skill levels were constantly changing so today's struggling forward could become a solid contributor within the confines of a single month or two.

When it was Jim's turn to address the team he spoke of something deeper.

"You guys are pretty good hockey players . . . ." he said. "But today we are playing the first place team. They expect to win. Now, I don't know if they win simply because they are so skilled or if they win because they've learned how to win. There is a difference. In fact even the best teams can lose, and often do lose big games, if they don't know what it takes to win."

"It's determination while remaining humble. Never expect to win just because you showed up. Determination must come from everyone of you. Determination to be the best you can be. The weaker skaters can practice and get better but today they simply have to play the best they themselves can play - push hard to do their best."

"The best players cannot coast on their laurels, not on what they did last week or last month. They have to push to be the best they can be. Everyone on this team is counting on everyone else to simply do their best. We will make mistakes. If we learn from them then they were worth it. No matter what happens on the ice today, come back to this Room after the game and be able to say you did everything you could to help your team."

"Now, who's ready to play hockey?"

And with that the team rose as one, yelling and hooting and clumped out of the dressing room, following the rubber matt path to the freshly cleaned ice. They began their standard warm up as Jim and Bernie carefully short stepped their way across the glassy smooth ice to the players' bench with extra sticks, a few water bottles, pucks and a small equipment bag.

"Andy, I'm going to be looking for you in the high slot like last week," said Eddie, with a grin, "and you look there for me, or by the far post, or behind the net."

"I always get you the puck Eddie, just get open and put it in the net, will ya?"

The two boys had played on the same team, and often the same line for three years. They honed their skills in road hockey games and tried to translate their abilities to the ice. Eddie ran better than he skated so it was often Andy who finished the play as he was a fluid and smooth skater.

"This is the team with that big kid, the one that controls the puck. He's so big you can't get around him to knock the puck away."

"I'll get him," said Andy, "and you watch for the pass in the slot."

"Good idea," said Eddie. "Who is on wing with us?"

"It's Will. Just tell him to hang out in front of their net looking for a rebound. Remember - stick on the ice."

Will was new to hockey and was a poor skater, though he had improved a bit in the few weeks they had played. He loved the game and tried to learn from his more experienced line mates.

The puck was dropped and the boys struggled to get it out of their own end. Jim kept telling the wingers to get close to the boards for a clearing pass and then to move it out over the blue line from there. They were nearing the end of the first period when opportunity finally came.

Eddie was one of the few kids who grasped the principle. He collected a clearing pass from the defense and swung it over to Andy. His pass caught Andy in full stride. Eddie admired it only for a second. Then he pushed hard to catch up. Andy swung to the left where the ice was open, pulling a defenseman with him.

As Andy angled across the ice Eddie skated hard straight up the wing and cleared the blue line just after Andy crossed it. Andy swung hard back into the center and Eddie headed for the right post. Andy hesitated only a second before firing a hard wrist shot for the right post about halfway up the goal.

The goalie stopped it with his blocker but the rebound came right to Eddie who whacked it hard. It climbed the goalie's pad and landed behind him but he twisted and fell on it with his glove hand before it went in. Andy nodded at Eddie as he got ready for the face-off.

The period ended with the score 1-1 as the teams traded breakaway goals.

By the end of the second period they were losing 3-2 as the big kid managed to score twice on hard shots from about 15 feet away. Eddie had scored after an initial shot from Andy and a rebound shot from Will ended up on his stick.

Andy was happy but subdued about the goal. Eddie skated hard back to the bench whooping it up on the way looking to celebrate it with his team. Will was right behind him.

As the game wound down, the other team was visibly tiring. The boys managed a tying goal with about 4 minutes to play. The big kid was going hard but he had obviously lost a step.

Andy's line went on again with just under 90 seconds to play.

Jim had decided he would leave them out to finish the game. He figured their exuberance to get a win would compensate for the extra long shift. As they buzzed around the net the defense managed to get the puck out to center and Will took the opportunity to get off the ice.

The next player on the bench was the next line's center. He went out with about 40 seconds on the clock. They buzzed, unable to get a good chance but still holding the puck. Then a defenseman fell just as Eddie's shot caromed to Andy high in the slot on the right side.

Andy skated around the fallen defenseman and pulled hard to his left to get back in front of the net while shooting the puck to the near post before he could be checked by the other defenseman. The puck was in with only 19 seconds to play.

The boys trooped into their Room when the game was over, still whooping it up having knocked off the first place team.

"The season is not over boys," said Coach Jim. "You guys did it. You played like a team and everyone did what they could to help. I saw good stuff out of every one of you. You guys should be proud of yourselves."

"But, we play these guys two more times this year and maybe again in the playoffs. You guys have set the tone, they will come out knowing you guys are tough to beat. If they are any kind of team they'll do what you did today - I don't mean win, though they might, what I mean is they will battle down to the last man, give everything they've got and you guys will have to give a little more. That's the nature of competition boys, good teams and players are always making themselves better and you have to do the same. See you at practice on Thursday."

"Wow, what a game," said Bernie outside in the corridor. "I loved how everyone stepped it up. And they were going for the rebounds with their sticks on the ice like we worked on in practice. They were really winning the races."

"So what do we work on this week?" asked Jim.

Bernie thought for a moment. "The breakout. We still have trouble with the breakout," he smiled, they had been working on the breakout for weeks. "We need to repeat it, especially now as they actually seemed to be getting it on some of the shifts."

"Okay, but I'd also like to work hard on their skating. You saw how the other guys ran out of gas. That's why we won. They couldn't keep up with us in the third period. If we can get their stamina up, that's a big advantage."

The Room was noisy. Kids were laughing, and in many cases they had forgotten why they were happy. As they trickled out Jim had a good word for everyone of them, usually referencing a specific play or skill they had executed during the game.

The team was slated to play in a city-wide tournament during the weekend between Christmas and New Years. The tournament promised three games in one weekend, four if they qualified for a playoff. Teams were from their league and three other local hockey groups in the city. They would play in a division with teams from other organizations with two games on Saturday and one on Sunday with the winner of each division playing a semi-final game on Sunday afternoon. The final would be played a week later.

"Okay, I have the inside on these teams," Bernie told Jim. "The first team is from Scarborough and is last in their division. The second team we play is from North York and is in the middle of the pack at 4-4-2 this season. Our last game is against West Humber and they are good - tops in their division and they haven't lost or tied a game yet this year."

"Well, that's a good set up. We're right near the top of our league and still have a chance to win it. I'm guessing they set it up this way. Assuming we do well on Saturday we have a shot at the playoff and we might get there having knocked off the most dominant team in the tournament."

When the ice chips cleared that is what happened. Andy's team won their first two games - the first a nervous 6-3 win, the second a more confident 5-0 victory. They went into the third game against West Humber and emerged with a terrific 2-1 win as they managed goals on both of their good scoring chances and held their opponents to very few shots on net. West Humber dominated but grew frustrated with their inability to score and started taking penalties. Their players abandoned the team concept and tried to score by themselves.

The lone goal West Humber got came on a huge mistake by one of the defensemen who tried to hit the centre with a pass across the middle rather than play it safe and move it up the boards.

At the end of the game Jim waited until the room calmed down. "Good win today boys but I think we learned something even more important. Everyone makes mistakes. Cameron's pass up the middle was a mistake. Cam knows it. We all know it. But as long as we learn from mistakes they are actually good. Because we made one mistake and 17 kids learned something from it. I noticed that we did not make another one like it."

The team played a semi-final that evening and won 4-2 in a hard fought game but one that they were firmly in control of as they grabbed an early lead and extending it before letting their opponents back in late in the third with two goals.

That set up a tournament final to be played a week later against a downtown team. The boys found out the game was to be played at Maple Leaf Gardens, the storied home of the local National Hockey League Maple Leafs.

Andy was in awe as he entered the rink 90 minutes before game time. He had watched on television as the Leafs won the night before against Boston on a late goal by Darryl Sittler.

He and Bernie were directed to a small dressing room on the west side of the arena and stowed Andy's gear before coming back out to look around the nearly empty building. Walking down a back hallway, covered with photos, and other hockey memorabilia they heard voices and two young men spilled out into the main hall. Andy immediately stopped dead in his tracks - two Maple Leafs were laughing together.

"Hey kid - how'd you get in here?"

Andy was frozen, his mouth agape unable to speak. He recognized the two Leafs from watching the games on television.

Bernie spoke up. "Andy and I are here to play," he let that hang in the air briefly with a smile. "We have an All-Toronto tournament final game here today, in about an hour actually."

"No kiddin'. Wow, I remember playing tournaments as a kid. Man they were fun. You gonna win today?"

"Uh, I, I hope," said Andy.

"No. That's not the right answer. Of course you are going to win. You have to be confident. You're certainly going to give it everything, right?"

"Absolutely," said Bernie while Andy nodded. "The boys won some tough games to get here - they are going to have to play their best to win."

"Well, watch the boards at the away end - they are extra lively. Puck comes off them really fast. You can use that to save a goal."

As the two Leafs sauntered off, Andy still could not move.

"Wow, wonder if the other kids will see them going out."

Sure enough, as players arrived almost everyone said they had seen the two Leafs leaving the building together. They had offered every kid they saw a "Good Luck today," on their way out. The kids were awestruck.

The game was closely fought with both goalies making amazing saves and defenses giving up very few shots. Andy's team started the game in the home end. Early in the third period Eddie blocked a shot at his blue line and picked up the bouncing puck for a two-on-one with Andy.

The defenseman set up and knowing that Andy was the stronger player he shaded to Andy's side to prevent the pass letting Eddie move in on the left. Eddie had moved more to his left to try to draw the defenseman but he was looking to pass and realized too late that Andy was covered. Their line mate Will was trailing the play trying to catch up as fast as he could.

Andy had told his line mates about the lively boards.

As the play unfolded, Will could see clearly that Eddie had moved too far left and given the goalie a good angle, while the defenseman had played it perfectly, shading Andy but cutting off Eddie from getting a better angle. Will yelled out, "Bounce it."

Eddie glanced at Andy and then fired his hardest shot wide on purpose and true to the tip from the Maple Leaf the puck caromed off the boards behind the net and came out on the other side.

Andy heard Will and could see in Eddie's eyes that's what he planned. In a split second as Eddie shot he angled hard to the right side of the net to meet the puck. It came out right on the blade of his stick and he corralled it and shot into the open side in one motion.

Andy was overjoyed and said to Eddie, "I knew you were going to do that. I knew it. What a perfect play."

Back at the bench everyone congratulated the pair on their goal but both Andy and Eddie pointed to Will who had called the play at exactly the right time.

"You guys mean that you meant to do that?" Coach Jim was incredulous.

"Yeah, Will called it. Their big goalie had the angle on me and the defenseman was covering perfectly. The Leaf players told us about the boards before the game."

The team hung on to win the game 1-0 thanks to incredible defense. There were very few scoring chances of any kind allowed in the game as the team was able to count on all its members to play smart and without fear of making a mistake.

The team threw their gloves in the air and crashed into their goalie as the horn sounded the end of the game. Their goalie Jack was given the Most Valuable Player award which Coach Charles said was testimony to their smothering defense during the whole tournament.

"Jack made the saves when he had to - and a couple of really good ones - but everyone should take a piece of that MVP because it was our defense and goaltending that won us this tournament."

The dressing room door opened and the big Maple Leaf defenseman was there asking if he could come in.

"I heard that kid yell 'bounce it' and I knew that somebody here was particularly smart. You have to use everything you know to win tough games," he told the team. "I am particularly impressed with that kid. Where is he?"

Everyone looked to Will who sheepishly stood up. "Kid, that was one of the smartest plays I've ever seen in hockey. "Sometimes the most important play is an assist that doesn't even show up on the score sheet."

The Maple Leaf gave Will an envelope. "Since you didn't make the score sheet here's something for your effort."

Will opened it up and pulled out four gold tickets to the next Leaf home game against Boston. His eyes widened and he looked up. His mouth moved but didn't say anything. Tickets to Maple Leaf games were virtually impossible to come by and gold level tickets were almost mythical.

"Watch Orr. He's the smartest player in the NHL right now. Get here early and ask for me; I, I want to make sure you get here okay."

Will sat down with the boys crowding around him. The Maple Leaf spoke briefly to Bernie and Jim and left after shaking hands.

Will felt the glow of celebrity for the entire next two weeks when Boston was due to play in Toronto. The big day arrived and Will and his father, an industrial mechanic by trade, went to the Gardens. Will wanted to bring his line mates Andy and Eddie so they were there as well.

"You brought the whole line," said the Maple Leaf with a wide grin. "That's the kind of teamwork that wins games." He shook hands with Will's father. "Come back after the game," he turned to a locker room attendant, "Hey Chuck, let these nice people back here after the game. I want to give them a couple of pucks."

The Leafs battled the Bruins and Orr had a particularly good game managing a hat trick and an assist in a 7-5 Bruin win. The once lowly Bruins were the team to beat in the National Hockey League thanks to Orr and a superb supporting cast. They had won two Stanley Cups in the last three seasons.

The boys ended up back outside the dressing rooms after the game despite being buffeted by the crowd and having a bit of trouble convincing the guard they were supposed to be there.

"Here they are," said the tall defenseman turning and tapping another player on the shoulder. The player had his back to them, still in his pants and skates but without his shoulder pads or jersey and was talking to someone holding a microphone. He turned when he was tapped on the shoulder.

It was Boston's hero of the night. The kids and even Will's dad were speechless.

"I heard about your great play William," he said, tousling Will's hair. "And about the quick thinking of your whole line. Man, sometimes I wish I could get that kind of stuff going with Sanderson and Espo." He tapped them both on their shoulders and gave them each a Bruins puck that he signed. The Maple Leaf was not to be outdone and he too presented Leaf pucks with his signature and Darryl Sittler's.

"I told the guys about the play and Darryl insisted he get in on the action. But then he's in on most of the action around here . . . " the big defenseman laughed.

The Bruin kibitzed with the boys for a few minutes asking about their positions and why they liked hockey. He finally got pulled away by a man in a suit and waved goodbye to the boys - with a grin, "Keep up the smart play. Remember, you gotta win the races to the puck. It takes a whole line to score and a whole team to win."

And he was gone. The Maple Leaf too was being beckoned into the dressing room. "Now we gotta face the music. Coach wants to talk. You probably know what that's like. Good luck with the rest of your season."

The boys thanked him over and over again as he disappeared.

"Well, I think this calls for some ice cream and a long letter to these players to thank them for their time."

After dropping Eddie and Andy off at home - Will and his father headed for home.

"You know dad, I think this has been the best day of my life," said Will, wistfully. "Wow!."

"You know Will, it might have been the best day of your life, so far. But I am pretty sure it won't be the only best day of your life that you will have."

Chapter Thirty-Seven - 1974

It was cancer. He was 78.

Charles Stuart was always a little frail, not necessarily ill or weak, rather the type of man who worked with his mind rather than his muscles.

It may have come from his natural bookishness or his disinterest in athletics even as a child, or even his war wounds, but he was never robust.

The cancer had been working on him for a while before it was obvious that it had control of him. In the 1970s most cancer was a death sentence, having deeply invested in its victim before it could be detected.

People accepted failing health as the onset of old age. They didn't complain. There was little point as medical science simply couldn't cope. Cancer was not well understood, except for its finality.

Eventually pain drove Charles to a doctor and before the Stuart clan even knew he was ill, he was in hospital for a bevy of pointless tests, designed more to tell when he would die than if. His pants hung a little looser, his shirt seemed a size too big and his hat sat oddly on his head.

Pain medication actually made him appear to be much better when the truth was the cancer was eating at him ever faster. Two weeks in the hospital and he felt better but was infinitely worse. A weakened shell of the war wounded shell he had been most of his adult life.

He was a rock of stability for decades but in his latter days that rock was discovered to be like a movie prop that looked the part but would be displaced by the slightest breeze. With no natural defence against the cancer he quickly descended into a coma and died only a few weeks later.

In the few days or so that it became evident that he was slipping away, Katharine was the only one of the family that was with him. What they spoke of she never passed on, save some vague mentions of his pride in the family and his efforts to help all its members achieve their life goals.

What was between them was theirs alone.

He was buried in a solemn ceremony with all the right and necessary attendees - but it was without emotion, as if his taciturn ways were being reflected back at him in his memory.

"Well, that is that," Katharine said, as she removed her gloves and dropped them on the credenza inside the front door. "It has all been such a whirlwind of obligations, functions and people. I'm glad it's over, though the house already feels a bit lonelier."

Charlotte removed her coat and started putting glasses out on the table to build a small bar service for a few family members who were coming back to the house after the funeral reception.

"I can still feel him here, his touch is on so much, but there is a hole at the heart of this house that can never be filled," said Chas. "It reminds me of when Father David died."

Charlotte looked at Chas, still holding a glass in mid-air, her attention completely diverted from her task. "Yes, yes that's it exactly," she said. "I haven't thought of that for many years. I remember how the family felt - like there was a hole which could never be filled."

It was the first time all the Stuart brothers and sisters and their offspring had been in the house together in more than a decade. Everyone took their usual place on the furniture and their usual place in the pecking order. Nobody sat in Charles Senior's easy chair so as the last man on the totem pole Fred sauntered over to it and took up residence. The grandchildren were too afraid and Fred's siblings were too deferential to take the spot. Fred felt guilty and undeserving of the spot but he refused to let a perfectly good chair sit empty.

Given that Charles Senior operated at best in a distant orbit of Katharine his easy chair was actually a natural place for Fred. As the youngest the only way he'd been able to get everyone's attention was when he was thrust into the stage floor in the centre of the group. Now he could quietly watch the dynamics of Bill and Chas and Charlotte and Mary and Helen play out in front of him.

"I remember that day," said Bill with a laugh. "Mom and Charlotte were down for the count, and little Freddie and Dad were trying to revive them."

Charlotte scowled at him and he relented. "You only remember the story, you weren't even there. Of course it was a shock to everyone."

Fred looked at his mother while Bill recounted her fainting and she momentarily looked glassy eyed but said, "Today we should be remembering your father not Father David, even if he was a big part of our lives - especially yours Bill. He used to play with you for hours. He's been dead now for almost 30 years. That seems like another world."

"I remember that day too," Fred said. "Dad was able to remain calm even through the shock and tragedy of it all. I remember nearly fainting myself."

"Dad was so busy with the business in those days," said Chas. "He was working constantly. It was just at that time that the company got a couple of big contracts, one was for the Simpsons department store downtown and there were two schools."

"Dad was working the numbers on those jobs when Stuart Construction had only done smaller institutional projects and retail spaces before."

"I wonder if his wartime experiences prepared him for the shock of Father David's death?" asked Bill. "He never said, but I often wondered how he managed to stay so calm, when the rest of us were so stunned."

"He was a great man," said Charlotte.

Fred agreed his father was a wonderful, understanding, gentle man, but he too remembered the priest. "Father David really helped us."

Mary had remained silent during this whole exchange. "I liked him, a lot. He was nice to me." She was wistful. "Dad was so busy in those days."

Kate cleaned out Charles's things quickly. Bill and Chas put it down to her lifelong neat streak. They got much of the old stuff. Most of which they took with a smile and then quietly donated to charity. Old suits, shoes, casual clothes, some household goods were parcelled out to which ever nephew could use them.

While my father's stuff was moved on, his office remained almost untouched from the day he left it. My mother's sentimental side was evident as she refused to close the door on that room and often spent time there sitting in a side chair she often used when talking to her husband about household issues.

The household maintenance fell to all three Stuart boys. But ultimately it was an old, old house in a state of gracious decay.

Furniture, paint and wall paper hadn't been changed in years. Kate didn't want the cost or the disruption and all her children were so comforted by the place they knew as their home that nobody even suggest an update. As long as the furnace worked, electricity was maintained well enough to keep the house from burning down and varmints were kept at bay - everything simply continued along.

Without the head of the family occupying a piece of the house it gradually became less forbidding to the hordes of grandchildren who Kate courted from a very young age. She let them tingle the chimes as often as they wanted to. That they were loud and rarely with any musicality, was part of the charm.

She made them sit down and talk to her about themselves and their day to day lives. She became a confidant, confessor, advisor and most of all a comfortable pat on the back in the most dire of circumstances to all her grandchildren, struggling with their commitments or happily ensconced in their lives.

She had the magical ability to focus on each contact she had so that even though she might only speak to you for a short second, a snatch of comment or a quick direction, you felt as if you and her were in it against the world, or at least standing vigil over whoever was in the room at the same time.

Soon Charles's memory faded - and his squirreling away in his office became an endearing trait. His devotion to the church became a symbol of his community interest rather than a connection to a strange and distant cult that it had seemed in his lifetime to those who did not share his devotion.

As the years passed Kate eventually cleared away much of the debris from Charles' old office, collecting papers and filing them away so the desk was empty save for some blank paper and pens and stamps. Kate put a photo of Charles on the wall of the office and moved a photo of Father David into the room as well from a small bedroom Charlotte and Mary had shared, where it had been for decades.

Family gatherings continued at the Stuart home and most of them barely acknowledged the years slipping by.

The memories of those times were the day to day little things that added up over the years to form the framework of a life and the foundation of a family. Change is the least appreciated and the most consistent factor in the passage of years - it is dreaded, ignored and fought at every turn, and yet it is liberating, exciting and ultimately unstoppable. Many times it is barely acknowledged and then shocking to those who have disconnected from it.

Chapter Thirty-Eight - 1977

"I just consulted my diary, my unofficial diary of course and saw that I first visited you here on this very day October 15th exactly 20 years ago."

Helen's English friend had donned a light silk headscarf and wore a heavy overcoat.

"You say it isn't cold today but I cannot get used to that biting wind. Even in Scotland the strong winds have a bit of sweetness to them, even on the coldest of mornings."

Another visit with her long time friend at the McFarlane's Ottawa home. It was a quick visit and one carried out without very many people in the know.

Helen confessed to her visitor that her last visit two decades before had stirred a little curiosity from her neighbours who wondered to each other who was being ferried to the McFarlane residence in the middle of the afternoon in the small black limousine.

Helen's diplomatic background was well known. The neighbours did not appear to have noticed the other two conventional cars that parked on the street just before and just after the arrival of the limo. At least they never said. It had been the talk of the street for several weeks with each neighbour in turn trying to turn a chance meeting in the street into details.

Helen easily deflected their questions and never let on it was anything more than an old friend dropping by from overseas. Which in fact, it was.

"Last time I was here I remember the leaves were turning just like today. It's almost as if nothing has changed, except for the new government in Quebec."

"Unfortunately, after the success of Expo 67 and the Olympics last year, I think the Quebecois will isolate themselves from many business operations in North America," said Helen. "They think that France will embrace them. What they don't understand is that France is embracing the rest of the world and its Lingua Franca is English."

"Already several large head offices have moved out of Quebec to avoid the xenophobia and legal restrictions on language promised by the PQ government. They are determined to go from being the commercial heart of Canada to a provincial backwater," said Helen.

"I am not sure what to do, save to let the situation play itself out. Perhaps once they do not get what they want from France they will soften their position on such things."

"You know my middle boy wanted to stay at Lakefield College for this whole term. However it is nearly impossible to alter plans once they are made so he only stayed in Canada for a few weeks once the term ended in June. He did much as I am doing right now - just went off the grid for a little while. Fortunately nobody seemed to take much notice."

"Yes, I heard that he likely it - I heard through channels at Foreign Affairs. I hope he will find cause to take notice of us," Helen smiled.

The two women chatted amiably while sipping their tea. Conversation moved from family to world affairs to future doings and even the vagaries of husbands. Just as it was time for a second cup, Helen put down a plate of butter tarts. Her visitor brightened considerably.

"I was hoping you hadn't forgotten," she said. "These are wonderful."

Chapter Thirty-Nine - 1984

Chas looked at himself in the mirror on his way out the door. Not quite the same 21-year old he had been 40 years before. As he continued his gaze he realized that exactly 40 years ago he had been struggling trying to salvage the engine of a Spitfire that had been hit by anti-aircraft fire during the D-Day invasion.

Walking the beaches now 40 years later lost in his thoughts for the last few days, Chas had enjoyed the time with old mates and his brother Bill. He kept straying to thoughts of Ver Sur Mer and his friend, the pilot Gordon McAuly.

He had written many months ago to The Caen War Memorial to get information on the museum for his trip and inquiring after the final resting place of Bill's friend Frank Edwards and his own wartime acquaintance Simon MacDonald. The museum put him in touch with a Jacques Gaspareau, a member of the French resistance during the war and a local historian.

Mon. Gaspareau wrote back saying that he did indeed know the spot where Lieutenant MacDonald was buried as he had been on a patrol that day in 1944 with his Resistance fighters when he came upon the body of MacDonald. He said the resistance often came across Allied soldiers and secretly buried their bodies to keep them out of the hands of the Nazis who were known to take out their frustrations on the corpses or otherwise denigrate their service.

Mon. Gaspareau said he would be happy to escort Chas to the site and show him around the area.

Chas remembered the events that led to Simon MacDonald's death. He had known Simon as a fellow mechanic. They had become friends as Simon was from the small town of Streetsville, just west of Toronto.

Only a few days after the D-Day landings, with the mechanics busy keeping the landing forces mobile, there had been a late afternoon call from Division for a mechanic to go to the recently seized bridge head outside of Reviers.

Chas was head deep in an engine just as the message arrived. Simon was just making the last few turns with his wrench to finish up the job on his vehicle. He volunteered.

Chas only heard of the events of that day from some of the other boys he had contact with. Simon never returned. When Simon arrived the Germans were apparently in retreat and many Allied tanks and personal were across the river. So Simon ran across the bridge without too much concern to reach a tank that had stalled and partly blocked the bridge egress.

According to those who witnessed it, a squadron of German fighters swooped down on the bridge at that moment and strafed the column trying to squeeze around the stalled tank.

Simon was hit multiple times and knocked off the bridge and into the river. In the chaos of the battle, and not really knowing that Simon was officially there, he was overlooked until several days later when he did not return to the motor pool.

Inquiries provided the story and likely end of Simon MacDonald. His body was not officially found until the burial spot was disclosed after the war. French partisans, including Mon. Gaspareau, found him down river and buried him in a quiet place without much ceremony.

After the war they provided his dog tags to officials who were able to match him up with their records and officially record his burial place. Normandy is dotted with these types of graves, usually unobtrusive, peaceful and enough out of the normal ebb and flow of daily life to be almost forgotten.

Chas was pleased that his inquiries were able to produce MacDonald's final resting place and a guide to help him find it.

Chas called Mon. Gaspareau. Thanks to the Frenchman's very European ability to speak more than one language they were able to quickly agree to a time and place to meet. Chas gave his full name to Gaspareau and began to spell it but Gaspareau stopped him.

"No, no Charles. Stuart is a well-known name around here," said Gaspareau.

Chas expressed surprise. "Oh, well, then I needn't spell it for you. I'll be with my wife. How will I know you on the platform?"
"Do not worry monsieur I will know you – what tourists we get in Ver Sur

Mer usually come by car. You will be well known to me on the train platform. I can spot a tourist anywhere," he laughed.

As he hung up Chas smiled at the thought that Mon Gaspareau could see through his attempt to be more restrained than the average tourist.

"It's the running shoes, dear," said Anne, who had been eyeing him eyeing himself. "They give you away, that and the Toronto Maple Leaf jacket you've been wearing. Honestly, even with a few more cameras around your neck, a tour book in your hand and a map in the other you couldn't possibly look more like a tourist."

"At least they don't mistake us for Americans," he said.

"But they do. And if they don't it's because of the jacket dear, not because you don't look the part."

They ambled out of their hotel room in Caen and made their way to the train station where they boarded the train for Ver Sur Mer. Securing their tickets they settled in for a 30 minute ride. Stopping at a number of village cross roads the train never worked up much speed. Soon it was slowing again as they reached their destination. A few of the passengers began to gather their things to disembark. Most appeared to be going on to Bayeux or Cherbourg. Chas and Anne would return to Caen that evening.

The train pulled into the station and it was immediately obvious there was a major ruckus occurring on the platform. It was raucous and crowded. And what first appeared to be some sort of trouble, soon looked more like a huge crowd awaiting a movie star or something.

"There must be a movie star or singer or some celebrity on this train. Listen there's even a band out there."

"Perhaps if we moved up the train we'll get clear of all the commotion. I don't even know what Mon. Gaspareau looks like. I bet he was counting on a quiet day on which to find us."

So the two Canadians moved through a few cars trying to clear the crowds. Chas saw a young man trying to manoeuvre a large box through the now open door. He was carrying a television camera.

"Here, I'll give you a hand with that," said Chas picking up the equipment box and moving through the door onto the platform, saying over his shoulder, "You'll miss the big moment if you don't hurry."

As Chas emerged, the platform erupted in a big cheer. He looked down the length of the train trying to catch a glimpse of whoever the big star was that everyone was waiting for. Anne stepped off behind the camera man who struggled with his rig.

Chas looked at all the people to see what they were focussed on but they were all seemed to be looking at him or the cameraman. The band struck up O' Canada.

Everyone seemed to have a Canadian flag, and a banner was unfurled from the facing of the station wall, which said "Bienvenue, Charles Stuart, Hero of Ver-Sur-Mer.

"What? There must be some mistake," he said to everyone and no one in particular.

A man appeared at his side.

"Monsieur Stuart, welcome to Ver-Sur-Mer, or welcome back for the first time in 40 years. When Mon. Gaspareau told me you were coming, well, I was overcome with joy. Your efforts to save our town and your extraordinary bravery to alert Mon. McAuly to our need will never be forgotten. This station is named Gare McAuly and the street on which it lies is Rue de Charles Stuart."

And so Mayor Jacques Martin of Ver-Sur-Mer directed Chas and Anne down the platform and through the cheering crowds of people. It appeared as if the whole town had turned out for the event. Every child was in their Sunday best, the boys with ties and the girls with flowers in their hair.

Down Rue de Charles Stuart they marched with a band keeping the beat alternating between Le Marseilles and O' Canada. People hung out their upper windows of the small central section of town, straining over the flower boxes to see the parade. In the midst of it all was a still bewildered Chas who wanted nothing more than a quiet afternoon in a small French town. He had come prepared to mourn his comrades.

At the end of the street was an open square with a dais to which Chas and Anne were led. Beside the square was a neatly kept cemetery with rows of white tombstones and a number of larger stone monuments. A small group of war graves were clearly visible from the platform decorated with national flags.

Several dignitaries were seated on the platform and all, save one older man, rose as Chas and Anne ascended the steps.

"Bonjour Madams et Monsieur's," Mayor Martin boomed before switching to English. "I have often longed for this day – to finally have the chance to thank our liberators for their bravery – face to face."

"On that fateful day I was a young boy living on Rue Esmerelda," he waved off to his left and explained for Chas his story as many in town were already familiar with it. "Just over there about a block from the bridge over La Provence. The Canadians saved my life, my family, my town and our beloved France."

Mayor Martin paused remembering a few fateful moments that made up most of his wartime remembrance. A tear gathered in the corner of his eye.

He remembered the day . . . .

Shouts rose in the streets and the Martin family wondered aloud what the commotion was as the Canadians had taken Ver Sur Mer two days before. The Nazis appeared to have fled in the face of the onslaught.

However on this day a group of Nazis burst into the Martin home to forage for food and regroup as they waited for others to cross the bridge and help retake the town. The Martin family was caught.

Seeing the whole town had supported the Allied forces the Nazis had dispensed with even rudimentary manners. They quickly grabbed the elder Martin and asked him about any weapons in the home. Jacques could only watch. His mother gathered his younger siblings but he was in another room and the Nazis hadn't seen him.

He heard McAuly's plane roar overhead and the burst of cannon fire aimed at the church steeple. Hearing the plane the Nazis became agitated and started to ready their escape grabbing bread and some beer.

Young Jacques ran into the street but the Germans heard him and gave chase. He burst onto the street and turned immediately towards a group of Allied soldiers heading for the church. They saw the Germans chasing and lifted their guns – young Jacques flung himself down on the road and heard the fire fight going on both sides of him with the whistles of bullets flying just above his head.

The noise stopped but still hearing the reverberations he remained still. A rough hand lifted him by his belt. He looked up expecting to see an angry Nazi but he saw a Canadian still flushed from the violence of the fire fight. He could see two or three Nazis lying on the pavement, the others must have escaped.

He smiled in relief but realizing his family's peril he ran back home. The Canadian followed. Jacques burst in on the Nazi menacing his mother and brother with his father crumpled in the corner bleeding from his chest. Jacques Martin could still remember bursting into the room and the look of fear and sacrifice on his mother's face.

The Nazi thought it was his fellows coming back and on seeing Jacques grabbed him and roughly tossed him to the floor. As he raised his rifle to shoot Jacques a shot rang out and the Nazi crumpled to the floor his life extinguished like a candle.

Jacques remembered how the Canadian's shot ended the Nazi's life like the embers of a wick after it's blown out, with a last string of smoke rising away. He crumpled to the floor and the surprise and fear in his eyes turned to glass and then he was dead.

Jacques never forgot those last few seconds of the Nazi's life as his face showed surprise, fear and then a surprising touch of grace before losing the last spark of animation.

Mayor Martin came back to the present.

"These brave men saved us, they saved me, though I know only two of their names. McAuly and Stuart, whose actions are part of Ver-Sur-Mer lore." He gestured over the dais where the dignitaries sat toward the cemetery beyond. " Both of them are finally together here today."

It was Charles turn to speak. He awkwardly got to his feet and shook the Mayor's hand.

"I ... I ... I am overwhelmed by all of this," he said. "I wish I could express my surprise and gratitude to your show of faith. Above all I wish Gordon McAuly was with us to share in this moment. It was really his bravery, his determination to jump into the fight without a second thought that knocked down the Nazi hold on the town and turned the battle. As you know we never found him in the wreckage of his plane."

"But I am right here Chuck," said a voice behind Chas. The man who had not risen with the others was now standing behind him. There was a distant familiarity in his worn features.

Charles felt the wind leave his lungs - he was gasping for breath. His knees began to fail him. McAuly grabbed him firmly by the arm.

Chas heard a distant voice. "But Monsieur, did you not know? McAuly survived. He stands beside you. He has lived here since the war."

Chas recovered himself enough to give McAuly a big hug, an expression of joy that doubled as a brace while he recovered his wits. Tears started down his face as he tried to gather himself. His legs gave way but McAuly was able to remain upright.

Chas did not believe it. Martin quickly told him the story. A farmer from the other side of the river found the flyer in a hay stack two days after the battle. He had been thrown clear of the plane before it exploded and

285

miraculously landed softly thanks to a partly deployed parachute. He was badly injured. The farmer nursed the flyer for several days before sending word into the Allied camp to tell them of an injured man.

Realizing the gravity of his situation he was left with the farmer for a few weeks before army medics tried to move him. The invasion force moved on.

McAuly was evac'ed to England where he convalesced for several months and then back to Canada when it was determined his injuries would not allow him to fly anymore. He was awarded the Victoria Cross for his actions in Ver-Sur-Mer receiving the medal directly from King George in London. There was a civic ceremony in Winnipeg for McAuly after the war.

Personnel had been notified but with the movement of men during those dark days the miracle had gone unreported to those who most wanted to know.

Chas sat back down heavily. Too many surprises for one day. A few more speeches allowed him settle.

The mayor presented both Chas and McAuly with Keys to the Town and Croix de Guerre, at the behest of the Government of France. He beckoned them both to join him. Mayor Martin stood facing the crowd. He held each man's hand and raised them together on each side.

Mastering the emotional crack in his voice, Mayor Martin declared, "Citoyens, I give you the Heroes of Ver-Sur-Mer."

The crowd roared. The band, tired of playing national anthems, played the Theme from Hockey Night in Canada.

Chapter Forty - 1984

Everything was in place. Charlotte thought that Frank could pick up the pieces and answer the questions. After all he had fractured the marriage.

Charlotte knew all the tears and fears were necessary to arrive at this moment. Frank could answer her lawyer. In the mean time she had a little money put away and she had her job. She stepped out of the house and closed the door.

It had been a long road. Since she first was able to prove Frank's serial adultery she had travelled a long way. Actually it had started before the proof, when she began to doubt Frank's excuses, question his absences, and wonder about the odd bits of evidence that turned up in pockets, in receipts and on the telephone.

Too many things didn't ring true in Frank's doings - at first she just thought it normal. But after a few sly conversations with friends and family it became evident that Frank wasn't normal and that his doings were rather odd.

She began to dig a little deeper. Pretty soon the whole house of cards came down as she was able to expose his lies. He didn't get caught in bad weather downtown last year. He didn't get billed in error for room service at a northern resort. His dinner for two at a country restaurant wasn't a chance meeting with an old school friend.

Charlotte first assumed that he was having a fling with a woman from his office. Then it became evident that he had moved on from that and had had a several trysts.

A little digging and she uncovered a few more liaisons. The evidence came in so slowly she was able to document quite a dossier on her husband before the plan began to form in her mind. She would remain quiet until she was ready to move.

She contacted a lawyer, she handed over the evidence. She drafted letters to her children Mark, Catharine and Thom. She co-ordinated her move.

Thom got his degree from the University of Toronto on a Saturday in October. He had been working in the city since mid-summer and shared a condo with two friends. Frank left on a Thursday for a convention in Montreal. Friday afternoon the letters were in the hands of her children. The lawyer had filed a petition for divorce. The house was cleared of her things and she moved into her new apartment. Then the notices were sent to friends, colleagues and associates, the last of which was Frank.

He decided to stay in Montreal until Monday.

Charlotte waited until early evening for her children to call. "Mom what are you doing?" asked Catharine. "This can't be right. What does Dad say?"

"Catharine, it doesn't matter what your father says anymore. The evidence is overwhelming. It is in the hands of my lawyer. I'm sorry it came to this. In fact, might have been able to overlook a single fling, but I cannot overlook the routine and continuous betrayal of everything I've worked for. I will not remain with your father - our relationship is severed forever."

"Believe me you do not want to see the evidence. Suffice it to say, I will not go back. Of course I still will be involved in you and the boys' lives. I'm your mother. However, your father ruined our family. Perhaps it was for the best that I only found out about him and his doings after the fact - otherwise your lives would have been different. Now, except for a little disruption at Christmas and Thanksgiving nothing much will change. I've got a little job. The divorce settlement will provide me a good nest egg and I will survive."

Mark called next.

"Mom I got your letter."

"Oh."

"I'm not sure what to say. Of course I'm shocked and have trouble believing it."

"So did I at first Mark, but the evidence is overwhelming. I will not be treated that way, not knowingly."

"I understand. I tried to call dad but there was no answer."

"He's in Montreal, with who I don't know, nor care anymore."

"So now what mom?"

"I have an apartment and a job - I'm assured the settlement will be quite sufficient."

Thom's reaction was a bit of a surprise. "I suspected for a while but didn't want to say anything. I saw him doing some funny things," Thom told Charlotte, recalling as a teenager how he heard his dad on the phone with some lady, and watching him pack for a business trip when he thought he wasn't being watched.

"Don't tell me," Charlotte said. "I just hope you've learned something from whatever it was you witnessed."

"Of course I wish this hadn't happened," said Thom, "but I'm afraid it happened long ago. I kind of was expecting this day at some point. How long have you known?"

Charlotte explained that she had known for a while and had pieced together a lengthy and damning documentation of the evidence.

It was two days later that Frank called her at her office.

"Charlotte, I'm sorry. There is really nothing else to say. I never meant to hurt you but I know I have. I just needed something more."

They discussed arrangements - Frank appeared almost relieved to have be absolved of the responsibility for breaking the news. Charlotte's decision to divorce was never disputed, nor was her expectation of a fair settlement.

However, as the months passed Frank became bitter as he watched Charlotte's lawyers earn their fees. Frank expected an equitable settlement but was increasingly angry that he was unable to dictate the terms of that equity. The family home went up for sale, while Charlotte kept the family cottage north of the city - it had been in Stuart family for as long as she could remember.

Frank had to provide much of his portion of the sale of the family home to cover Charlotte's share of his pension credits. He did get much of the contents of the home, furniture, cars, electronics and sundry items gathered from years of family life. He had no savings, few investments and a five year old car he could sell.

He bought a small townhouse and gave away much of the contents of his former home. Charlotte purchased a condo, had money in the bank and a cottage she and the kids could share.

Eventually the divorce decree became final. The children gravitated to Charlotte who spent time and effort maintaining the heart of her family.

Frank would show up at his kids' events from time to time, usually unannounced, seemingly unable to connect with them in any organized way.

Frank faded while Charlotte flourished. Most of their joint friends and neighbours sided with Charlotte and included her in their annual events. She sparingly took them up - largely to remain connected to her community even while letting parts of it go.

Charlotte remained unattached while Frank bounced from short term relationship to live-in girl friend.

Charlotte frequented a coffee shop on her way to work each day. She grew to enjoy the banter with the young staffers who quickly recognized her.

"How was your holiday?" she enquired of one.

"Oh it was nice to get away but every relation I have in the world was there - it was more than a little crowded, but maybe that was half of the fun."

"Oh I like it when everyone can get together. There are so few opportunities as everyone gets older," Charlotte said with a sigh.

"I know what you mean," said a voice behind her. She turned to see a nice looking man smiling. "I love it when we all get together, the dynamics are really fun, especially with the youngest generation."

Charlotte had seen him many times before. He also frequented the coffee shop. They had often exchanged smiles and nods as part of their morning caffeine ritual. She had even seen him turn into an office building just down the block as she made here way to her building next door.

"Do you have a cottage?" she asked. "Or are you talking about Thanksgiving and Christmas?"

"Both actually," he said, "I try to get the kids up to the cottage with their families and then I usually join one or more at holiday times. Trying to find meaningful rituals as family dynamics change is really a challenge."

Charlotte nodded. And then it hit her. "Can you sit for a minute and tell me how you do it?" She motioned to a table with her full coffee.

"Sure," he said. "But I'm not sure I'm any kind of an expert. I'm still trying to figure it out." He lowered his voice, almost embarrassed, "I've only been trying for a couple of years, since, since my wife, I mean former wife and I split."

He shrugged and smiled.

They sat down over coffee.

Chapter Forty-One - 1988

"It used to be that a picture or bit of video was sacrosanct. Sure, you might not get the context but you definitely saw what you saw. A picture was worth a 1,000 words. Now most of those words are lies."

"Some predict a time in the future when images can be entirely created in a studio or on a computer - like a movie but in real time. If that happens what value does any photo have other than as a piece of art?"

The class squirmed. It was late Friday afternoon and everyone had a drink waiting for them and a party to attend. Not too many students were listening.

The class worked diligently on their campus news program using old equipment and learning all the standard techniques. They did try new approaches when time allowed or their assignments required.

"Remember the footage of Cronkite and Rather, I want 500 words on their presentation style and its affect on the audience for next Wednesday. If you refer to actual things in the video the 500 words will get written very quickly. I hope everyone is proceeding well with their term project - if you are having trouble I'll be here or in my office for a while."

As the professor wrapped up the class, the students began to pack up and leave. Soon there were only two left.

"Can we write more than 500 words?" Julia asked.

"I'm not going to hold everyone to exactly 500 words but part of the exercise is to be succinct. Journalism is the art of getting as much information as you can to people as quickly as possible - especially in hard news."

"You didn't answer my question," said Julia. "Can it be more?"

The prof laughed, "You are going to be a good reporter. Yes it can but the grade is based on quality and brevity. The 500 words is a guideline. If you have more to say, say it, but don't draw it out just to make it sound impressive. Papers are not graded by length."

It was Julia's chance to smile. "But that's standard academic- speak. How can I be expected to deviate from the norm?"

"You can write that way in other classes if they let you get away with it, but not here," the prof turned to the other student. "John, what's up?"

"Sir, I have already completed the Cronkite assignment. I am working on my term project and running into a bit of trouble. "I'm doing a front page and I am having trouble stripping in the copy, I can't get everything to line up."

"We talked about that a couple of weeks ago. Did you miss the class?"

"I had to leave early and only got the basics but I'm guessing I missed the detail stuff on how to get things right. I saw the page dummies, the waxer, the copy generator and the headline machine. Then I had to go."

"Have you not been working on the student newspaper?"
"No he hasn't," said a still loitering Julia, just a bit miffed. "I thought everyone had to."

"I'm studying meteorology and journalism. We don't have to work on the paper as our course load is heavier."

"Well, I suggest you offer to help out a bit in paste up. It doesn't take as much time as the reporting and editing for the paper and you know exactly when you are needed. It's mostly done on Wednesday afternoons as the paper goes to press late Wednesday and is available Thursday mornings on campus."

"Just come in and look for me," said Julia. "I will let the editor know you're coming. You'll learn all the little things pretty quick. I actually help out sometimes in paste up. It's pretty neat."

John dutifully showed up the following Wednesday. True to her word Julia was waiting for him and introduced him to the editor.

He gave John a knife and put him to work immediately cutting up name, date and page numbers to be inserted on every page.

John started cutting and then took the tiny slivers to the waxer. The first one went through and he was able to take the waxed piece and stick it to the page mock up, the soft wax acting as a bit of glue. He went back to the waxer and inserted the 'Page 2' sliver. It stuck to the wheel and John couldn't pluck it off. The hot wax made it painful to try. His fingers burned. He stopped the machine. And then started and stopped it again to get the waxing wheel to stop where the sliver of waxed paper was more accessible.

He plucked it off and trotted into the paste up room where all the pages were set up on easels. Just as he put the piece in place he heard a screech from the other room.

"Who the hell stopped the waxer?"

John ran back in and admitted it was him.

"It takes a couple of hours to get the wax melted and at the right temperature. If you stop it, the wax will harden and we will miss our mock up deadline. This paper has to be at the printer by 8 p.m. or we don't get a paper - our advertisers will be angry, our readers will be confused and generally everything goes to hell. Got it?"

John swallowed hard and nodded. "Sorry."

"The mock up editor let out a deep sigh. "You're new. Who put you on the waxer without explaining how it works? Never mind. Come with me."

When she saw John's pile of tiny slivers of page numbers she let out a sound between a wail and a caterwaul. The approach was absurd.

"No, no, you take the whole page of page numbers, run that through the waxer and then cut it up as needed."

"Nobody told me."

"Nobody told you how to breathe either but you appear to be managing it well enough. Use your head - ask if you can't figure it out. We don't have much time for foolishness."

John finished his task and then decided to simply watch as the pages were pieced together. The paste up regulars were quick.

Janine the mock up editor was like lightning. She managed to get things on the page so fast that John didn't even see her do it. He was left to inspect the work and try to figure out how it was done or ask. He decided to go back the next week to learn more and to see if he could help out.

John told Julia how impressed he was.

"Yeah, it's a dead skill though. Big papers are moving to computer paste-up. They position everything on the page through a computer program and then send the completed pages to the printer through telephone lines."

"So when do we learn that?"

"We don't, except in theory. It's too new. Newspapers don't all have it yet and probably won't for a while."

"What about all the jobs?"

"Well some people will be needed to operate the computers but most people in paste up will lose their jobs. Who knows how long it will be before we move to that type of system here. Probably not until after we graduate."

"So some people will graduate with useless, outdated skills."

"Not sure if anyone has thought that far ahead, but yes, they will have to learn computer paste up or they won't get jobs. A lot of the principles are the same on managing space on the page, it's just the tools that are different."

Chapter Forty-Two - 1990

It was his 69th birthday that June day.

A sports fan for life he especially loved baseball – the game of his youth.

Chas Stuart still got around, including teaching business part time at the local community college three days a week.

Chas' eldest son Peter put together a Triple A / Major League double-header for his father's birthday bringing along his oldest son Jakob.

The three generations of Stuarts took to the road to attend an afternoon game at Pilot Field in Buffalo, home of the Triple A Buffalo Bisons. Their plan was to finish that game and drive two hours to Toronto to see the Blue Jays take on the Boston Red Sox at SkyDome that night.

They crossed the border at Buffalo without incident and made their way to the nearby stadium, parking just east of the left field fence. The parking lot wasn't the closest to the stadium gates, nor was it the easiest to get to but it had the extremely good quality of providing a quick escape from the crowds back to the highway, the border and ultimately Toronto.

Chas cackled about his perfect parking lot as he swung is old Buick off the highway and negotiated the nearby streets to find his lot. He didn't know his way around Buffalo but he knew every nook and cranny of free parking within walking distance of either Pilot Field or the nearby Aud where the Buffalo Sabres played. He also knew every place within walking distance to get chicken wings and beer.

As they glided into the lot, a parking spot came open immediately adjacent to the exit. Chas manoeuvred the car in backwards to allow him to join traffic more easily.

"Grandpa, I never understood why you like getting out so fast when you love coming here so much?" asked Jakob.

"Access, my boy, access; I like to come and go when I please. It's worth a little extra effort to keep your destiny in your own hands."

Jake smiled, "If your destiny is to avoid a traffic jam, okay. But if your destiny is to be in a traffic jam I'd rather just go for dinner. Remember those wings we had the last time?"

"If you're in the traffic sooner, your destiny is to get through it quicker," said the old man with a twinkle in his voice. "Plus we have a second game to attend."

Pilot Field was a great place to watch a ball game. Nestled downtown it was comfortable, intimate and a fun place to be. Various characters sold beer in the stands, making a general entertainment of their job.

Chas delighted in watching the parade of soon-to-bes, has-been's, wannabes and never will bes playing for their own reasons. It took the elegance of professional baseball into a whole different place.

Since minor league teams were raided for players at the major league team's whim, minor league championships were not terribly important. The importance was more immediate. Each game and every play had significance beyond today and tomorrow.

Every play was linked to the past and the future often in ways the players themselves didn't understand.

As it happened that day Jerry Reuss was pitching for Buffalo. Reuss had enjoyed an 18 year career in the majors and success as part of the 88 Dodgers and their wonderful pitching staff. Which included future Hall of Famer Don Sutton and Mexican sensation Fernando Valenzuela.

Valenzuela had first impressed scouts with his youth and ability. He earned a spot on the team with his arm. Even though it became obvious after a decade of success that Fernando likely wasn't as young as he claimed, his ability was real. His career was short but memorable.

As Fernando's career was running down Reuss was staging a come back, and tooling through the minors in hopes of being called up. He had an impressive record through April and May but he was knocked out in the third inning of his last start.

In contrast, Louisville sported first baseman Sammy, Boom-Boom Turner, who was still in the minors despite impressive hitting stats because his defensive limitations reduced his usefulness to the parent team. The big league press was baying for his call up.

In the bottom of the first Turner arrived.

The leadoff hitter walked on a close pitch on a full count. The second batter, a left hander, cue-balled an infield single through the gap between the third baseman and the shortstop, who was leaning toward second to cover the bag.

Turner advanced to the plate with two on and no outs.

Reuss threw a fast ball to try to get ahead of the count. Turner hit the ball into the parked cars beyond the right field stands. It was as quick and efficient as that. A pre-dramatic home run.

Chas, Peter and Jakob were sitting in the 10th row between home and third. They watched as the ball started low, as it was very well hit, and then began to climb, lifting off like an airplane. It stayed close to the ground at first and as it gained altitude as it slowed only to hang in the air, framed by an elevated section of Interstate 190 in the background, before it slowly descended into the parking lot. The right field crowd rose as one, slowly tilting their heads up as the ball gained height and then twisting to watch it land as it went over their heads.

There was no doubt about the home run from the moment it started to rise. But the majesty of the ball's flight left the fans in awe so there was a noticeable quiet in the park for a few seconds before an unusual hubbub gripped the fans as they discussed the flight of the ball.

The ball hit the pavement and ricocheted off a concrete wall before bouncing high enough to be visible from inside the stadium.

While everyone was marvelling at the monster home run and getting settled Chas watched Reuss. The old pitcher knew two things, the ball was long gone, so he motioned for another before it even landed. As he turned from the crowd to look at centre field while he rubbed up the new ball, Reuss' puffed up his shoulders, but Chas could see from the slight upward tilt of his head that the old pitcher knew his comeback was over.

Reuss would take the mound a few more times but age had finally caught the old warrior.

The game ended with a Buffalo win 7-3 behind good defence and a few timely hits, including a bases clearing double in the eighth.

The Stuarts made their way quickly to Chas' 88 Buick Century and true to the old man's word, were whisked onto the highway in time to see the grounds crew rolling the protective tarp over the infield.

Within minutes they were across the border and on the QEW heading to Toronto with time to spare.

"We'll be in Toronto by six and the game starts at 7:05 p.m. Are we eating at the stadium or before?" asked Jacob.

"Restaurants near the Dome will be full. We can grab a hot dog from a vendor on the way in and then get some peanuts and drinks once we're in the Dome," said Peter. "That okay with you, dad?"

Chas hated paying the high prices inside the Dome, and even though he was there as a guest he still couldn't bring himself to in anyway support that thievery.

"You know how I feel," said Chas.

The Stuarts followed their ritual and settled in their seats. They sat about 15 rows up opposite first base.

"I remember the old Exhibition Stadium," said Chas. "It wasn't very good; small, cold and smelly but it was better than this place."

"Every time we're here you say that," said Jacob. "How come everything old was better? If it was better why did they tear it down and build this one?"

"Well Jake, old things aren't better always. I just remember the ones that were. All those things I don't mention, rest assured, the new ones are better than the old. I liked the old stadium because it was smaller, we sat closer to the game and it had more leg room. It was cold and spare and pretty ugly but that was part of its charm. Here you're always assured of getting the game in – no weather problems. That's a big advantage. But my knees have never been good, you know. With the way I have to crunch up my legs this stadium reminds me of it every time we come. Some of the sight lines are poor, especially if you are sitting down the foul lines. The seats aren't set for baseball, they are turned too much into the outfield. Probably to satisfy the football crowd. I never understood why they ruined 82 games of baseball for eight games of football."

After the game they made their way to the car and the inevitable traffic jam. They had to make their way out to Mississauga where Peter lived. Jacob had moved back with his parents for a time, having just finished a finance and accounting degree at Western. He was working on his CA exams.

Charles eased the car through the jam before they began to pick up speed as they passed the Lakeshore ramps which entered the highway on both sides and creating additional lanes to handle the traffic volume. The jumble of traffic was sorting itself out when they were nipped along the back of the driver's side rear quarter panel. It happened quickly. The contact pushed them slightly into the right lane before the back end spun out taking them sideways. A truck, moving left out of the way of traffic coming onto the highway, crashed into them at full speed.

The cab engulfed the driver's side and rode up on the top of the car. Chas was crushed, Peter was thrown so violently by the spin and the impact that he broke his neck and was killed. Jacob, who was behind the front passenger seat, was thrown about, his back and right leg were broken. As the rig spewed fuel on the crushed car below, only Jacob remained alive enough to be killed by the smoke and flame, but thanks to his injuries he never knew it.

The driver of the car that broadsided them immediately corrected his mistake, got back into the left lane and drove past the spinning car. As he looked back into his review mirror he saw only faint lights of the Stuart car facing perpendicular to the direction of traffic. He didn't see the rig smash into them until the fireball appeared in his rear view mirror many seconds later. By then he was more than kilometre away from the accident scene and convinced himself that his apparent near miss had nothing to do with the accident in his rear view.

He touched his brakes as if to stop but realized he would have to run more than a mile back down the dark highway.

"The people behind can take care of it," he thought. "It wasn't me."

He pulled off the highway at his first opportunity, looking in his mirror for any sign of the car he had brushed. The highway remained dark, except for the fire raging far back along the road. Then he saw a trickle of traffic advancing down the highway and he drove on.

He crossed over the bridge to see back down the highway. There was a cloud of thick black smoke silhouetted by the raging fire. It was already getting smaller as he looked down the highway.

Eastbound traffic was backed up almost to the exit he had taken. Some cars pulled over on both sides of the highway and there appeared to be movement on the road. A few cars made it past the accidence scene to continue westbound.

The trucker was sitting on the guard rail having been pulled, dazed, from the wreckage just as the fire was taking hold. An explosion of the truck's fuel tank rocked the area and blew apart remnants of the Buick. The car's fuel tank exploded as well but with only a loud pop as there was little fuel and no pressure in the savaged tank.

The instigator crossed the bridge again trying to convince himself he had not caused the accident. He knew there was nothing he could do. After inspecting the passenger side of his care he resolved to wait for any appeals to the public for clues as to the cause of the crash before he would volunteer to come forward.

However, those calls never came. His resolve to come forward faded. Even as he drove to another city to have the damaged right front bumper repaired, he clung to the belief that he would come forward should there have been a public appeal by police who suspected a third car was the cause.

His secret undiscovered, his life resumed and soon eroded the memory of his guilt. It was just an unfortunate accident - only an expensive repair, though he took care of paying for it himself rather than notifying his insurance company.

The Stuarts however, had to bury three generations of their family. Chas had been in the process of getting his affairs in order – but he was not much past the good intention stage.

Peter had life insurance and other baubles of modern tragedy in place. Jacob had only a fiancée, a legacy of friends and a lot of student debt. Life would go on, but the scar on three generations of Stuarts was there, and it ran deepest in the young.

Chas' wife Anne wasn't prepared for the shocking manner of passing. However, in her late 60s she had begun to come to terms with the idea that he would not always be there. That she would likely outlive him she already knew to be inevitable.

Peter's remaining family, his wife, younger son and daughter were profoundly affected. Their grandfather, father and brother were dead in an instant.

Everyone coped in their own way. Anne took her husband's death as a blow, but not one she couldn't recover from. However, her eldest son's death was difficult. In fact, while she soldiered on at first in automatic pilot, then with even a degree of mirth in her day to day, she could not shake her grief at Peter and Jakob's deaths.

She blamed Peter for letting Chas drive. She blamed Chas for agreeing to such a taxing trip. She blamed herself for letting Jakob tag along. She never recovered entirely – though those who knew her only after the tragedy would never know the extent of her personality change.

Months later she took to the task of reordering Chas possessions. She gave his clothes to the Salvation Army Thrift Shop. She gave away the accoutrements of his life, some for the usefulness they had, others so they could be used and not wasted. As she went through his possessions, she left the box he kept on his desk until last.

The box was decorated with travel motifs. She had given it to him for their 10th wedding anniversary. He used it to store important papers, passports, stray coins from their travels and a few oddments.

She had seen these items before and even knew what they all meant to Chas. There were a couple of chestnuts from their trip to France half a dozen years before. There were his service medals. There was a postcard he had sent home telling his mother that he had married and was bringing Anne to Canada after the war.

Anne sorted through the things, things that had meant something to Chas. She was unwilling to break up the collection, but looking at each item and thinking of how she might display the bits of Charles life that he treasured.

As she picked through the coins and pins and medals she found a piece of unadorned gray steel. It was slightly concave with two parallel edges bent back into quarter-inch wide flanges. Most curiously it featured a perfect hole in its center.

She looked at it closely. It appeared as if the hole was the result of a piece being cut out, even though the edges were fairly smooth. She had no idea what it was.

"Well that appears to be nothing, I can start with it," she thought as she set it aside to be tossed in the recycling.

She made her way downstairs as the phone rang. She put the metal piece down on a table while she took the phone call.

Chapter Forty - Three - 1994

He typed with a pen. It was in his hand, between his lips, on top of his ear. Sometimes he chewed it. The pens were not tossed because they ran out of ink. They were tossed when they became too unpleasant to be handled.

Sometimes it was in his mouth held like a bridle, other times it dangled like a cigarette. Much of the time he merely juggled it while he typed with two, three or four fingers in practiced movements writing, adjusting, editing and reworking computer code.

Sometimes that code came in stattaco bursts. Other times he'd hunt and peck, thinking about each bit in the string as he methodically built it up.

Once in a rare while his pen would rest length ways between the keys on his board ready to be snatched again and moved around as he worked.

An ethnic Russian, Neved Bolishkoi was born in Ukraine and decided at

22 that he'd rather be a Russian in another country than a Russian in a country that really wasn't his.

He eventually immigrated to Canada with a bit of computer savvy, a quick wit and his skates. He figured he could buy a stick once he arrived.

He settled in Ottawa, the center of Canadian computer business and quickly found a job.

The first few months were difficult. Vacillating between exhilarating and lonely, Neved changed his name to Ned on the advice of an immigration officer. He got a job easily in a small software company that specialized in web-based financial applications and security, but he struggled with North American systems. It was like he had no background at all.

It irritated him that his degree in computer engineering was treated like a certificate from high school. And yet he had to admit he was only remotely prepared for the code requirements of his new job.

Fortunately for Neved, he was a quick study and very determined. He took to working all day and half the night, sleeping at the office, and living out of a small carry bag for several months as he slowly mastered the new coding language and improved his speaking one.

Most of his colleagues didn't know he slept on the reception couch, they only worried that his early mornings and late nights made their efforts look poor in comparison. Some took to pointing out their greater accomplishments in shorter amounts of time.

Neved's boss was concerned about the lack of productivity and teetered on the edge of firing him, however praise from one of his office mates who knew what Neved was up against kept the hammer from falling.

Neved gradually cut back on his hours. Showering at a local gym, with no rent to pay he had saved quite a bit of money after a few months. Enough to find an apartment, buy a hockey stick and seek out a place to play.

It wasn't long before Neved found himself playing hockey Wednesday nights with a co-worker's team, becoming a valuable team asset at work, a quality right winger and taking a little time for himself on weekends.

His English was improving and television helped him improve at things other than computer code.

"Hey Ned. What cha doin' after work?" Dave McMaster asked him when they both went for a morning coffee.

"I am playing hockey with you. It's Wednesday," he said with a grin.

"Before hockey. We don't play until 9:30."

"Getting ready for hockey, Dave."

"Do you think you could spare an hour or so? I need a little help. It pays."

"For you Dave, and for money, I am able to help. What is the job?"

"I've been running a little computer 'consulting' business on the side. And, well, frankly it's getting too big. There are so many people out there who use home computers but who have no idea how they work. Half of them can't turn them on. And when something goes wrong . . . well, they call me. I've got some easy jobs that need doing. I can pay you by the job or by the hour."

"Okay, what do I have to do?"

"I'll give you the work order – name, address and computer complaint – you go a fix it. Simple."

"Simple. Okay."

So Ned got into making house calls to fix sick computers. And it was simple, ranging from those who forgot to plug in their machines or people who didn't know to defragment their hard drives to people who pushed the wrong button and had to have their machine rebooted. Most of the fixes took less than 20 minutes.

After realizing that people's constant references to his house calls were likened to a doctor, Ned took to wearing his lab coat to these visits saying he was coming directly from his office job, even on weekends.

He and Dave devoted more and more of their time to these calls until Dave quit the software firm to run the repair business full time. Ned kept his day job and did most of his house calls in the late afternoon and early evening.

One evening Ned was ushered into a home and sheepishly asked to hook up a new system.

"My son said I could do it, but it's just too overwhelming," said Helen McFarlane. She escorted Ned to a wood-paneled den with a desk and boxes of computer items piled high.

Ned started to assemble the computer. As he mindlessly opened plastic bags and untwirled wire he looked at the framed photos on the wall.

Seeing one photo he moved closer until he nearly fell over in shock. The framed picture was of a much younger Helen Stuart and several other officials.

"That photo was taken in Lvov in 1952," said Helen, returning to the room and seeing Ned looking intently at the picture.

"I know. I have seen another photo of the same event," said Ned pointing to the center of the photo. "That man is my grandfather."

"Oh my. He was the mayor of Lvov. We were photographed after a speech where we promised development and reconstruction aid. The Russian official assigned to our party was so angry, our tour was cut short and our subsequent attempts to help were turned aside."

"We have a similar photo which includes you, where my grandfather is holding his child, my father. He was only two years old at the time."

"I remember that photo being taken. Your grandmother didn't want to be in the picture, she held onto her other child, a small baby. Your grandfather insisted that your father be in the photo."

Ned was still holding various bits of cord and wire. The colour had come back into his face. "My grandfather disappeared a few years later. My father always said he was taken to the gulag for insisting that the Americans would help if we only let them. The Russians promised to help but it was always too little and too late. My father said they were very difficult times – little to eat and few jobs. We are Russians so we managed to survive."

Helen's mind was swimming though a torrent of memories of those times, that tour and the promises she conveyed to so many displaced people during those years.

"Your grandfather . . . and father. Would you like to have the photograph," she asked?

"I'll configure your computer for free if you'd give it to me," said Ned as he dove into the parts and began to connect them in earnest.

Ned could hardly believe the photo existed. And yet it was ephemeral. Mrs. McFarlane didn't really know any more having only travelled through the area on a diplomatic tour. Ned didn't know much more, but realized the photo was surely one very few of both his grandfather and father. He thought back to the photo of the same event that was displayed in his grandmother's house in Lvov. Perhaps it wasn't strange that his grandmother would choose to display only the more official photo with his grandfather posing with members of the foreign delegation rather than the more sentimental one with his father in it as a child?

As he pieced together the computer he was already writing the letter to his mother about this event seeking some other connection, something more profound than what appeared to have happened.

Ned wanted to see more in this event than mere happenstance. He wanted it to lead him. To be a stranger in a new land and have his own life so abruptly reflected back at him must mean something. The photo of his two immediate ancestors suggested more than a whiff of destiny, but there was nothing to grab onto, just an old photo of a long ago minor event.

And yet, the photo had angered the Russian diplomat, who made sure that Ned's grandfather's days as a rising public official were ended. The decline in his family fortunes sparked by that photo had eventually led Ned to leave the Ukraine and move to Canada to forge a new life. Perhaps, he thought, the photo did display a ghost of his destiny.

Ned wanted to know more about Helen's travels and her jobs and her connection to his family, however tangential. The computer was running perfectly, printer, scanner and internet connection all humming. As he made ready to leave he offered to return a few weeks later to make sure the computer was still functioning.

Chapter Forty-Four - 1995

"Who is that guy?"

"You hired him and you don't know?"

"He's always here. I get here in the morning - he's hunched over a desk. I leave at night and he gives me a nice wave. Doesn't the guy have a life?"

"He sleeps here. He gets cleaned up at the fitness place around the corner and essentially works all the time," said Marko Gubic, lead analyst at Byte Me, a software company operating out of a converted warehouse in Toronto's post industrial east end.

"Is he good? I mean, is he alright, like in the head?" Chris Williams was the vice president and day to day operations manager. He was a partner in the company which largely ran on his experience and connections.

Byte Me wrote operating software designed to make the newest computer chips work more efficiently. It was cutting edge stuff, constantly changing and fast paced. Marko was one of Byte Me's best employees, he understood the industry, understood the constantly changing dynamics of technology, theory and manpower.

Right now the industry was flooded with wanna-be's; guys who knew a little, pretended to know a lot, and sank or swam by how adaptable they were. Things were changing fast.

The Information Technology industry was so desperate for help that they would hire guys who demonstrated the least bit of competence and keep them employed for many months even in the face of total inability in the hope they would transform into productive employees.

Talking the talk got you a job. Walking the walk allowed you to keep it long enough for a better opportunity to come along.

It made for a crazy work place atmosphere - as each place of business was as much a workplace as a school. An Information Technology business of any size was a bit of a merry-go-round with employees constantly shifting and the focus of business in constant flux. Quality employees were gold and were well compensated. Byte Me was typical.

"Hell, he's our best guy. I gotta admit he likely got hired on wonky qualifications - he's from Russia or something - but he's had experience there and is translating it here pretty quick. In fact, now that I think of it, his attempts at translating their ways into ours is probably what gives him insight into new approaches to programming. He's taught our guys a few things."

"Russia? Is he some kind of security risk? How the hell did he end up here?"

"I'm not entirely sure. He said he left after the Soviet Union collapsed. I guess it wasn't just hockey players who came over," said Marko. "He spent some time in Turkey or someplace and then emigrated here."

"Well, tell him not to sleep here anymore, we're a business not a hotel."

Marko nodded as Chris headed back to his office with a fresh coffee and a newspaper. He knew that Vladimir, the former Soviet citizen, lived in the office to save money and to put a maximum effort into learning North American computer programming. He wouldn't leave willingly and Marko did not want to lose him - his effort alone lit a fire under all the other programmers who had to show significant effort or superior knowledge just to keep up.

Vlad stayed but made a show for management of leaving in the evening only to return after dinner with a key Marko had made for him. Vlad was no spy, or anything as crazy as that. He was just a regular guy who wanted to get ahead and was doing it with a mix of determination, effort, adaptability and smarts.

Byte Me quickly evolved. It kept its core business of systems development and started a division where the programmers went after institutional operations - mostly inside operating systems for companies, back office applications in accounting, word processing and pagination.

Chapter Forty-Five - 1995

"Holy crap, you're kidding? Everyone?"

"Yep, the announcement will be made Friday after paste-up is done."

"Everyone?"

"Everyone - except the two proof readers and Chuck - he's been dabbling in desk top stuff for a while and he's going to do the paste up on computer."

"One guy can do it all?"

"That's what they say. He'll be training the editors to do the paste up so there's back up if he goes down sick and apparently there will be a couple of paste up artists hired for advertising. I'm sure it will change but that's the plan right now," said managing editor Artie Manassis.

"It's no change for the photo guys anyway. They've had those bloody expensive cameras for a couple of years now, eh?" asked lead columnist Frank McRae. McRae and Manassis were long time friends whose roots in the newspaper business were deep.

"Remember, we made those guys bolt lock boxes for those digital cameras into the trunks of their cars," Artie smiled at the memory. "Those things cost $15 grand a pop. Now you can get a better one for a few hundred bucks. We're almost afraid to buy them as they get better and cheaper almost every day."

"A couple of those guys even soldered the boxes in place as they didn't want a hole in their trunk that might rust out."

Newspapers were early adopters of software applications for pre-press, photography and printing. Adoption of these applications occurred quickly as there were huge savings in the costs of photo processing which were quickly translated into colour photos. Colour used to be special, now it was becoming routine.

The switch over was planned for a month after the announcement. The grumbling was loud and the upset was enormous as younger computer-savvy reporters suddenly got editor jobs because they could do the pagination. Older editors struggled with the new technology knowing if they didn't adapt they would be cast aside. All of this was happening in the middle of a deep economic malaise caused largely by a socialist response to a free market correction.

Layoffs were common. Industries were dying, shifting and adapting and employees were finding new roles which were advantageous to some and a death blow to others.

"This is great stuff - the money we'll save is astronomical."

"Somehow I doubt it will make its way down to us. Everyone just feels lucky to have a job, even the management guys are stressed."

"I gotta go, I've got a meeting on some of this stuff."

Artie had received a call from the newspaper's publisher who said he'd received an interesting letter from a young computer programmer. He wanted Artie to meet with the guy and report back.

Vlad waited nervously in Artie's office. He had borrowed an office laptop computer from Byte Me and taken an early lunch in order to be at the meeting.

Artie walked in and shook Vlad's hand noting his fairly thick accent. He was trying to place it when Vlad introduced himself.

"I'm Vlad Kositanov. I'm a computer programmer originally from Ukraine, though I have spent some time in Bulgaria and Turkey."

That explained why the accent was difficult to place, thought Artie.

"I wonder if you have heard of the internet?"

"Not really, well sort of. There are some of our guys posting news items there."

Ned was pleased that what he was going to talk about was not a new concept to this newspaper man. " I want to show you something. Do you have an open telephone jack I can use." He hooked up and quickly called up a 'chat' post that he had flagged for use.

"Here is one of those news based chat posts," he said, pointing to white characters filling up the screen. See here, someone is adding information as we speak." A line of characters describing an industrial fire magically appeared as Ned was speaking.

Artie's eyes widened but he didn't say anything.

"But with new software I can do this . . . " Ned said dramatically as he hit ENTER to switch to a new internet address that he had pre-programmed.

The page quickly filled and a photo began to fill in rapidly, line by line. It was a picture of a cruise liner on a sunny sea surrounded with some advertising copy about taking a holiday cruise. Artie's eyes stayed open. He didn't blink.

"Wow. You can do that?"

"That's what the internet can do," said Ned. "Now watch." He clicked enter again and explained to Artie what was about to happen. Soon the still photo turned into a very short video with the ship bobbing on the waves and slowly sailing through the frame. Ad copy filled the sea and sky behind the ship as it moved.

"Holy crap," Artie blurted out. "You know how to do this?" Artie was shaking. He could immediately see the transformative power of this new technology. "This is unbelievable."

He tried to discern what to do next . Would this sweep everything in publishing aside or would it merely add another wrinkle to the industry? It was too shocking a demonstration to allow him clear thought.

"Yes, I can do this. It requires a program in HTML, Hyper Text Mark Up

Language. How would you like to sell a newspaper advertisement to a travel agency where the cruise ship is actually moving?"

Artie nodded. He was stunned. He simply could not express the transformation which had just taken place in his mind. He made a major effort to slow down his thinking.

"Can I see more of this HTM-L?"

Ned improvised and went to a one of the few corporate sites that existed. The screen slowly filled up with corporate brand information.

"That filled out a bit slower."

"Yes, there are technical reasons for that but the speed is improving all the time. It will not take too many years before the networks will be able to produce content as quickly as a television."

"Well, what do you want young man? How can I use this?"

Vlad explained that the web could be used for information purposes and that soon it would be a two way communication with subscribers using it to contact the paper, and with the paper providing a internet publishing presence both as a corporation and as their product.

"There are so many applications for this I cannot predict all the ways that it will be used, only that it will," said Vlad.

Artie asked Vlad for contact information. "I'd like to call you in a few days to set up a demonstration of this for my colleagues. Can we do that?"

After Vlad left, Artie simply sat at his desk - his mind filled with the sweeping change that this visit promised but absolutely blank on how it was to be achieved.

Vlad left the meeting elated. It appeared that his demonstration had had the dramatic effect he sought. A window of opportunity had opened wide. He had stumbled on the web a few years earlier and had made understanding it his business, often conducted after hours at Byte Me. It changed rapidly. He had taught himself HTML and followed developments in the new technology.

New websites were popping up every day and he had recently downloaded Netscape, a program that allowed users to access and translate websites into interactive media rich environments. It was a major jump in programming from Mosaic, a similar but earlier program that was unwieldy to most home based personal computers which had been purchased for individual use without network considerations.

Ned realized that hardware and improvements in computer chip speeds would be required to operate the new network approach. His job at Byte Me was likely secure for the foreseeable future. Now, with Marko on him to work more conventional hours, he could do that while using the time to pursue his own path.

The phone call from Artie never came.

Vlad waited for two weeks before he began to wonder about Artie's response. He called his office and left a message. Then another, and another. Finally he went to the newspaper and stood in front of Artie's office. Artie's secretary tried to shoo him out but Ned stood firm.

"Mr. Manassis said he would call. Is his phone broken?"

"He will call you when he is ready," said the secretary.

"I'm ready now," he folded his arms and stood firm.

Artie popped his head out of the office and invited Vlad in. He did not ask him to sit down.

"I mentioned your demonstration to my colleagues. They declined to be interested. I think they are short sighted and foolish. Probably they are just overwhelmed."

It was Vlad's turn to be shocked. Here was the mother of all opportunities and main stream business was unmoved. Perhaps they were too shocked to move. Artie broke the silence.

"However, I am interested. I haven't called you because I have no idea how to move ahead and frankly if my bosses aren't interested then officially I am not interested either. Can we meet somewhere else and talk about how we can move forward and use this technology?"

"We could start an on-line newspaper," said Vlad.

"We can't talk about that here, Vlad. Can I meet you at your place of business? Obviously not, if we are going to talk it has to be somewhere else. Frankly I'm not even sure about what to talk about."

They made arrangements to meet for coffee the following Saturday.

Chapter Forty-Six - 1995

UR/TO started up almost immediately - first as a copy only web bulletin board service but quickly morphing into pictures and even short motion video content.

Artie was able to get Vlad in touch with a freelance army who would feed news info and provide articles, photos and other content which Vlad posted in twice daily updates to the site.

Word quickly spread and the site grew. Vlad found himself occasionally using computers at work to update the site but he did most of his work on it in the early morning and late evening.

He received his first offer to advertise from a computer hardware store and then he got another and another, pretty soon he had a classified page for computer related sales and service and was bringing in several thousand dollars a month in revenue.

Artie remained his very silent partner, giving him inside info on stories to pursue, pointing out where he might find freelancers and even directing him quietly to potential investors.

After six months UR/TO hired its first employee - as Vlad was unable to keep up with the demands of updating the growing site. UR/TO had a news page and a classified page. It sported banner ads displayed and paid for monthly, and it had a number of specialty pages for sports, business, local events, comment and anything else that freelancers were willing to post new content to. Vlad found many people who were happy to get their articles published and only a few who he had to pay, mostly for hard news stories that Artie insisted he continue to publish.

UR/TO was updated often, but it fundamentally changed every few weeks as ideas for content floundered or floated. Vlad soon began flipping his banner ads to create more income - he programmed the site to change the ad every minute - that way he could sell several banner ads for the same page and advertisers actually liked the fact that the ads were dynamic as the changing banners caught people's eyes.

Vlad tried desperately to keep as much financial control as possible, however the need for employees, computer hardware and eventually an office location made it difficult. He went to his bank for a modest operating loan of $100,000 to purchase hardware and to use for cash flow as some of the advertisers were hard to pin down, as their businesses were growing but financially unpredictable.

Three of Canada's big five banks turned him down. It was obvious to Vlad that the loans officers and bank managers simply did not understand the nature of the business. One cited Vlad's existing growth rate as impossible and Vlad's five year projection of users and ad revenue as unrealistic.

Another banker spent the entire two hour interview trying to understand the internet. Ned felt like a TV pioneer trying to explain television to natives in Borneo. Within 10 minutes he knew the banker would never provide the loan.

Vlad's final attempt at a bank loan was a bit more promising however in the end the loan's officer declined to provide a business loan saying that while there was definitely a business case, the changing nature of the business suggested that if Vlad was successful he would be back in for much more than $100,000. The banker said he simply wasn't comfortable getting involved with a business that was so unpredictable for a much larger sum.

Vlad thought that the banker might well turn out to be right - however, if the business remained successful, there was a lot of money to be made.

In the end he was able to get some private money through a tip from Artie who knew some potential investors. Artie remained a silent partner in the venture, with a 25 per cent stake based on his connections, advice and several thousand dollars of his own money invested.

Vlad took 25 per cent as a co-owner and another 25 per cent as the CEO to pay employees and operations costs. As the sole employee he had a few very lucrative months before hiring. The final 25 per cent was held as capital with stock issued in the company and held against any payouts to investors.

Artie and Vlad owned this jointly and as they accepted investor's dollars they exchanged those shares for the capital.

All in all it was proving a lucrative arrangement with several thousand dollars coming in each month in revenue. By the end of 1995 Vlad was ready to quit his job at Byte Me but felt he needed to take UR/TO to another level, which would also give him something to do with the time he gained by dropping the paid employment.

He undertook an extensive search of the web and found infant versions of search engines, a couple of web comics, which he republished on UR/TO and an obituary site where people posted memorials for their dead relatives. Vlad was intrigued with the potential for music being streamed across the web but realized that download speeds were still too slow.

He quickly added a movie listings page and memorial site to UR/TO and managed to make them pay modestly.

Vlad moved into his new office, 800 square feet in an industrial park west of Yorkview Mall near the 401. He lived in a large storage closet in the back equipped with a bed and a small armoire. A couple of shelves held his personal items and he used the employee kitchen and bathroom. He rose early, updated UR/TO and left for his morning workout which provided time for him to clear his head and get cleaned up for the day.

UR/TO's two employees suspected their boss lived in the back but never worried about it too much as Vlad kept it pretty quiet. He took most of his meetings with potential freelancers, advertisers and investors at a nearby Tim Horton's always buying the coffee and Timbits in advance of the meeting and having them delivered at this table when his meeting commenced.

The web was exploding as was personal computer use. Email use had risen exponentially after America On Line connected their system to the internet.

New providers were popping up and company adoption of the form was ramping up in some sectors. It took another five years before it was essentially universal in business communications.

Chapter Forty-Seven - 1996

Artie was reasonably cocooned in his job, watching his co-creation grow.

At Christmas 1995 he attended the annual full staff meeting at the newspaper. It was there that he saw the future beginning to unfold. Management staff were provided the raw business numbers, sales, revenue, and subscriptions. For as long as Artie had been in the business, subscriptions had always risen. This year they were down about three per cent - the newspapers comptroller was puzzled at the reduced numbers.

"Strange that our subscriptions are down but our revenue and bottom line have risen significantly as we begin to come out of the recession. The expected change in government has already had a positive effect on the economy. Perhaps our subscriptions are down as many newcomers to Toronto are unfamiliar with the language - those numbers should rebound."

Artie had a sneaking suspicion it wasn't language issues with immigrants that were causing the numbers to drop. It was UR/TO and some of the smaller, more local imitators that were springing up.

Vlad was on the leading edge of the web and he introduced a search engine of his own invention called Find It! It wasn't long before practicality had him posting a link to the Lycos Search Engine and eventually Yahoo.

"The trick is how to make money off this stuff," Vlad told Artie at one of their meetings. "It's the internet providers and hardware guys that seem to be getting all the cash. The content business is difficult because it is so easy for people to start a site - the only trick is having the time to populate it with content and continuing to do it without a business model."

"So we can't get anything for a subscription to our site as other sites provide much the same stuff for free, even if we do it better and are much more organized?"

"Right," said Vlad. "All we can do is charge for ads and any content that someone is willing to pay for as what we really have to sell is the number of people who use our site - they come to it because it's good, it's all in one place and it's free."

"Should we be branching into internet hosting or something?"

"That's a thought, but it is hardware driven and fairly expensive. Getting into the service provision end is difficult as I think the big boys will eventually swamp the smaller providers," said Vlad. "Bell and some of the cable companies are getting into this now in a big way. They can charge for their services and they already have the wires going to every home. We can't compete with that."

"I think that there is money in distributing music and other digital media, however the web isn't fast enough yet to make that practical. It's worth keeping up on it though as anything that can be digitized will eventually end up on the web, including regular phone service and even television sometime in the future."

"Television? Wow, still pictures on the web take a while to load. Television will require huge increases in speeds."

"It's coming. You've probably seen a GIF or two on UR/TO - that's those short video bits, essentially a few still frames strung together to simulate movement. Cable companies transmit by cable now, transmitting video through a web connection is just a technicality. I hear that it is possible now, it's just that chip manufacturers and hardware guys realize they have to ramp up the hardware to match the software - and for most business applications the cost point of new hardware has to be kept down - or it will not be adopted."

"So we sit tight, keep watching the industry and make our decisions when the issue presents itself?" asked Artie.

"Yes. So far the industry appears to provide a lead on where it is going and our readers have no trouble letting us know what they want. The key for us is to remain number one on the web in terms of local information and move when moving makes sense."

"I did investigate the possibility of using 900 telephone numbers to require subscriptions. Since most people connect through Bell lines I thought we could get them to connect to UR/TO through a 1-900 line, on which we set a connection rate, say $2. Then they download our entire site and read it at their leisure. That is the equivalent of a subscription. But, is that the future? Would it shut us out of the free net? That's where everyone wants to go. The Bell guys told me in order to use the 900 service we had to provide uploading capacity within a certain distance of their technical centers. The cost for that is just too high and too cumbersome - so I dropped the idea."

Artie mulled it over. "It sounds like they are just trying to shut us out. It would be nice to set this up like a newspaper where we get revenue in two streams, through subscriptions and from advertisers. You are right, it seems like a road not taken if you think about how this internet stuff is going to play out."

"I've integrated a comic each day and I've seen some of the other sites do this - they post links to other websites - essentially they make a comment and post a link to the other website for people who are interested to explore."

"A link?"

"Yeah, it's a bit of code. If you click on it will take you immediately to another web address. It can be posted raw as code or associated with a key word."

Vlad demonstrated links for Artie.

"But doesn't that mean people leave our site?" asked Artie.

"Yes, but they can easily return, In fact the few times I've used it I've seen more than half return after going to a link, the rest I guess move on or shut down. Other sites will link to us - especially given our size."

"You can track that?"

"Oh yeah, it's pretty rudimentary but you can see how long people are on pages, where they jump off from and where they go. We also get people coming to us from other sites. So this sharing of links isn't really hurting our numbers. Again, we have the best and most comprehensive content so most people come to us eventually and they stay."

Artie was intrigued. This type of information was gold to newspapers and they paid a lot of money to polling firms to get it. The web provided it as a matter of course. That certainly gave websites a leg up in terms of planning. He mulled over how UR/TO might make that kind of information profitable.

UR/TO was morphing into a portal. AOL had done it and newer services from the larger providers like Canoe were doing it too. The portal was an entry page into the web, with all of the most of the basic stuff people wanted and a site that was a jumping off point to more specific information such as movie showing times, retailer sites and entertainment.

Chapter Forty-Eight - 1996

Vlad was contemplating his lengthy conversation with Artie at the gym the next day. He was on a stair climber equipped with a small television screen on the handlebars.

Conversations were going on around him as friends who worked out together often swapped stories and even spoke about personal things as if nobody else was there.

"So, are you a big fan of MTV?"

Vlad was thinking about where UR/TO should go next. He also was wondering when he should put some time into looking for a new car, as his old one was becoming a bit small to hold all his things that didn't fit in his closet space.

Vlad felt a nudge on his arm, "Are you a fan of MTV? You have it on but you don't seem to be watching it."

Vlad turned to see Natalie finish her question. She was looking over her shoulder at her friend Amanda and gave a shrug of her shoulders with a twisted smile. She looked back in time to catch Ned looking at her.

"Sorry, I was wondering if you could hear me."

"Well, yes, I heard you. That's why I looked over," he noted that the screen on her handlebar was blank. "If you want to watch MTV you can use my step climber, I'm pretty much done." He slowed it and stepped off. "There you go," he said as he walked towards the locker rooms.

As he walked away he heard an awkward "Ah, okay, thanks," come floating back to him.

The next morning Ned followed his same routine. Today he was going to go to look at a few cars at some local used car lots. He flicked on MTV and let the sound drown out the noise from the gym machines.

"Hi. Thanks for letting me have your climber yesterday. Look, MTV again, but you aren't watching it."

"Ah, no," said Vlad in his heavily accented English. "I'm thinking about things. I need to buy a new car, well, new for me."

"We're you thinking about that yesterday too? It might be your lucky day. I work at a car dealership and could show you a few models."

"Well, I was looking for used."

"What you want is new because it hasn't been broken in by anyone else. These days you get any used car without much of a price break on its status as used and you give away the best operating years of the vehicle.

344

It really boils down to how long you want to drive it for. If it's short term, buy used. If it's long term to get the best value, buy new."

Vlad was intrigued, here was the same careful analysis of an issue that he liked to do.
"Okay," he said. "Where do you work? I will be there in the late morning."

Like most auto dealerships it was a brightly painted, striking building from the outside, sporting a large showroom floor. Natalie was behind the reception desk and quickly spotted Vlad coming in. She handled the reception duties in the sales area and took on the full sales job some evenings and weekends.

Vlad was dressed like most computer programmers, more like students than corporate or even office types - the army of IT workers were so desperately needed by companies that they had relaxed the already declining standards for office dress. Many programmers dressed so shabbily that they were occasionally mistaken for homeless.

Vlad had quickly grasped the need to dress up a bit for financial meetings and down significantly when talking with his programming employees. His unconscious approach to fashion put him firmly in the office casual mode which he needed to be taken seriously by his staff. He even would occasionally wear a tie with blue jeans and a nice Oxford shirt. Today he had purposely dressed down to try to get a better deal - however, he couldn't resist wearing his nicest shoes.

"Hi - I've been looking for you. I'm Natalie Stewart. I handle the main desk and have been helping customers select their vehicles for about a year. We have a range of cars and utility vehicles both new and used."

She leaned in conspiratorially, "Some of the used ones are really good deals. Our General Manager doesn't like to price the imports too high because that makes our models look inferior by comparison."

Vlad introduced himself, " I am looking for a larger car, maybe a Jeep or something where I can keep things," I don't drive a lot and I don't want to spend much money."

Natalie took Vlad to the back lot of the dealership - it was full of cars in long lines, grouped by size and style. The Sport Utility Vehicles were in the third row.

"Compacts are popular so they are up front, then the sedans and family cars," she explained as they walked through the lines of parked cars. "And then the SUVs which are gaining in popularity very fast. In fact they are almost as popular as the family sedans now. The ones at the end down there are the newest ones to have come in."

The vehicles were all aligned with their windshields facing forward and a price displayed prominently, sometimes with additional financing offers attached. Ned was a bit overwhelmed as he really hadn't given much thought to the purchasing process.

There were a range of Ford Broncos, GMC Suburbans, a few Jeep Cherokees, and a couple of Toyota 4 Runners.

Vlad scanned the line, "What do you recommend for me?"

Natalie had already given this potential sale a lot of thought - she saw the shoes and knew that Vlad was a member of her fitness club. With the strange accent and downscale clothes sense she had pegged him as either an electrician, an academic or a computer programmer. She settled on the latter as she figured an electrician would not be looking for extra exercise at a fitness club.

"The Jeep is the nicest looking - in a sporty kind of way," she said, hedging her bets, "but the Toyota is the most practical. It is priced a little higher than the others because it's a Toyota, but it should be much higher due to the low miles and general good condition. It just came in on a trade in from one of our fleet customers. The guy who gave it up wasn't too happy, but with his company taking on his auto costs he managed to get over it quickly enough."

Vlad climbed in and motioned to Natalie to get in the passenger side. He wiggled his shoulders, reached for the controls, asked a few questions and then repeated the process with four or five more vehicles.

"The 93 Toyota. How much do you charge for an upgraded sound system? And can you hold it for a few days, I never buy anything without thinking it through."

"Are you going to arrange financing with your bank? Can I show you our options?"

"No and no. I'll be back in two days, same time, and we can talk specifics on the price then. I'll be paying cash. I'd like to get something on my current car - it's a 1980 Datsun 210."

Vlad was true to his word returning to cut a deal. He was firm and direct, and stood up to leave when the sound system upgrade he wanted was priced higher by the dealership than it was at an aftermarket supplier. Natalie fought with her manager and got Vlad the upgrade but only if she took the car on her own time to have the sound system installed.

On top of the sound system Vlad insisted on $1000 for his Datsun, a complete detailing, a full tank of gas, a year of oil changes and a two year guarantee. Natalie priced it all in and sealed the deal with her manager by cutting her commission by $100, the cost of the two oil changes.

Vlad picked up the car on the weekend but did not speak to Natalie who was talking to an older couple looking at a new car in the showroom.

Vlad tried to catch her eye but she didn't acknowledge him. She saw him at the club two mornings later. "How is the 4 Runner, Vlad?"

He nodded that it was fine. For the next two weeks Natalie vacillated between a cheery good morning and asking after Vlad's new car.

"The 4 Runner is no longer your concern," he said. "It is my responsibility now."

After that Vlad didn't see Natalie at the club for a week. When he saw her again she noticed him on the step climber and then moved to the other side of the room. In a flash he realized he had acted poorly and he immediately wanted to fix the problem. He went to her.

"Have you been ill, or away on holiday? You no longer want to use the step climber?"

"No, I didn't want to bother you," she said. "After all it's my responsibility to find my own step climber. I had to wait a bit, but this one works very nicely."

"I see."

"I have upset you. Can I buy you a coffee and Timbits before work? There is a Tim Horton's two blocks from here near the Mall."

Natalie thought for a second, "I know the place. I have to go directly to work from here, though I can meet you there at lunch. Do you work nearby?"

"Yes, I do work near here. I will be there at lunch. Goodbye until then."

Vlad was meeting Artie at the Tim Horton's. Artie usually didn't meet Vlad so close to RU/TO's office but he said it was urgent.

"Vlad, the newspaper's subscription numbers are down. Management thinks it's an aberration due to large numbers of non-English speaking immigrants who haven't got the language skills to read the paper. I think that might be some of it, but checking through the IP information you gave me, it's obvious that most of it is coming from people who get their news on-line, from us or other sites."

"I saw a site in California which they call an aggregator - in simple terms they are using links almost exclusively for their content - they don't do anything original."

"We have moved in that direction - I'd say that we now have about a third of our stories connected by link rather than posted by us coming from our freelancers," said Vlad.

"Well the newspaper isn't saying anything yet but I can hear it in their voices when they talk about the net. So far I haven't heard any references to RU/TO but once I do, I'm going to have a decision to make. I don't think I'll be able to live a double life - in fact I was thinking of letting it slip that I've got some involvement here. I don't want it to come as a shock when RU/TO becomes a major competitor. It's better if they know now when we are still small and almost unnoticed."

The website may have been lurking below the surface of the media business but it had not gone unnoticed. The advertising sales guys had difficulty selling newspaper space to any computer related business. They knew why. The ad managers had never had much computer ad business because it had not previously existed so they did not notice that an entire retail segment was largely missing from their ad portfolios.

Artie had been struggling with his decision to come clean with his employers. He thought it was only a matter of time before he heard his colleagues refer to RU/TO. He had dropped hints that he was sympathetic with the on-line phenomenon and even enthusiastic about its potential but he had been careful not to reference any specific site.

As 1996 crawled on, the wheels of technology spun faster with personal computer sales, internet usage and email becoming common if not yet universal.

Vlad had been dating Natalie for six months and they spent much of their free time together. They both had little free time. Natalie had taken on more sales responsibilities filling in for one of her colleagues who was off on maternity leave while maintaining her reception duties. The truth was Natalie had a knack of getting sales leads through the front desk and was reluctant to let those duties go.

Vlad had been working hard just keeping up with the massive changes in the on-line world. Growth was exponential and money flooded in but was reluctant to settle anywhere in fear of missing the next big thing. Those fears were not without foundation as changes in direction were rapid and masked a growth in business connectivity and home use that seemed to increase in the shadow of business. People were talking about working from home remotely through computers but few actually did it.

Chapter Forty-Nine - 1996

Natalie's parents had met Vlad. Her father Fred was cool to the relationship while her mother Madeline was less concerned. They were both careful to hide Fred's concerns from the young couple.

"It's his accent, that's all it is, isn't it?" asked Madeline, more commonly Maddy to close friends and family.

"No, he hasn't got any roots. He's practically a communist for God's sake," said Fred.

"Oh Fred, give it up. The Wall fell, communism is dead," said Maddy. "He seems to be a hard worker, always at his office. Nat says he's the general manager of some computer thing and even a part owner. She tried to explain it to me but it's all new. It's computers though and he's very busy."

"At least he's not a Paki or some wacko Asian that eats dogs," said Fred.

"He's some form of Christian and vaguely European, I think. Didn't Natalie say he came from Turkey? Or did she say he eats turkey?"

Fred grinned a big grin hoping to draw his wife into his pun.
"He lived in Turkey for a time," she said trying to suppress a smile. "He hasn't said much about his family even to Natalie. She says he'll tell her when he's ready. She thinks they might be dead. He told her they had to move after the Chernobyl nuclear accident. I guess they lived in Ukraine."

"Well, maybe they all got radiated or something - it just seems funny that nobody knows anything."

"Look she's bringing him to Easter dinner this weekend, see if you can get him talking," said Maddy.

Fred tried but got very little out of Vlad. Vlad tried to explain his business leaving Fred with the impression that he was into networking computers. Fred had seen his own workplace struggle with their own small network to tie manufacturing together with warehousing and sales. Everything now had to come with a bar code - it was those bars that allowed the computer to catalogue everything once it was scanned.

As logistics manager Fred was moving from a paper-backed arrangement for keeping control of parts, storage and sales deliveries to a computer based system, and was learning the advantages of just-in-time parts and stock deliveries. He found Vlad knowledgeable but he provided nothing too specific. The same came to his background where Vlad was quite forthcoming with his movements from Ukraine to Bulgaria to Turkey and then Canada but only said that his family left Ukraine after being displaced by Chernobyl. He didn't give any more detail.

Fred was determined and asked Vlad directly.

"Son, you are getting serious with my daughter and I'd like to know more about you and your family," said Fred.

"Well, there is not much to tell. I have been on my own for a while now. My father was radiated at Chernobyl, he was an engineer at the plant and died shortly after the disaster. My mother took my brother, sister and I to Bulgaria to live with my aunt. My mother had difficulty coping and died of cancer in late 1989. My sister and brother stayed with my aunt, they are younger than me."

"I took advantage when the Wall fell and moved to Turkey for school. It was inexpensive and my uncle helped me. I think he figured it was worth the expense to get rid of me permanently. I think he thought the Wall would close up again - he was a police captain, who had used his Russian background to rise through the ranks. He was a good man but overwhelmed with three new kids to house and feed. So I left. Of course we were not close. But I do send my aunt, my mother's sister, some money when I can."

"The education in Turkey was good but the country was not. Too much family favoritism and community networking. When you aren't in their circle you can never get in. So I tried to get into the United States, thinking of graduate school and the opportunities that would come after. I also applied to Canada and Canada accepted me first."

Vlad explained that he had enrolled at York University but quickly realized he'd gain far more practical knowledge and necessary finances by working - so he took a job and worked long hours learning as he went. He had to learn the language and the computer protocols - and that took him a year - he pointed out that he was still learning English, as it is spoken in Canada.

Fred was overwhelmed. Vlad's background was a lot to take in and Fred now understood why the young man had been unconcerned about telling anyone. He made Vlad promise to tell Natalie the story.

Chapter Fifty - 1998

"Natalie, I sold RU/TO."

"Really. Did they make you a better offer."

"They offered five times what they offered last time and I almost took it then. I had to hold my face together before reluctantly taking it. They want me to stay on as general manager for a year while they groom one of their people to take over. I agreed but for $200,000 extra."

"So when does it go through?"

"We shook on it today and they said they would have the paperwork together in a week. I'll have a lawyer go over it and then sign - maybe another week after that," said Vlad. "I am interested in the logistics business - tagging or chipping goods, and how to make it more efficient. I expect to take some of the sale price and buy into that business. Even if I don't stay with it personally, it's a good place to park some of the money

- a good on-going business for a good long while I expect."

Vlad also explained his interest in the cell phone business, more as a developer for smart phone applications. He said that the development of cell phone applications would be the next major growth industry in IT.

"Wow. I hope we can use this to remain financially secure even as we move into other things," she said cautiously.

"Absolutely. This sale is perfect as I believe the portal business is peaking and all the big companies will end up controlling the market anyway - they want an instant presence and the good will of an existing site and I don't want to take them on long term. Everybody wins."

"Business has finally understood the power of the web. In fact, I think they are over-estimating its value and forgetting how rapidly technology can make changes. But I'll take their money and wish them well."

The sale was completed and Vlad remained in his role but rapidly handed control to News Corp.'s hand-picked CEO. While Vlad felt some fondness for the company he founded he knew that the rapidly changing industry would have wrecked havoc on his creation so practicality dictated the smart move.

As 1999 approached he was only venturing into the RU T.O. offices for appearances sake and because he felt he couldn't cash their paychecks unless he fulfilled the terms of the contract they had arranged at sale time.

The market had taken news of the sale especially well creating a significant increase in the stock price of News Corp.

Vlad purchased a number of warehouse facilities in Milton, Pickering and Vaughan, all on major highway routes and surrounding Toronto on all sides. He started contracting with various businesses, food, auto parts, containers to move their goods into the city. In order to beat his competitors Vlad purchased an abandoned factory building in Toronto's east end just south of Lakeshore Road. As a former factory site he purchased the land cheaply as environmental regulations required the owner to remediate the pollution on the property cause by the lengthy heavy industrial use. As Vlad wanted the property for a warehouse he was able to use it while undertaking a slow but steady clean up of the site.

The city warehouse location provided him with a jumping off point for deliveries in town. He was able to move product in bulk from his suburban locations at night to his city warehouse and then move it to restaurants and hotels during the day in much smaller trucks. The computerized tracking and sorting of goods made his operation extremely efficient and profitable.

Vlad took on Fred as a partner and as general manager of the operations while he acted as a hands off partner. It freed him up to investigate the cell phone business.

Chapter Fifty-One - 1999

The endgame.

My mother was very old and was fading. Her breathing had become laboured, she barely acknowledged visitors and hadn't really recognized even close family for several weeks.

As her youngest I had been preparing myself for these days for many years, like an actor trying to feel my way into this future role. I knew it was unbecoming to feel like an orphan but it was hard not to feel it.

Real orphans at least have only the smallest memories of their mothers if they have them at all. I was all memory. Years of events, shared rituals repeated endlessly, bred in my bones my essential 'Stuartness'. It was the Christmases, birthdays, events and family vacations of a lifetime that provided my experience.

The loss of my father had seemed natural, if a bit premature. As Dad's years ran out, his influence had waned. He was never able to translate his experiences into the more esoteric vagaries of modern life. He remained a rock on the important things - that bedrock on which us Stuarts built our lives.

However as my mother began to slip away, first into a lack of recognition, and then into the altered consciousness immediately preceding death, I began to get claustrophobic, like the wall between my brother and sisters were closing in. I would no longer be able to plead my case in family disputes to an authoritative arbiter.

In these final days, already the shift was occurring in the relationships between the Stuart siblings.

My older brother Bill was the natural decision maker. Since Chas' death he had stood alone in the lead role. My sisters, who had borne so much of the burden of our mother's final months, and who needed time to come to terms with their lives after our mother died, had battled with Bill. Bill was pragmatic in the extreme, which was his way of dealing with his grief.

I left my mother curled up and in a drowsy semi-sleep like a cat. I promised to return the following evening. I did return, this time with Jeremy, my oldest, who had surprised me by wanting to come.

Jeremy had been very detached from the process of his Grandmother's failing health for almost a year; it was evident especially once my mother had turned the corner from an aged angel to a wizened and forgetful gnome.

"Grandma's going to die soon isn't she?"Jeremy asked on the drive over to her ramshackle house.
I sighed audibly, not really wanting to acknowledge the truth out loud.

"Yes. Unless you come again before the end of the week, this may be the last time you'll see her."

Jeremy sat in silence, only the hum of the tire treads on the cold road could be heard.

"It's the same for me," I told him.

"I'm not sure I want to see her, if she isn't herself. I don't want to remember her in any odd way. I don't really know how to feel," Jeremy said. "It's like I have to project my feelings of losing her onto this experience. Why doesn't it make me feel something more obvious, more concrete?"

"Maybe because it's so many conflicting things all at once - loss, fear, your own mortality, new family dynamics. I just feel lonely - like an orphan."

"But you're over 60. You can't be an orphan."

"But I am, or will be shortly and I certainly feel like one already."

We sat in silence for the remaining few minutes of the trip. As I pulled the car into the driveway, I started to explain what Jeremy was going to see.

"She's in bed and has been for a while," I began to explain. "I wonder if your aunt Charlotte is here." I looked around for her car.

"She doesn't know anybody. In fact it's been weeks since she's even tried to pretend that she knows people."

We entered the house and began to climb the stairs. Jeremy was slow, not really keeping up with me, like he wanted to ease himself into a very uncomfortable situation.

I turned the corner of the upstairs hall and turned my head back to speak to Jeremy.

"She's right in here," Charlotte said and I swung my head back to enter the room.

I stopped.

"Mom? Mom?!"

"Is she all right, is she alright?" stammered Jeremy, bravely pushing past me into the room.

I was transfixed. My mother was sitting upright in bed, taking a few spoonful's of soup from Charlotte. She turned to look at the commotion of our arrival.

"There he is," she said to Jeremy, holding her hands out in the familiar gesture to cup his face. He was quizzical but compliant. I was fixed to my spot, completely stunned. "How nice of you to visit with your father."

She took some more soup. "Charlotte dear can you please get me a bit of water?"

Charlotte left the room and shot me a look a surprise and exclamation.

"Mother's had a very good day today, a very good day," she said quietly as she slipped past me, to leave the room.

Kate chatted amiably to Jeremy quite lucidly speaking of Charlotte, a previous visitor and the day's weather. She even slipped in a few references to previous days, when she had appeared to be almost in the next world.

Gradually it dawned on me that she was constructing the conversation from snippets that had passed in her presence over the last several weeks. She wove in tiny reminiscences about her house, her parents, my father, her children and grandchildren.

I began to realize she had gathered her strength for one last visit. Even as we called my brother and other sisters she wearied.

"Mom, tell me about your life. Tell me something I need to know."

My mother looked at me, and the smile on her face faded.

"Your father was a good man, and then he died. It was terrible. So many years ago. I felt like it was my fault when God took him. He was going to go anyways and leave me. But your father picked up the pieces," she said, staring into space. "He knew, I think, but he never let on, he never did, he was a good man too."

She fell silent. Charlotte had come back into the room.

"Dad was a good man," she repeated. "He did everything he was supposed to; he fulfilled his obligations, but never seemed to enjoy it. I always thought he was a bit broken because of his war experiences."

"Yes, the war caused his problems and God answered our prayers."

My mother motioned for the water and another sip of soup. Charlotte scrambled to comply. As she took the soup she slid back a little deeper in the bed. "That's enough for now dear."

I was shaken. "Mom, what are you saying?"

I had always wondered about some odd references to my childhood but here at the end I wanted something concrete.

She closed her eyes and sighed. "He was a good man and then he was gone."

"I think tomorrow I'd like to go for a little walk. I'm awfully stiff. Can you come back then and help me?"

She slid even deeper in the bed. "What's on television tonight? Is it Sunday? Is Ed Sullivan on? I like Ed Sullivan."

Charlotte shot me a look as she rose to turn on the TV.

"What?"

"Later," she said as the television noise filled the room.

Bill arrived but the moment had passed. However, there was an animated discussion in the kitchen.

"She said what?" asked Bill.
I repeated the essence of the conversation again and asked if anyone knew anything more. Bill looked uncomfortable. Charlotte looked at Bill not wanting to catch my eye.

"What's going on here?" I demanded.

"I think you know," said Charlotte before abruptly leaving the room. Bill looked after her, clearly uncomfortable facing me. He raised his eyebrows. He didn't want to say anything.

I didn't want to ask but slowly I pushed the words out. "Who was my father?"

Bill only stared at him.

"I think you know already," said Bill. "Dad was a good man, but the war damaged him, left him reflective and distant. Father David filled the void for Mother. You were so young when he died you never really knew him and nobody was going to put those questions into words. Nobody wanted a concrete answer. In fact I'm not sure I ever really knew until just now. It was never voiced, only surmised due to voice and evasive, scripted answers when his name came up."

"It was never spoken but somehow we all figured it out," said Charlotte re-entering the room. "I always just knew. I guess there were enough sly clues that it just reinforced the idea over the years. I'm not wrong am I?" she asked Bill, suddenly agitated.

"No, you're not wrong. I remember the same hints."

So now that the truth of those years appeared to be within reach, there were more questions. They would have to wait. The ground, already soft beneath my feet at the imminent loss of my mother shifted again.

I remembered Father David only in a few vivid moments. The priest gave me a quarter once when I was four and only barely knew what it was – blissfully unaware of its enormous value in 1939. My mother insisted that I give it back. I refused. My mother manoeuvred me into using it to buy food supplies which she used for her charitable meals.

He taught me how to throw a ball and shoot a puck. He seemed to fill in whenever my father was unable or unwilling to take up my need.

I arrived the next afternoon expecting to see my mother so I could ask her the unspoken questions. It was not to be. As the day wore on she wore out. Her breathing was forced and then stopped all together. In the stifling heat of a Toronto summer day, she was gone.

The world had long before passed her by. And yet her footprint on the future was larger than most. My father had never been able to reconcile his value but my mother knew her value instinctively and lived it to the end.

Chapter Fifty-Two - 1999

Soon after she died we began to dismantle the old house. It was painful and heartbreaking. Nothing could ever be the same again. Familiarity of things and purposes led back decades for my family and with my mother's death they were rendered memories. I realized that soon I would never have reason to visit my family home ever again. The memories would be lifted and distributed and the shell sold. That chapter, lengthy though it was, would end forever.

We split up the furniture. Some went to each family and some pieces sent off to grandchildren who needed them. I moved the beautiful old dressing table into my home. It had doubled as a desk for my mother. My father had built it as a wedding present for my mother. I thought it the finest piece available and a significant heirloom of my family.

A man who built countless desks, armoires and shelving units for his children and grandchildren, it was unquestionably the finest piece he had built. It was as perfect as he could manage, as elaborate as its size allowed and as classically conceived as he knew how. Inlaid with multiple woods, it was detailed and functional and had stood in my parent's bedroom for decades.

As I eased it into place I began to exploring it. I knew of one hidden drawer in the front facing. I had spied my mother opening it one day when I was little.

I reached up and pressed on the center of a decorative section. Just as it had many years before, it popped open, leaving a shallow shelf in the upper frame. In it there was a copy of my father's death certificate.

Knowing there was one secret compartment, I knew my Dad well enough to know there would be others. I started to push and tug on different facings, various knobs and pulled at corners. The design of the desk made for a multitude of potential hidden drawers or slots. I found another small cubby but it was empty. And another.

I took hold of a decorative knob along the top frame of the upright desk. I twisted it. Nothing.

I tugged gently on it. Nothing. I twisted it one way and pulled and felt the knob shift slightly. Without releasing the knob I pushed it back and then pulled out - and then it slid out - it was the facing of a very shallow drawer several inches wide and less than an inch deep.

There was an envelope in that drawer.

I took the envelope out knowing there was much more exploring to do with the desk. The envelope was open. I carefully extracted the yellowed paper inside. It bore the letterhead of the War Department, Ottawa.

December 10th, 1940

Dear Father David O'Riley:

It is my pleasure to inform you that your application for a Commission in the Royal Canadian Army has been accepted.

You will report to Army Command at 5195 Sparks Street, Ottawa, Ontario on Monday, April 15, 1941. You will be commissioned with the rank of Captain and serve with the Canadian Medical Corp as a chaplain, as your faith guides you.

You will undergo a modified basic training and ship overseas with your company once arrangements have been made in England.

You have the next few weeks to make what personal preparations you require. Please acknowledge this letter to the above address.

Signed,
(Major) Gordon Hiller, CAC, War Department, Ottawa

Scrawled in the margin were the handwritten words, "It's difficult - but for the best. D"

I held the letter. My eyes glazed over. Father David had received a commission but had died before taking it up.

I sat down, my eyes swimming and as unfocussed as my thoughts.

"Who am I?" I thought. "Who am I."

A phone call broke my reverie.

"Hello."

"Mr. Stuart?"

"Yes."

"Mr. Stuart, I'm Scott, the real estate agent your brother hired to sell your mother's house. Bill asked me to give you a call to let you know that the house will be listed for sale today. We are planning an open house, as I believed you two agreed, this weekend. If you have any questions I'd be happy to answer them."

"Questions? Yes, I have questions but I haven't really had time to think about the house. Ummm, ummm, yes go ahead. Do you need anything from me?"

"No. Everything is in place. I just wanted to call to let you know."

"Thank you. I appreciate knowing."

"Goodbye Mr. Stuart. Don't hesitate to call if you have any questions."

And as the sun rotated beyond the horizon, from my chair by the phone I looked out the window into the gloaming. I could see the silhouette of tree branches against a bluish black sky.

And above the uppermost branch, a little pinprick of light. As I stared at it, it seemed to grow, to glow, to flicker, then it disappeared only to reappear a moment later.

A strong storm wind stirred up the leaves and then the branches of the tree brushing up against the sky to cover the bit of light, in a pattern but without a predictability beyond my ability to comprehend. It was gone and then visible again.

I thought of all the distance that bit of light had travelled only to be blocked from my sight by a tree on a planet that may not have even existed when the light began its journey. All that time passing without anything getting in its way only to be blocked by a leaf. And yet, of all things, that leaf could use that bit of light for life. To me it was just nice, enjoyable and something to muse on.

I sat there in the dimness of my room, gazing at the bit of light as it flickered, thinking about nothing in particular, but letting the recent changes in my life organize themselves in my mind.

Then it came to me, bumping up against the edges of my thoughts in one of those moments of heightened lucidity that thrill with their sharpness. So sharp that you can never quite grasp a hold and claim the truth as your own.

As the moment faded I was left knowing my life had been lived in significant moments, sometimes small and seemingly inconsequential and others more grand, events that impacted the direction of my life.

Some of those moments I controlled but most, and their consequences, were thrust upon me. Some must have occurred without me every recognizing them as important, and others I saw clearly only years later.

So my life was a blurred jigsaw of the momentous and the plain, and of the dance between choice and chance.

All the while the leaves kept swaying in front of the window, now obscured by a scatter of rain drops.

42650325R00207

Made in the USA
Lexington, KY
01 July 2015